I0628815

ellis kross

the hate train

a novel

Sinclair Leprieur

First Edition, June 2016
Written by Ellis Kross
Edited by Sidonie Lailler

PUBLISHED BY ELLIS/KROSS

ISBN: 978-0-9976453-0-9
Kross, Ellis, 1983—
The Hate Train
I. Title. Fiction. Apocalyptic Fantasy

ISBN: 978-0-9976453-0-9 pbk.

Story by Ellis Kross
Book Design by Izzy

Front cover includes photographs from istockphoto.com

Written at the Crow's Nest.

Printed in the United States
10 9 8 7 6 5 4 3 2 1

the hate train

I HATE a lot of things.

I pretty much hate every little thing that gets under my skin. It's the blood. It's aged and bitter and at times, boils to the surface, resulting in my skin to thin.

For example: I hate the way Bill used to pick at the leftover food stuck between his back teeth with his tongue before he discovered a toothpick. The annoying noise he'd make sounded as if he was giving his teeth blowjobs. I hate his mannerisms; actually, I hate *a lot* of them, but that doesn't mean I hate Bill, the person. During that weird phase in my early teens when we never talked—I mean, not even a "hi" or "hello," or even a gesture when I was standing in the same room with him, and we were like these two primordial beings occasionally shooting seedy-eyed glares at one another whether it be passing each other in the kitchen or going to our separate rooms or whatever—I think I might've hated him to the bone, but I don't hate him anymore.

I hate the color yellow, too. I'm talking about mustard yellow, that kind of intense nastiness that stains everything it touches, like my skin whenever it's prone to sharp objects, which cut, scratch, or lacerate the surface, inviting in the outside world. On the contrary, I *like* the taste of mustard, especially spicy mustard, on a turkey and Swiss cheese sandwich. It's fair to say I like gold as well, yellow's distant and yet, strangely cool cousin. I like tagging things around Spartacus with hella-gold. *But* yellow, I despise it. I also can't stand it when people wear yellow: yellow T-shirts, yellow ponchos, yellow shorts. It hurts my eyes. If people only knew how tacky they look wearing the same color as a sticky note. Reminds me of that goofy, ogreish, dyed lab mouse from *5th Avenue*. Mousosaurus is his name. I hate Mousosaurus too, for unmindfully rolling around in the spilt vials of turmeric, for all his gibberish in a children's educational TV show, which—now that I think about it—was state media peddling propaganda. Who the hell put a giant mouse in charge of educating the youth? Same goes for that clumsy bastard B-Rex, the pink dinosaur. I don't like him either. He gives me the creeps.

I also hate the way people look at me sometimes. The expression alone makes me feel as if I'm some unwanted creature that was dropped off in the woods when I was a baby and then, later, mothered by wolves. I don't exactly hate the people who look at me in a way that clearly advertises disgust. Can they really make it that obvious? The rolling of their eyes. The smacking of their gums. The furrowing of their brows. The cocking of their heads. That Elvis half-snarl of their lips. I hate their expressions, every one of them, intended for "my eyes only," as if it's their own little way of expressing how much *better* they are than me—I take that back—I hate the people who look at me that way. What's their problem?

Like the Vet, who used to look down on me, I hate her, too, and how she used to rip me off and take advantage of me. She did this with my first cat, Alexander The Great, a Russian Blue, who died four years ago from kidney failure. The Vet wanted to do all these tests on Alex, which would've cost over thousands of dollars, and when I asked questions and demanded the reasons why Alex's kidneys were failing him, she said it was "environmental," which was another way of saying "I dunno." I wanted the Vet to explain what she meant but she sounded more like a saleswoman than a quack. As much as she hated cats, Peggy suggested buying a new one, a "prescribed cat," to rid any lingering thoughts of Alex, the memories we shared, hit delete, erase them, cover them up with another cat, as if Alex never existed, but unfortunately that one didn't work out as planned. Life has a way of tripping me from behind and telling me, "You're not supposed to be happy."

I hate it when people ask me how I'm doing. If people wanted to know how I was doing and not just ask it as a natural response to acknowledging a fellow member of their species, they'd totally freak out and run away. You run into a lot of these insincere questions in Spartacus, I've noticed. People will ask how I'm doing, as if it's no different than a hello. They ask it, only expecting to hear a simple one or two word answer, like "Good" or "A'ight," which seems to be a popular answer, or "Pretty good," or "Not bad," or, for those smug dopes out there, "Great" with three exclamation marks! Are these the auto-replies society has agreed to? So you really want to know how I'm doing, I'll tell you. But don't say I didn't warn you.

That makes me think: I hate it when people tell me what to do. Or, how they act as if they know what's best for me when, in fact, they're equally as screwed-up as me—or worse.

I hate holidays.

And birthdays. I hate them as well, so much that I don't even celebrate them anymore. Every year since Peggy can never find the right gift for me, she slips a hundred dollar bill inside a cheap birthday card that she bought at a drug store, the card being written by a staff writer; however, at times, I wish Peggy would never give me any money. Worse, I hate whenever I talk about traveling somewhere, like overseas, or share my future plans with her, like visiting other countries, like Sweden or a place where it's really cold, which costs money and her reaction is one of complete dismay followed by those witchy words *"With what money?"* The demoralizing response alone makes me feel subhuman, as if she thinks I'm so pathetic that I can't even earn a penny on my own. If she only knew the damage that she's inflicting on me.

I hate anniversaries.

I hate award shows, for instance, like film award shows. Dolled up assholes jerking off one another. Award shows in general present themselves larger than they are. That pretentiousness under one roof can, at times, be nauseating and hard to watch. The way I look at it: One man's "Best of" may be another man's "Worst of." What makes a film, song, or play worthy of an award? It reminds me of that one scene in that film with *Dead Poets* in the title, which Bill begged me to watch with him after convincing me that Debbie Harry from *Blondie* made a cameo—which was a lie. In the scene, the teacher-character has each one of his students rip out the introductory pages of their poetry textbooks, most importantly, the section that explains the most effective ways of writing a poem according to a silly chart or graph. Unlike competition, there are no winners or losers when it comes down to creating a piece of work. Did the piece mean anything to you? Did you *feel* anything when you read or saw it? To most artists, most *true* artists, it's like breathing. Is it not?

Peggy would send me to church after this one: I hate thy neighbor, truly, and his noisy power tools, which he uses at all hours of the day. I'd never resort to calling him one "evil son of a witch," a bona fide asshole for sure, definitely inconsiderate Euro-trash, who has no respect for any of his neighbors, which is probably why he chose to live out in the county. Which begs the question: Why did Peggy move us all the way out here? I'm pretty sure the neighbors are god-fearing people, like Peggy, even though they don't act like it, especially when they pump out country music from their garage like a sound factory or rev their muscle-car engines in the middle of the night. One night, I'd like to sneak over to their house, when they're sleeping in their tombs in the basement, and run a very long key with lots of grooves across that Carolina blue mustang or throw a brick through the windshield, show him how to responsibly play with his toys. I especially hate it when he burns trash in his backyard, and that smell clings to everything for the entire week.

I hate appreciation days. For real, *they* even created a National Do-nut Day—and by the way, who exactly is "they?" I mean, who exactly creates these ridiculous days? Is there a secret underground committee who comes together in the back of steamy alleys while we're sleeping and designates a perfect day for donuts?

I hate these foodies who share fancy pictures of their food on the Internet. I hate it when they try to turn their food into art. Didn't your parents teach you not to play with your food, you degenerate?

I might as well confess: I hate dill. More than anything, I hate the way a cook slips it into potato salad or some other dish without telling me, like a salmon burger—*What's the green stuff in there? Oh, by the way, that's dill. Enjoy, fuckface!*

Speaking of surprises, I hate gender reveal parties. Why exactly do I give a flying shit whether or not your baby is a boy or girl?

Oh yeah, and I hate it when you open doors for people and they don't say thank you in return and you just want to grab them by the ears and scream in their faces, "You're welcome!" Same goes for driving, which I hate as well. I hate it when you've been waiting in a turtle-slow line of traffic, then, out of respect for your fellow man, you kindly let another driver merge in front of you and they don't give you a thank-you-wave. Instead, they go about their merry way like a turd sandwich. I swear every time I show the least amount of courtesy to drivers and receive nothing in return, I want to slam my foot against the gas pedal and rear-end the back of them and really prove a point— *You're welcome!*

Did I mention that I hate driving, too? Man, do I hate driving or what! Not because I'm another lousy driver like most drivers on the road (in fact, according to my driving instructor, I'm considered a su-perlative driver for my excellent awareness of the road—that's right, Ms. Teague, I finally used the word *superlative* in a sentence, so chew on that, you uppity bitch!), but because I absolutely hate being on the road with *other* drivers. I make sure to follow the rules: I flip on my blinker when I'm making a turn; I never run a stop sign; I never make a left turn on a red light; I let people in if they need to squeeze into traffic even without a thank-you-wave; I don't talk on my phone while I'm driving; I don't text; I don't stuff food in my face; I don't do anything but keep both my eyeballs on the road and make sure the weapon I'm driving is as tame as a sedated zoo tiger. Lately, this has been an issue with me: that hot rage, so much of it coursing through my veins, unable to control it at times, especially when I'm the one acknowledging drivers when they pull dick moves like cutting me off or stopping short or failing to use the turn signal and these drivers are fully aware that I know what they did, then they shake their heads as if they're in the right and I'm in the wrong or worse, mouth off at me in the safety of their own cars. Be-cause look at me: I'm just another ungrateful, entitled, piece-of-shit (enter generation cattle brand here) kid. Another waste of space raised in the unholy wasteland of the WWW. I don't know any better, right? I don't know anything, remember? I'm completely ignorant of the world around me, except for the digital one eight inches below me. Because I'm worthless. Because I'm afraid to make direct eye contact with people, right? Because the dark, sinister makers of technology have highjacked my body and infected my brain with a million mind-controlling parasites. Because because. If that were true, then they'd never see me approaching from behind. The crippling thoughts prod at me, as if it's daring me to turn these noxious, nefarious images into a wicked reality. I'm not a violent person, and I don't want to be violent; but sometimes, I feel as if there's going to come a day when those images come to life. I feel as if one day I'm going to do something really, really awful. The only thing preventing me from crossing that line are Bill's words: *"Be responsible, Josh,"* he says. I'm trying, Bill. But I'm starting to lose control.

Don't dare get me started on social media. I hate it with a *passion*, and perhaps it's one of the reasons why I've been so unhinged lately. As much as I want to unplug and live a life without a time-consuming app like MyCircle constantly redirecting me to the latest "Friend suggestions," it, that unholy Beast, sets the traps and continues to lure me back in as if it knows exactly what's going on inside my head. I hate how it has sent us back to the Stone Age and how one day it'll wipe out the human language and our dysfunctional way of communicating with one another and how it'll revert us back to cavemen with all of our emojis, emoticons, hashtags, filtered animal-face facials, lengthy tirades, our slams and zingers—DESTROYED!—our meltdowns, our spats and piss contests, convenient GIFS of other people's reaction to convey our very own, an entire Hallmark card society that takes what others have written and filmed and pass them off as our own or worse, stealing images created by other people, using them out of context and replacing them with our words, and not to mention, never-ending clichéd attempts to seek "approval" of a declining society where it's more acceptable to post the most repulsive, humiliating garbage imaginable than it is to post something thought-provoking and dare I say, an "original" idea. We, as in the ones hooked and wired by the big IT, are, essentially, wanderers of the junkyards drowning with rusty parts and used widgets in an endless wasteland which has infiltrated and permeated our dreams and desires, like a living entity, a parasite to its host, collecting dreams and desires to produce its own beautiful collage of chaos. Imagine for a hot minute: the entire human population catalogued away like files in a filing cabinet, modern day cave paintings carved into internal databases of the Internet. Millions of years from now when a *more* intelligent species comes along in their super high-tech spaceships, they'll peel open the ash-covered processors like crinkled pages from a hardback and there, our pathetic little broken lives will be on display, each one of our sorry lives explained through a dizzying matrix of laughable ideograms. A gray-skinned, melon-headed intergalactic nomad will turn to its genital-less counterpart and say bemusedly, "What in the name of Science is an eggplant?"

I also hate these people who follow me on an app, like Chatterz, then unfollow me if I don't follow them back and I just want to visit them at their work or pay them a visit at home and ask them why they unfollowed me. Even worse, I hate it when people follow me, then un-follow me once they "receive" my follow, like it's all a popularity contest to see who has the most followers or a highest to lowest follower-to-following ratio. I recently encountered one of these star-hungry fiends on Chatterz. He was an aspiring filmmaker who liked and *rechirped* one of my chirps about how the latest actor to play Stargazer Blazer sounded as if he was constipated when he spoke in costume. He followed me. I followed him. He had over a million followers on Chatterz, which I found odd because I've never heard of him before or seen any of his work. Two days later, he *unfollows* me. I don't know his reasons—frankly, I don't care. But as I was scrolling through his Chatterz page, I skimmed through his followers. They were all bots that he bought from a bot-farm.

Also, while I'm on the subject, I hate people who use a person's death, mostly, a "celebrity's," which, these days, in order to be considered a one, you must have at least fifty-thousand followers on Chatterz, bots or no bots, to benefit from their own personal gain, in particularly those who use "R.I.P." in a chirp. If they only knew how insincere and superficial they sounded. Who are these people talking to exactly, the one who recently died? Wouldn't that be the definition of hell, after you die you still receive notifications in your Chatterz feed? Strange how when scrolling through this opportunist's timeline he or she doesn't mention a single word about the recently deceased person in previous chirps. Does it make them feel taller or more self-righteous to comment over the eternally silenced? Do only some deserve "R.I.P." while others do not?

And TV, a device I'd like to send to the grave, hate it.

Even though I find ways to get sucked into it, if it's from catching a screen grab in the corner of my eye or simply something to do to pass the time, I can't stand how television always manages to lure me in. That seductive black hole.

I hate comedy clip shows, the absolute worse, especially the ones that exploit people's pain and suffering. Then, judged or criticized by a cartoonish-looking host. Peggy and Christian get a kick out of them. Every now and then, I'll hear Peggy cackling her ass off at a poor schmuck racking his nut sack after a failed nosegrind from the other room. I think the real reason why I hate these shows so much is the fear of one day winding up on one of them, having some loser whose life is so bankrupt that he spends his life waiting to capture a moment of misery film me getting injured, or worse, killed while I'm in public, like getting run over by a car. Or, just someone capturing me on their phone while I'm having a bad day. Aren't we allowed to have bad days anymore without fear of being filmed, then having that video posted on the Internet? The thought alone of having an injury or even worse, tragedy, being the primary source for someone else's idea for entertainment, makes me never want to leave the house ever again or show my face in public. If you think our need for violence is out-of-hand, during the Middle Ages people used to burn cats over bonfires or beat them to death as a form of zoosadistic entertainment. At the time these horrific acts were even sanctioned by the Catholic Church, considering most believed cats were associated with witchcraft. Have we really changed from those times?

I hate copycats, too—even though I need them as much as they need me.

While I'm on the subject of copycats, I hate musicians, not all, but some, except for the ones who can actually play music. I guess, in a way, I respect most musicians, even if their music isn't my taste. I also hate these puffed up shit-bags who think they're so forward thinking and call their music groundbreaking when, in fact, they're repeating what their idols did decades before them and claiming it as their own. I can't stand the phoniness, how they blindly mistake arrogance for self-confidence. Most of all, I hate mainstream musicians, which, these days, falls under the category of those who can play music and those who can't but would have no problem dancing on a stage like a puppet: I'm talking about corporate auto-tuned hand warmers who can't carry a note to save their lives or greedy flakes who make their money off exploiting others for the sake of a new clothing line. Those desperate rent-a-lyrists shamelessly standing atop the shoulders of icons like parrots. I sometimes imagine these iconic figures, basking in cold moonlight, translucent like the Ghosts of Music's Past, repeatedly crooning the words: *Get the hell off our shoulders, you parrots.* Sometimes, I just want to cradle an ego in the palm of my hand as if it's some kind of precious egg, and then squeeze my hand into a fist and let all that yolky mess ooze through the cracks of my fingers until my hand is dripping wet with death. Having said that, I might as well confess that I also hate the undiscovered musician—I'm talking about a modern day musical genius who comes around every decade or so, and who, out of the blue, becomes what society labels as "mainstream." Like when you find a local band in some hole-in-the-wall record shop and buy its debut album and the album turns out to be one of the greatest things you've ever heard and you want to share it with a couple of friends, and then, BOOM! The band blows up, an overnight success; that one song you were jamming out to in the car, the song which you declared "My Song," even though the song wasn't really your song, but still, it felt as if it was all yours, becomes "Everybody's Song." You hear *your* song in a lame TV commercial for a treadmill from the same brand that once used an Ad agency to create controversy right before Christmas, which caused the Internet to lose its mind—but, in reality, the Treadmill company hired a bunch of advertisers, who used thousands of bots to trash their own product, saying the Ad was every kind of "-ist" in order to generate controversy or discussions—as if we don't have enough discussions already, and that juicy controversy ended up, of course, of all places, in the Headlines, who gave the Treadmill company free advertising and now, the whole world is straight up like: "THAT'S MY JAM!" Now, the world is rocking out to the same beat, and I hate it. I hate the song, I despise it, because it was once, not even a decade ago, living comfortably numb inside my head, replaying like a first kiss; then, after the song's success, I desperately wanted to grab a pair of tweezers and rip the song out of my head and then stomp on it over and over until it was reduced to pulp. What's worse: Ads playing older songs I used to listen to with Bill when I was younger, ones that had sentimental value to them. To me, those songs felt sacred; and now they aren't anymore. I often wonder if it's the record labels or ad agencies or the artist themselves who desecrated these songs.

I hate how mega-corporations have taken over the country, and how expendable we are to them. I hate it when they look at us and all they see are dollar signs, as if we're nothing but these flat-faced, two-dimensional cardboard cutouts lacking any substance whatsoever and the only noise we make is the sound of a cash register going *Chi-Ching!*

Also, I hate gym rats, especially the ones rocking out to "My Song" while they spend hours perfecting their already perfect bodies, which will one day turn to natural compost. You know the extra-motivated type I'm talking about. Creatine-for-brain dickwads who take up way too much space, constantly consuming, consuming, consuming in order to look swole. Sometimes, I want to walk up behind one of these circus freaks while they're doing dead lifts and pop their muscles with a very long needle and watch them spin round and round in the air like a deflated balloon, and then once they're all flat and flabby, stand over of them and scream in their goofy face. Most importantly, I hate it when I'm trying to get my scrawny ass in shape and I'm curling a twenty-pounder in front of the dumbbell station when all of a sudden a sweaty, heavy-breathed dick with legs, who looks as if he has his own line of action figures, plumps his sweaty dick-self inches away from me, and he's dressed in a skintight wife beater and Daisy Duke-coochie cutters, and he's obnoxiously grunting like an over-the-top tennis player as he does power lunges, and the only thing I can think of is the horrendous stench emitting from every gaping pore of his giant dick of a body, and I want to turn to him and put it as nicely as I can without hurting his feelings: "Brah, you smell like dog shit."

Oh yeah, and I hate sports, as well. Once, I gave sports a try when I was in middle school, not because I wanted to, but because Bill insisted it'd be good for me. I tried out for basketball, had a decent jump shot but eventually, I lost interest. I even tried football for like a week or two until I got blindsided by a two hundred and fifty pound linebacker who nearly knocked my head clean off my shoulders. It was a harsh example that Bill, who might've had his best intentions in the right place, often misguided me into a direction that fit better for maybe himself instead of his own child. Besides, back to the whole more intelligent species invading the earth millions of years from now, imagine what they'll think of us when they study what we did during our leisurely hours. How insignificant and meaningless they must think of us: bouncing or hitting a ball around for the sake of competition or a display of dominance. How barbaric we must look to them. Sports may be an escape for most, like Christian, for instance, a sports junkie who's obsessed with the Carolina Stompers, but whenever I think of the general concept of a sport, I can't help but laugh at the absurdity and especially how these are the same athletes who get paid millions of dollars. And, also, other words like *prima donnas* come to mind. Take away all the millions of dollars athletes get paid, I say, see what happens. Take away the pretentious advertisements. Sponsors. Their absurd merchandise that turns people into tribalists by dressing them in colorful animal decals. Pay 'em in pennies, I say. Bill was the same way. He was never fond of sports either, which makes me wonder why he pushed them onto me in the first place.

I hate the word *G.O.A.T.*, as in the abbreviation for "Greatest Of All Time," which is mainly used when referring to athletes. You often hear this saying in the sports world, especially ones who've recently beaten a world record. How arrogant does someone have to be to use a term like that, being that time is infinite and we are only here temporarily? G.O.O.T., or "Greatest Of Our Time," would make more sense. I guess the word *goat* is more marketable. Has a catchier ring to it. But even so, who gives a damn? You know how to run faster or jump higher or handle a ball better, but so does the thousands of other kids on the street or out in the country who'd leave G.O.A.T. in the dust, who'd make G.O.A.T. look like a fifth-stringer, but he's too smart not to sell his body to his corporate masters whose mission is to wring every drop of his soul into that holy dollar and would gladly put him down like a horse at the first whiff of disobedience. So play nice, loyal one, a diabolical, red-eyed man says in his deep, devilish voice over a glowing orb. Here's a lollipop and a smiley face sticker and make sure not to make a fuss and obey your sponsors or else we'll take away all of what we have given you. Mooh-ha-ha-ha!

I hate the word *inclusion*, too, and how everybody wants to be included in everything, like, for example, take that kid—yours truly—who was the last one to get chosen in a pick-up game during recess. The captains didn't want me on their team, not because I looked or acted a certain way, but because I sucked at basketball. I couldn't play defense. I couldn't dribble like the other kids. Sure, I might've had a decent jump shot and trying out for middle school years later was, despite Bill's convincing, my last attempt at pursuing extracurricular activities. But sometimes, you just have to move on. Which is something I'm still trying to work on. Obviously.

I hate people who throw around the term "pro-tip." Enough already. I don't need to take advice from someone who can't even hold his or her own shit together.

I hate hand-me-down expressions used time and time again like "under the bus" or "dragged through the mud." Can we not come up with better expressions or are we going to recite the same bullshit we see in the movies?

I hate it when Christian tells me "I told you so" after schooling me on whatever and he does it as a way of rubbing his intelligence in my face. I swear, if he says that line one more time, I'm going to snap.

I especially hate people who tell me that I should smile more. I can't tell you how many times I've run into these comments from complete strangers, who act as if my business is their business. Why should I smile for you? Do I look like a trained monkey?

I hate going to the dentist's office, not because of the discomfort from having my teeth cleaned—I have a high tolerance for pain— but because of trying to come up with small talk with the hygienist. Having to answer questions about what I do for a living, if I'm in school, my hobbies, or worse, "How about this weather, huh?" then followed by waves of awkward silences. That goes without saying: I hate going to the barbershop or any other place that requires me to respond to statements regarding the current climate conditions as if I'm a complete idiot who can't distinguish a stiff breeze from a fart.

I hate human beings who call themselves "human beings" as if it's an excuse to be a straight-up asshole. You know, like for example, sorry for running over your cat with a car. It was dark outside, and I'm only human. Where the hell did these human beings come from? Are they really human beings as they claim they are? If so, then why do they keep reminding us that they're human beings?

I hate irresponsible gamers, who sometimes act as if they're *not* human beings, especially the ones who play online while some two-year old is screaming bloody-murder in the background but they're too busy playing a video game to tend to the child.

It makes me sick. And I hate being sick. And the way people treat you when you're sick. I hate going cold turkey. I hate it when you're waiting in a checkout line and you're waiting to buy a nicotine patch after spending a lazy week in bed with the flu and you're starting to feel better and hungrier, your color is finally back—that glow—however, you're making sure to keep a distance from people for the sake of others getting sick and then, out of nowhere, a cough slips from your chest and you manage to catch it with the crook of your elbow and then you turn around and witness a mother of two children staring at you as if you have the black plague. Then, she shields her children from you like a lion protecting a cub. God forbid that little ball of snot, that walking germ, baby dust buster who eats everything off the carpet, the bacteria trap, the anal tickler, the poop sniffer, the little booger eater, from getting sick. I hate all these overprotective, speedy-van soccer moms who smother their children.

On the contrary, I hate parents who leave their little booger eater baking in a sun-beaten van in the middle of summer, and when they realize that they left their child suffering in a van while they're shopping at the Depot, their only excuse is that they "forgot," as if their own flesh and blood was not even a glint in their mind. Yet, that special bargain on a new cordless Black Hawk power drill for $39.⁹⁹ was more important than the very creation they brought into the world. On that note: shouldn't the punishment fit the crime? Instead of locking up these incompetent parents, shouldn't we stick them in a steaming hot car, roll up all the windows, lock the doors, and let them roast for hours? That should be enough to teach them a lesson. Shouldn't it? Same with rapists, who should pay a visit to the chop shop. And the murderers. Screw wasting the taxpayers' money by keeping all these savages locked up in cages like animals. Once you've killed another "human being" with the exception of, say, an eye-for-eye revenge killing, then you've lost the privileges of being a "human being." Do them a favor, do *everybody* a favor, and take them out back in front of the firing squad. Actually, I have a better idea. Instead of locking them in some prison or putting them to death after years and years of waiting on death row, move these murderers to a zoo that is funded by these mega-corporations, not taxpayers. People from all across the country can visit the zoo and take photos and videos of the prisoners' confinement, post them on the Internet for the whole world to see—*Oh, honey, look, look! It's an endangered serial killer rapist! Let's get a selfie with it!*

And doctors. The slow killers. Not the surgeons or the ones out there saving lives everyday. I'm talking about the ones destroying lives. I hate everything about these quacks, how they label us and as they always do, put these absurd names on our disorders.

I especially hate how people toss around the word *crazy*, as if it's normal, but it's not. I can't stand everything about that word, its baggage, its complexity, or its many definitions. Most importantly, I can't stand what "the word" has become.

I hate lithium, as well. I don't like the way it makes me feel. I hate the way I feel sometimes. I hate how I'm *always* looking for the next fight. I hate fighting. I can't stand it! I hate what it's doing to me. I hate the way it's churning my insides like butter—*another idea!*

How about this: why don't people start posting pictures of their own feces? Nobody posts food that goes into making a dish, which will go straight into your mouth, which will then be digested, which will then be defecated from your anus; people post the product before the final presentation, the food, as it would be perceived on the plate, not in the bowel. Give me a plate and I'll "share" with you what food really looks like. After all, food is shit in waiting. It's inevitable.

I swear, I hate some people—I hate *a lot* of people.

Like I said, I hate a lot of things.

And that's why I must destroy the world.

PART ONE
THE CONDUCTOR

1

The murder: 9-to-5 - Childhood Memories - Trophy - Small beginnings - The backlash - Peanut gallery - The march of the pigs - Vultures swirling overhead - Horrible nightmare - Lonely world - The sign

HE wears a caramel-colored sports coat, which is made of corduroy, with a powder blue dress shirt underneath, the top two buttons unbuttoned, no tie. He's not a detective, or at least, he doesn't look anything like the last guy. His wavy dirty blonde hair is too neat for a detective, as well as the Ivy-League grin, which is slightly crooked. He could be a cop. The other kind. The closer. He reminds me of Bill's friend, Paul, a history teacher, who used to make sarcastic remarks to me all the time. I couldn't stand him; in fact, it's fair to say that I hated him.

Before I can ask him why I'm here, the nicely dressed man first introduces himself. He says that his name is Samuel Glasser, goes by the name "Sam," says friends call him Sam, but he's in no position to be my friend. I don't know whether or not to believe him. He shows me his credentials and says he's a psychiatrist, who's been appointed to me by the state. He wants to help me with my case. I want to trust him, but right now, I don't even trust myself. First off, he wants to know my relationship with Mary Ryder.

I honestly don't know what he's talking about nor have I met anybody named Mary Ryder.

"You might know her by the alias Mayhem," says the shrink.

May—?

He takes a seat across from me at the table, and all of a sudden, the gray walls feel as if they're starting to close in. Next, he places a leather briefcase on the table. All I can think about is what's inside that briefcase: *What kind of information does Sam have on me? My background? My grades? My browser history? How did I wind up here—*

What happened?

"Listen, Joshua, do you mind if I call you Joshua?" he asks, but I know he's going to call me Joshua anyway. "Are you aware of the charges against you?"

"I don't know what you're talking about. . . ."

"You've been charged with the murder of Mary Ryder."

Murder?

"Her body was found inside the basement of Meme's, a restaurant that you've been frequenting for the past couple of weeks. According to the owner of the restaurant, you and a group of friends play a video game called *The Hate Train* inside the basement."

"She's not dead," I say. "It's impossible—"

"—How so?"

"Whatever happens in the Hate Train stays in the Hate Train. It's one of the rules!"

"Well, the coroner would beg to differ, Joshua. According to his report, Mary Ryder—Mayhem—died from a severed carotid artery along her neck. She bled out within minutes. The weapon used to kill Ms. Ryder. . . ." He pulls out a photograph of a bronze swimmeret with one end blackened, jagged, and sharp, ". . . a piece that was recently stolen from an iconic statue. Do you know what statue I'm referring to, Joshua—"

"—That's bullshit. . . ." I say, the words escaping me.

"Then, tell me the truth," says Sam.

"I can't—"

"—Why? Because of the rules?" Sam pauses. "Let's start over, shall we." Ready to listen, he intertwines his fingers together. "Tell me, Joshua, what do you remember?"

I shrug: "I dunno."

"Why don't you start from the very beginning, Joshua?" he asks.

"The beginning?"

He asks again, "When did you first lose control?"

The answer to the question is simple yet complex.

"At Phantasy Worldz, I guess," I say suddenly.

"Then, why don't we start there," he says. "What happened at Phantasy Worldz?"

#

Centered at the entranceway of **Phantasy Worldz** towers a twelve-foot tall bronze statue of **Raymond Chancellor** holding hands with one of his most beloved dreamatures of our time, the humanoid crustacean, **Sir Spur**, surrounded by a hexagonal bed of fireball-red roses. Three hours before the theme park opens at seven AM, each petal is meticulously prepped by an army of perfectionistic landscapers who work like mongrels for very little pay. Each blade of grass cut precisely four inches. Every single iota of trash ridden from the property. A mantle with Raymond's quote, *"Dream beyond the skies,"* is carefully scrubbed and cleaned before the gates open, giving way to kids and adults alike. To some, it's like a utopia.

When I was younger, I was one of those goggle-eyed kids. Every summer we went to Phantasy Worldz. There was one time—I believe it was six summers ago—when Bill decided we'd spend a summer vacation in Charleston for a week. "Switch things up a bit," he said with a smirk creeping through one side of his cheek. "Take a year off from Phantasy." We left early in the morning when it was still dark outside, mainly to beat traffic. Bill made sure to install the deer whistles on the bottom of the grill to ward off deer. I dozed off during the drive. Christian was feeling under the weather at the time, which was a good thing because he wasn't bugging me, like he does on road trips. By the time I woke up, we were driving through Limely—Bill mumbling his complaints to Peggy about the horrible Floridian drivers. Minutes passed and half-awake, I was still wondering whether or not I was dreaming. Bill's eyes turned to the rear view mirror and said, "Surprise, boys! We're here. . . " Phantasy Worldz was our family tradition—that was when we were still a family. When we arrived, we'd take a moment out of our hectic schedule of mapping out rides and stop by the iconic statue, google-eyed and slack jawed, my hand locked with Christian's, Christian's locked with Peggy's, Peggy's locked with Bill's, as if we were a paper people chain, all four of us gazing upward at Raymond Chancellor and his shrimpy friend. The statue was tyrannical in scale and size and grandiose in its remarkable detail, a truly massive thing, which, for years, seized my child-like wonder—surprisingly, Bill's as well. Like a god welcoming us into His masterpiece of awesome. That was back then, the innocence, that endless wonder, unencumbered by any doubt or dismay. Now, the statue looks like any other one, small and insignificant, a distorted symbol.

The next morning when all of the visitors arrive at one of the oldest theme parks in the South, they'll find Raymond defaced with the word *thief* spray painted across his chest and his cute and cuddly friend missing a valuable appendage, carried out with what the cops will later determine as a butane blowtorch, which, at first, melted away the bronze at twenty-four hundred degrees Fahrenheit, then crushed and chipped away by what is called a firmer chisel, similar to a bench chisel, only without any bevel on its sides. The firmer chisel is not only the ideal chisel for heavy-duty work, but it can also withstand the repeated blows of a mallet.

Why would anyone even contemplate desecrating one of America's greatest visionaries, as well as the dreamature whom millions of people have grown to love—and hate?

Last spring, the boneheads in charge of Phantasy Worldz received pressure by small people to change the dreamature's original name, Sir Spur the Shrimp, to Sir Spur. The majority of the small people community thought the word *shrimp* was offensive, and they had the audacity to label Raymond as a bigot toward people with smaller statures. Raymond Chancellor, who welcomed everyone, big, thin, tall, or small, into his theme park, now a bigot? Eventually, Phantasy Worldz caved in to the demands of an extremely charged group of protestors and planned to change the name next year. Over three decades of Sir Spur cartoons, toys, action figures, stuffed animals, video games, Tee shirts, coffee mugs, all waiting to be recalled or modified because of one word; then, from there, they would be archived to a wasteland of raw, uncensored material. These products will only exist on the Internet, and I imagine they will sell like diapers. Not only that, they'll probably sell for a lot of money, too, double, even triple the retail value.

But, again, why would any individual desecrate one of America's greatest visionaries, as well as a caricature whom millions of people have grown to love—and hate?

The answer: Because I can.

I remove the blowtorch from Sir Spur's oozing, once finely detailed face, and move the flame toward each swimmeret protruding from its trademark bib overalls and then, once the bronze starts to melt, I take my firmer chisel and give a brisk whack with my mallet, severing the swimmeret. I do the same for each swimmeret, as well as the two antennas projecting from its hickory pinstripe engineer cap like rabbit ears. The appendages are the easiest: swift strikes with a mallet, and then the appendages rain down like pocket-sized meteors and titter over the ground below.

Once I'm done defacing Sir Spur, I reposition the ladder, then work my way to Raymond.

At the last second, I think over the word *thief*, the most fitting word to describe Raymond, a man whom I had once admired, now grown to hate—I'm sure I'm not the only one who feels the same way. One side may say: Raymond was a brilliant man, an innovator, and, of course, a visionary. He might've been those things. He *was* those things; however, the ones who had succeeded Raymond after his death took advantage of what he had created. Soon after Raymond died—me being around the age of seven, I believe—the theme park, on the contrary, had literally begun the slow process of raping the rest of my childhood.

As I finish the last remaining touches to Raymond, I gather the appendages and whatnot from the ground and split before the sun rises.

2

Usually, on a good day, it takes a little over seven and a half hours from Limely, which is around twenty-two miles south of Orlando, to Spart-acus—that is, if my car, a 2004 orange, or what the sleazy, yellow-toothed car salesman referred to as "radiant ember," Nissan Maxima, or "Maximus," as I like to call it, doesn't overheat.

I take I-95 N and keep to the speed limit.

I stop twice to stretch my legs. I listen to the radio, but the story hasn't broken yet. It will, though. Soon. Give it time, I tell myself. I expect cops are examining Raymond and his shrimpy friend right about now. I expect a cleanup crew to arrive shortly afterwards to wash the paint from the statue. Perhaps the park officials delayed the opening or, even covered up the statue like a coroner does to a corpse before the hundreds and thousands of visitors showed up at the park.

3

Not too hard to miss our house. Pea soup green. I don't mind the color. Bill hated the color. As far as I know, the only color he saw was red. The porch light is on, I notice, which means Peggy has more than likely already left for work. If so, then that gives me an entire day to de-compress and tie up any loose ends in my story. I pull into the driveway and the first thing I do before walking inside the house is check the ga-rage window. Good news: Peggy's Crossover is gone. I grab my things and head straight to my room where I remove the curriculum guide, as well as the pamphlets and brochures from Southern Technical Institu-tion—STI. I place all the school junk on my bed, then hide my book-bag behind a dusty pile of vintage keyboards, samplers, and drum ma-chines in the back of the closet. Then grab a gutted speaker from the top shelf, unscrew the back of the speaker, and place the recent trophies inside: two bronze swimmerets; two bronze antennas; and a miniature figurine of Sir Spur that I stole from a gift shop. I tighten the lid and place the speaker back on the shelf with the other speakers. The story should've broken by now.

First, I open up the menu, which consists of a well-balanced diet of processed news and start with the 24-7 hour news channels, like Your News Now (YNN), the branded "vitamin-rich" TV dinner of news, which, according to my ex-shrink, can lead to cardiovascular disease, or The Progressive Channel, the sugar-free breakfast bar of news, which can lead to an early onset of dementia, or Century, the gooey, nutty, nugget-centered, chocolate candy bar of news, which can lead to severe depression and at times, intense waves of nostalgia and euphoria and, vice versa, plentiful amounts of unnecessary rage—the "rage bait," channel, it's often called. Over time, all of these diseases and ailments

listed above can be exacerbated if the following programs are not consumed in moderation. But what the hell did John the Shrink know?
Lastly, there are three major networks: the Communist Broadcasting
Channel, American's Broadcasting Station, The National Broadcast,
which can be accessed on my phone throughout the day; however, I
keep a steady eye on the program, *Live News*. Today's anchor is Carolyn
Russell. Nothing out of the ordinary: Carolyn sinking her teeth in for
the kill as she riffs back and forth about insider trading with a sprightly,
quirky senior editor from *Washington News and Facts*, as well as three
other snarky analysts and a contributor from *Collection Magazine*. I don't
care much for Carolyn. She's always interrupting her guests on her
show, *always*, and at times, acts as a corporate *shill*, a word that has been
used often by YNN's competitors. She plays a bitch on television, but I
know she's only playing a character. Based on surveys, she's a favorite
among unfiltered, unapologetic women, as well as—believe it or not—
the fellas. Carolyn is a visual feast, naturally brunette with blonde high-
lights, full yet chiseled brow, and most importantly, a great eye for a
good story. Beauty and brains. Carolyn graduated from Topp University with a major in journalism. She doesn't have any children. The
news is her baby. Then, I flip the channel to *Right Hour* on Century.
Then, try *The Bob Shuler Show* on The PC. Nothing burger. Then, try
the local news—mainly, WSS on Channel 3—and watch loops until the
time inches closer to high noon. A nothing burger with a side of nothing. I make my rounds through each channel once more. Then, I
checked the other three major networks on my feed. Not one mentions
the story. Then, by the time I go back through the channels a second
time, it's the top of the hour. I start with *Midday with Stacy-Kay* on YNN,
Century, *News Today*, then, *Rundown with Jean Foulard*, then, finally, The
PC and YN4U. The story has officially broken; in fact, it's one of the
headline stories alongside the latest "controversial" chirp by movie actor, Sebastian Birch, which has caused a major backlash of protesters
boycotting his latest film, *Graphic Nature*, a cell phone video of a reality
TV show celebrity falling from the stage, two terrorists blowing themselves up in a populous square somewhere in the holy city, Ka-boom,
somewhere in the asshole of Who-Gives-A-Shit-istan, resulting in the
deaths of over three dozen innocent bystanders who didn't worship the
right god, and an orange tabby name Sourpussy doing the rumba with a
one-legged parakeet, which has gone viral.

But first, the breaking story: ICONIC RAYMOND CHANCELLOR
STATUE VANDALIZED.

The media circus is at Phantasy Worldz. Frantic reporters from
other news channels are running around everywhere. The parking lot is
full of distraught visitors. Protesters are blocking the streets.

A close-up of the vandalized statue on TV: Raymond's genitals
melted off, the word *RAPIST* spray painted in red across his chest. Rap-

ist has a better zing to it, I think. Sir Spur appears unrecognizable, a once beautiful sculpture reduced to a burnt candleholder.

As of now, investigators have "no leads," Stacy-Kay reads from the teleprompter, except for a young male who was spotted carrying a briefcase. From a distance, it may look like a briefcase; however, for your information, it's actually a collapsible ladder.

I catch a few Z's before checking the news again, YNN, Century, The PC, then their sister networks.

By the time I make my rounds, it's a quarter past three and I'm starving to death. I go downstairs and head straight to the fridge. I sort through a neatly organized Tupperware of food, each one labeled and arranged in alphabetical order, starting with the apricot salad on the top shelf to zucchini fritters on the bottom shelf. I'm in the mood for protein. I find two containers with leftover Chinese food. I cautiously take a sniff before heating it up. Chicken, I notice. Peggy doesn't eat chicken; in fact, she's a vegetarian—at least that's what she claims to be—even though she makes a living cooking chicken. I don't think too much of the chicken. Perhaps she had a girlfriend over last night. *Perhaps.* I nuke the chicken in the microwave and when it comes out, it's steaming and talking to me with pops and hisses, a telltale sign it's ready to be devoured. I let it cool off a little and check the news on the 60-inch. College campuses around the entire country are holding "Anti-Hate" rallies—which are anything but peaceful. More protesters are standing outside Phantasy Worldz with showy signs saying, "Raymond is a rapist," or "Stop the abuse of small people" or "Rape Worldz." For a moment, it looks as though there are hundreds of protesters from the angle of the camera; then the camera pans back and only shows a handful of people; nonetheless, a couple of protesters are burning PW merchandise on Phantasy Lane and screaming and demanding for Phantasy Worldz to change Sir Spur's name, "not tomorrow or next year but today," and they're not leaving until their demands are met. Fights have broken out between protesters and visitors, as well. According to YNN, two people have died from stab wounds. Two less people in the world. It's a start.

4

I purposefully set the curriculum guide from Southern Tech on the kitchen table before Peggy comes home from work.

I turn the channel from the news to the first sitcom I can find on TV—a phony one with a lot of audience laughter. Peggy calls out my name a few times, but I don't answer.

"Hello," Peggy says, her voice worn and drawn out.

"Hey," I say, making sure not to show any emotion.

"You're back," she says, as she sets her set of keys on the kitchen counter.

"Yeah," I say quietly.

"So," Peggy sighs, "how'd it go?"

I make sure not to look Peggy in the eye when I answer: "It was a'ight."

"Just all right?"

"Yeah," I say, flipping through channels. "I don't think it's for me."

She fires off questions about Southern Tech—questions that can easily be found in the brochures—and I answer them to the best of my knowledge. I reword my answers and put a personal touch on each one, as if I've been there in person and breathed the air every Southern Tech student breathed. I tell Peggy that I didn't like the professors. They seemed unprofessional—that's the word I use, *unprofessional*—which, in the back of her mind, I can see those words creeping into her thoughts. *Told you so!* Then, she returns by telling me that a lot of those techie guys are unconventional. I return with the icing on the cake: "I didn't have a good feeling about it."

"Well, you have to trust your gut," Peggy says, as she makes her way to the fridge. She opens the fridge door, searches through the shelves, and stops for a moment.

Then, after a long pause, she grabs the Tupperware of pineapples.

"You should've stopped by Phantasy Worldz whenever you had some spare time."

"Phantasy Worldz? I think I'm too old for *Phantasy Worldz*."

"Nobody is too old for Phantasy Worldz." She places a cube of pineapple in her mouth and gives me a closed Joker-smile with her lips stretched thin. "Besides," she says through the corner of her mouth, "age is just a number, Joshua."

I hate it when she calls me that.

5

I place the curriculum guide on top of the stack of other curriculum guides in my closet and watch the news in my room with the volume turned down while I spend the rest of the night blogging on my website, *Beyond the Pale*.

6

They're after me. The little devils. I'm fighting off each and every one of them, but there are so many. They're crawling all over me, as famished as wolves. Their fangs are barred and biting at me. I search through the darkness, but I can't find any resolution to ease my mind. The sweat feels heavy over my body. I eventually wear myself out after hours of switching from one position to another. Peggy's alarm clock is chirping downstairs as soon as I slip back into the dream riddled with dreamatures. The alarm chirps a couple of times followed by a *thud* from Peggy slamming her palm against the snooze button. Three more times she'll do this, I know, a vicious game of back and forth, from alarm to snooze, inside the vampire-tomb darkness of her bedroom. Each time, the alarm will go off in shorter spurts before she quickly hits snooze.

The smell of coffee lingers in the air, kindling my senses. I roll out of bed, zombie-like, and slam the door. I slither back into bed and drift into sleep. The dreamatures are back. They're not cute and cuddly like they appear in the movies and cartoons. They're demonic, and they're out to get me. I sleep for about three more solid hours before deciding to roll out of bed. Peggy has already left for work.

I find a note on the kitchen counter. Of course, it's a reminder for me to turn in the job application—as if I didn't hear Peggy the first time around. Five times Peggy told me before I left for Florida: once, when I was on my computer—I can hear Peggy saying, *You're always in front of that computer*—another time while I was playing the game, *Flip-A-Bird*, on my phone; twice Peggy told me while I passed her in the hallway, me trying not to make eye contact with her both times, then that redundant sequence of words: *Make sure to turn in your job application by the end of the week.* Then, the second pass, me blurting out, "A'ight!" Lastly, she told me while I was packing all of the things I needed for my next project. I was placing a mallet in my bookbag when I heard a *knock* on the door. She poked her head inside like the curious cat she was, then, of course, those words cutting right through me. My lower teeth grinding like a saw against my upper teeth. I often wondered if she was reminding me on purpose, as if she was trying to get under my skin. I head back to my room and grab the job application from my desk. A boring position for Sales Associate is available at the Shoe Company, a shoe store that recently opened up about two miles from the house. I fill out the application while I'm eating a snack from post-breakfast, then stop by the Shoe Company where I hand in the application to some ornery cashier who then places the application on top of a stack of other applications. As I'm about to leave, she says shortly, "We'll call you." Liar. I put on my very best "thank you" smile and shoot for the exit, relieved that it's all over. Then, as I open the door, I see an associate—around my age— helping a guy with a yellow pair of Kixx. The associate asks the older man how the shoes fit on his feet, if they're too tight or loose—Well, what is it, you old bastard? Too tight or too loose? The older man, who can pass as the white-haired colonel, paces around the aisles and tests out the new sneakers. My stomach stirs with nausea.

I leave the Shoe Company before I get sick and stop at a sandwich shop called Freddy's. Best sammies in Spartacus. I order the famous cheese steak and charge it to my credit card instead of using the money Peggy left me. I'm waiting for my food to cook and my vision starts to narrow and my chest is turning into a fist because it's taking longer than it normally does. I can feel the panic spreading through my shoulders, then my stomach lurching. I'm not going to puke, but I know it's in the mail. If I think about it any longer, Freddy's is going to look like a crime scene. I look around the place and try to keep my mind busy. I keep my eyes on a family of four sitting next to a soda machine. The dad and mom character have their heads in their phones while their two little pissant kids throw french fries at one another across the table. The snack from earlier has made an express delivery. I feel sick by looking at them, more so than watching that Chicken Guy trying on a new pair of kicks. I hear the server call out my name over my shoulder—*Josh?*

Relieved, I turn to the beady-eyed server, and the tightness goes away. She hands me the bag of food. "Have a nice day," she says, doing a double take at my face.

"Thanks," I say in one breath and leave.

I walk outside, only to be greeted by a nasty waft of funk in the air. I turn to my left and standing directly in my path is an inkblot of a person, a smudge of walking excrement polluting the air. I feel even sicker.

The mailman's on the way. Two houses down.

I try to ignore him, but he smells like an infection. Even his skin is coated with a layer of street grime, and it's hard to make out his face. He approaches me, his right leg dragging behind him like a dead tail. I already know what he's going to ask.

I do what my body tells me: I ignore him.

After I dodge him, I make it back to the house, super-relieved.

I stop at the mailbox in front of the driveway and grab the mail.

I flip through the junk mail, glossy-looking Chinese food flyers and whatnot, until I come across one piece of mail that catches my interest. It's an envelope from Bill.

I open the envelope, but I already know what's inside.

2

Good intentions - *A Decent Man* - Modern family - Cold
Feet - Poisoned by society - Lake Poe Oakee - The blood
of a Lamb - The Pale Boy - Peggy is growing incredibly
suspicious - Breaking News Report - More night terrors -
Carpe diem - Sparks Outrage - Small town on fire -
Countdown to zero

FOR the past year, Bill has been mailing me these different fly lures. Inside the envelope will be a handwritten letter (Bill is the only person I
know who writes letters). After all, he's a writer—I mean, *was* a writer.
As I'm sure like most starving artists or writers, he struggled to find an
audience in the beginning of his career. Although, I never understood
why, of all careers, he chose that one in particular. *Writing.* A breadless
profession, as Peggy once called it, where the chances of not only reach-
ing millions of readers, but also captivating millions of readers are as
likely as getting struck by lightning during a thunderstorm. *The American
Pipedream.* Everybody from Savannah to San Fran wants to publish that
next Great American Novel. For a while, I sort of felt bad for Bill.
He'd receive a weekly rejection letter in the mail. I remember he kept
all of the rejection letters. Every single one. He had some two hundred
rejection letters, mostly impersonal letters, typed out, not by an agent or
publishing company, but probably by a secretary who hated her job. A
couple of agents and independent publishing companies nibbled at a
few inquiries; and then, Bill did the whole back and forth thing with
them, but nothing that landed him that book deal. He kept trying,
though. Every day, Bill mailed a query letter, hoping to receive an advance. He'd bring his lunch home with him and wait by the window for
the mailman to show up. Then, he'd spend sleepless nights in a cold garage, typing away on a boxy laptop. I'd hear him typing away whenever I crept downstairs for a midnight snack. His mind was like a machine; his fingers like robotic arms pushing keys on the keyboard. Each

letter was a product being transported down an assembly line, *clicking* away throughout the dead of night. I'd make sure to keep any noise to a minimum because I knew he was in that cold garage regurgitating his entire mind on paper.

The first book he submitted was called *A Decent Man*, a mystery about a writer named Charles Fogg (Charles being the name of my pet turtle) who faced an extreme case of writer's block while in the grip of a looming deadline. Depressed, frustrated, and doubtful about the future, Charles drowned himself in booze one night. The next morning, while fighting off a serious hangover, Charles woke up to a freshly printed manuscript on his work desk, which apparently he wrote while he was drunk off his ass the night before; however, he had no recollection of how the story came about, let alone writing it. Then, as the days barreled on, miraculous events started to transpire in Charles's life, ones that had taken place in the story that he *allegedly* wrote on the very night he was intoxicated. After a while, Charles didn't know what to believe anymore.

Was it coincidence?

Or, was it something beyond the realm of science?

Or, was he merely searching for these things because he had already written them in a book?

Parts of the story weren't as PG-13, as Bill explained to Peggy. I read it years later after its publication, after I learned how to read on my own. It took me six days to finish; and initially, I was surprised, not by the story, but by the fact it was created by a man who acted as if he didn't carry one creative bone in his body.

After Bill's second book it became evident that he named some of the characters in his books after real people in his life or in Charles's case, my pet turtle.

In the second book, Bill named one of the protagonists, a lonely, mysterious librarian, after Francine, who was a neighbor of ours. I don't remember much about Francine, except for her always smelling like menthol from cough drops that she used to eat like candy.

In his third book, Stubbs, a charismatic man who worked at the postal office. He used to give me free comic books—which I never read—and every time I saw him days later, he'd ask how I liked the comic and I remember lying to him.

I think the reason why Bill chose certain people in his circle for the names of characters in his books was that he needed an anchor to reality.

In Bill's seventh book, he used the name of Peggy's distant relative, which didn't sit well with her. However, Peggy never read any of Bill's work. Before Bill and Peggy divorced, she made it clear to him that she didn't feel comfortable being in a position of having to critique his writing. She felt as if it was too much pressure on her.

Bill was eventually published—*hurray!* He quit his teaching position at North Chester University where he taught a creative writing course after he signed a two-year contact with Peak Street Publishing. Even did the whole book tour thing. I was too young to remember any of this, but I do, however, remember traveling to various cities all over the country and staying in hotels and having one of Bill's assistants chaperone me while he was off signing books for fans.

The following years after Peggy and her son, my stepbrother, Christian, who's three years older than me, were welcomed into our house, the book tours weren't nearly as enjoyable as they were when it was just me and the rent-a- assistant who allowed me do whatever I wanted. After a while, we stopped going and we stayed home while Bill was off signing his life away. It was never Bill's intention to become rich or famous, but I guess there was a moment when he thought he "made" it. Who would've thought? A poor kid from Port Landia, South Carolina, turned *All Time* Best-Seller.

Around the time Bill's tenth book came out, which, to him, was a milestone, the industry changed. Because the Internet. Because e-readers. Because a snowball of things. All accumulating to our impending doom. Society hadn't changed, yet it had taken on another form. People were, more or less, adapting in ways this new beast could only predict when introducing the first desktop to the world.

One time when I was younger—maybe when I was around the age of twelve—we were driving home from Blowing Rock and we stopped at a B-rated horror movie diner somewhere in North Carolina.

A loudmouth waitress with a thick Long Island accent asked Bill what he did for a living.

Bill told her that he was a writer.

She let out a throaty laugh and asked Bill, "What do you write? Smut? How do you make a living?"

It wasn't until years later that I realized Bill's profession was in jeopardy. Bill was stuck living in a past that only existed among a small group of people. Paper was no longer the primary medium for publishing. Paper was out. Electronic, in. The change diluted Bill's blood with poison.

I once remember him saying while working on an outline for a new book: "This is the one."

Each book he wrote was "the one."

At least, in Bill's mind.

After each failure, another one would come along. *The One.* If the tenth one (X) didn't make it into readers' hands or make an impact on their lives, then Bill was going to hang up his writing hat on that ole thorny rack, which had a tendency to swallow all kinds of hats. Halfway through drafting his eleventh book, Bill did exactly that. He threw in the white towel and retired that heavy hat.

From that point on, I saw the change in everything Bill did: the way he spoke, ate, talked. Everything about Bill was reptilian, in a way. The change was like watching a force *slowly* suck away all of that glowing positivity. The Hashtag Generation squatted directly over his head and took a loose shit all over him. According to Bill, it was the *Death of The Writer*. The Death of The Writer was—I believe—the death of my father. At least the greatest part of him. Bill claimed that we had been reduced to an *entitled* species, pitiless freeloaders and piggybackers waiting for handouts, a nation divided between the doers and nondoers, haves and have-nots. I didn't understand what he meant until he stopped writing. Taxes were rising every year. Each year, health insurance was becoming more expensive. A visit to the doctor resulted in soup and sandwiches for the rest of the week. Raising a child became more of a burden than a necessary expense. Bill worked at tons of crap jobs on the side to keep a roof over our heads. I felt guilty. I can't tell you how many times I've downloaded a book without paying a penny or illegally downloaded a song or ripped a movie from the Internet. Not once did it ever occur to me that I was literally stealing bread from someone else's mouth. It never occurred to me that I had become exactly what I said I'd never be: a *thief*.

Eventually, Bill went back to teaching at North Chester, but by then, Bill was a different man. He quit teaching right before he and Peggy's relationship took a turn for the worse. Peggy, being a strict petite woman from a small island in the Philippines, whom he tried to convince me that she was "sweet," if I got to know her, even though most of the time all I saw in her was sour, had given Bill multiple opportunities to salvage the relationship: counseling, planning date nights, or *trying* multiple times to birth a child together but ending up leaving the doctor's office disappointed about Bill's infertility. Afterwards he spent his days lounging around the house, feeling sorry for himself.

While Bill was down in the slumps, Peggy's career took off. She became an entrepreneur, a lady determined; and like every entrepreneur, Peggy knew that, in order to be successful in the 21st Century, one most learn how to camouflage to one's surroundings. She ran a company, "Bitchin' Kitchen," a catering service that specialized in already-prepared dishes (fresh or frozen—you pick), casseroles and whatnot, like Chicken Tetrazzini, Chicken Green Bean casserole, Mexican Lasagna, or Baked Ziti to name a few, and, of course, Filipino cuisine, which used to stink up the house, all ready to be thrown in the oven or left in the freezer for another day. She knew her clientele. Peggy's business was primarily focused around working class mothers and fathers who didn't have time to cook for their children. She also catered to other demographics with single-serving dishes, as well as the food she grew up eating, which drew in foodies who, in return, would take photos of their food and post the photos on PhotoBag.

Despite how much I resented the frog-faced judge for allowing Peggy to gain custody over me, I learned to accept her as a mother figure. She had her moments, I guess, and I believe parts of Bill—especially Old Bill and his polished work ethnic—rubbed off on her and now she had become like a moving slot machine always wanting more, more *money, money, money! Money!* You know how the song goes. More money meant more security. Better car. Nicer house. *But* the damage was already done. Their marriage was in shambles. Peggy was in charge of a successful business. Bill was clinging to the past by his fingertips. I think deep down inside the two still had love for one another even though they couldn't stand being in the same room for more than a few minutes at a time. I remember they'd go days without talking. Peggy would threaten Bill—*I want a divorce*, she'd say then storm out of the room and slam the door behind her. Those words were routinely passed around in our household during my adolescence. Then, after days of silence, I walked downstairs and they'd be at the kitchen table, talking and laughing over breakfast. Then, one morning during breakfast, I saw Peggy sitting alone at the table. Bill had left in the middle of the night and checked into a motel. Peggy pulled me aside, sat me down at the table, and broke the news to me. After twelve years of marriage—fourteen, if you include the last two years going through a torn separation where I'd occasionally catch them together at strange hours of the day—Bill and Peggy *finally* decided to "legally" unbind themselves from one another. During the separation, Bill, who, according to the judge, was unfit to financially support me and at the time, was staying in a crummy apartment. My mom, my real one that is, before Peggy, who abandoned me after birth, was MIA and last I heard, was somewhere over in Belize with another man and could've been six feet under, for all I knew. The judge, who was a prick, allowed Bill to visit me once a month. Peggy and Christian returned to using their surname, *Dagohoy*, which, I think means "talisman" on the island where Peggy was born. I kept my last name: Lamb.

Since Bill was currently on what he called a tight budget, I was stuck with Peggy and Christian. Three people sharing one household. Two last names. Except for holidays, I hardly saw Bill after the divorce. Eventually, I stopped seeing him altogether. I'd get a birthday card in the mail. Apparently, Bill changed career paths since writing hit a dead end. He enrolled in online courses and received a bachelor's degree in Counseling. Didn't take long for him to find a job as a guidance counselor since he already had teaching experience.

Just as things were starting to go well for Bill, Peggy received a phone call in the middle of the night.

She woke me up.

I knew it was bad because she never wakes me up.

"Your father was involved in a car accident," she told me.

T-Boned.

He was in bad shape.

Broken ribs.

Broken femur.

Severed spleen.

The left side of his body receiving most of the impact.

He surprised doctors, and made a speedy recovery; however, he was left with a limp when he walked.

The accident brought us closer. For a while, I saw shades of the Old Bill. He'd visit once a month. I thought maybe Peggy would give him a second chance after the accident, but she already moved on with her life. Which brings me to the lures.

Bill and I spent most of our time together fly-fishing along many of the tributaries that fingered off Lake Poe Oakee before our innovative power company, Trade Power, dumped coal ash into Dunleigh River, polluting all of the surrounding towns' drinking water. I didn't mind fly-fishing. Didn't mind, which, to Bill, meant I enjoyed fishing.

A week after we first fished together, he started sending me different kinds of fly lures in the mail. He always did this: whenever I showed any interest in something, like fly-fishing, he'd latch onto it and revolve his entire life around that one particular interest.

One year, I was into skateboarding. Every paycheck, he'd buy me skateboarding stuff: T-shirts, shoes, new decks, elbow guards, knee guards, helmets.

Then came the game systems: first, his hand-me-down Nintendo consoles, Turbo Graphics, Sega Genesis, which were like these prehistoric artifacts. Then, he decided to upgrade by buying me consoles from my era: Playstations and X-Boxes. He'd latch onto that one interest until I eventually grew out of it. I have an entire closet full of discarded interests. I seriously could open a store called *Discarded Interests*.

Christian, on the other hand, was the total opposite of me and if you compared us to, say, shopping carts, he was the shopping cart that did exactly what it was intended to do while I came with slight resistance, like that one cart with a lopsided wheel, which had been bent after either hitting the side of a wing stack and whenever it was pushed, it'd flutter like a fish out of water, or being crushed by the tire of a car while it was left stranded in an empty parking lot and whenever it was pushed, it'd drag along the ground and force the other three good wheels to do all the work. For Bill and Peggy, Christian was an easy kid to raise; he found an interest in airplanes and pursued a path that would further his education in electrical engineering. Despite Bill's failures as a father, I always knew he was trying to make me happy. A part of me felt bad for not sticking with only one interest like Christian and his engines and airplanes. Not until a few months ago, I started to see a change in Bill; in fact, the last time I saw him, he seemed not all there. Like the time he he stopped writing and drifted from one job to another. He was a stranger yet again, a man possessed. I sometimes wondered if this was what the real Bill was like, this miserable sap who not only hated the paths that he chose for himself, but also hated himself, and throughout my childhood, I was living with an imposter, an incredibly brilliant writer who was destined for greatness. Instead, it was all a front, and he turned out to be a fraud, a hack. A flawed man who was anything *but* decent.

I sometimes wondered if I had the gene, too. Not the creative bone. The mean bone. Wrapped in skin so thin that it could easily tear. The blood of a Lamb. I often ask myself: Are these the gifts our fathers leave us, not fly lures, but their misery?

I skim over the letter. Bill tells me that he misses me and looks forward to our next fishing trip. I go to my room and place the artificial fly inside the frame of other flies.

2

I check the news again.

More protests.

How come those who advocate for love come off as the most violent, abrasive, loud, and aggressive?

I love hearing such good news.

Another person was killed. Pulled a gun on a cop. The cop unloaded on the man. The man was pronounced dead on the scene. Later, they found out that the gun was empty. I return to my blog and tell the people of the Internet what they want to hear.

3

Peggy's running late. It's twenty-three minutes past seven when she arrives home and I've already filled up on what she'd call junk food. She's complaining about the traffic, which isn't out of the ordinary.

Over the past two years, Spartacus started to lose its small time vibe. It's still a rather small town compared to the surrounding cities, like Atlanta, Greenville, Charlotte. The census three years ago was in the ballpark of twenty-five thousand, and I'm sure the number has grown quite dramatically since then. More trees have been cut down, making room for more housing developments and shopping malls that'll inevitably go under. More construction, blocked roads, and detours, more traffic. Every now and then, a new bank will pop up on the street corner. A new fast food joint. And every now and then, a new fast food joint will be forced to close or delay opening due to a shortage of employees. If Spartacus had its own flag, it'd have a cartoon caricature of a drunk redneck with a cigarette hanging from his mouth while hanging out the window of his monster truck with a "Jesus Saves" bumper sticker and buck horns tied to the front grate and the tailpipe spewing thick black cloud of exhaust fumes, and speeding to a worksite while trash flies from the back of the tailgate, littering the highway. Lately, on the contrary, I've seen more locals on street corners, holding up signs like "Need work, not money." I've seen less small businesses around the town. The ones that have been here since the beginning remain thriving; however, a couple of them, like Henry's Bar and Grill, had to relocate across town to make room for a food-chain restaurant where the food tastes like it was nuked in a microwave. Henry could've taken the money and left Spartacus, but, like most locals, he stayed. It feels like Spartacus has been recently added to a level in the *Sims* game. Just another cut and paste town, which was once special but now looks like any other town infected by corporate greed and the arrogant display of power. They're also building a shopping center directly behind the Shoe Company. A movie theatre. Not like the old and majestic Paramount I frequent downtown, but a massive box with over twenty screens. Coffee Hut. Another Super-Mart. Like we don't have enough of them already. It's almost as if Spartacus is preparing or—dare I say—in the works of becoming a city ready to welcome in corporations that consume everything they touch. Most locals who have grown up in Spartacus are ready for the fight. I'm ready for my popcorn. But make sure not to destroy the reels.

As Peggy sets her things on the kitchen countertop, I notice she's brought home one of her bestsellers, spinach and mushroom quiche with a couple of sides, special mashed cauliflower and a pasta salad with chunks of red pepper and eggplant.

Despite being somewhat full, I fix a plate while Peggy washes off her day. I grab the food and throw it on a plate before the scripted line comes out of her mouth. Peggy doesn't say a word. I pour myself a drink and as I'm about to take the food into the living room, I stop at the doorway. I don't hear anything from Peggy, not a word. She keeps to herself.

"I dropped off the job application," I tell her as she dries her hands over the sink.

"That's good," she says and lets out one of her trademark sighs. "Well, how'd it go today?"

"It was fine," I say.

"That's it." She crosses her arms—an old gesture I haven't seen in a while, one that she used to give me whenever she was upset or talking to the obnoxious neighbors.

"Yeah," I say. "Fine," I repeat. "The manager wasn't there. So, I just dropped it off. I talked to some girl who worked there. She was nice."

"Good." She grabs a bottle of Chardonnay from the wine rack and pours herself a glass of wine.

I take the food to my room and eat by myself.

4

I wait until Peggy leaves the kitchen before bringing down the dirty dishes.

I quietly place the dishes in the sink, hoping not to attract Peggy or lure her into a conversation. I check the wine bottle next to the sink, and it's half full. So far, she has already worked through two, or possibly three, glasses of wine. I also notice the quiche. A wedge is missing, and it happens to be from the wedge I've already eaten. The sides only have a scoop missing. Untouched since I last saw it. I place the food back in the fridge to keep it from spoiling.

As I leave the kitchen, I catch a glow in the corner of my eye. Peggy sits in front of her computer, a glass of wine dangling from one hand, bloodshot eyes glued to the monitor. The office is dim, too, as if she didn't even have the stamina to flip on a light. I stand in the hallway, waiting for Peggy to acknowledge me. She doesn't.

5

I'm watching a live feed from Phantasy Worldz when all of a sudden I hear a voice from the doorway—*Whatcha doing?*

I turn my shoulder, only to find Peggy standing at the doorway as if she's been there for a while.

"Knock much," I say, flipping through channels.

"Sor*ry*," she says.

The room goes silent. I land on a movie where someone is getting hosed down by a machine gun. Lots and lots of screaming involved. Gallons of blood spraying everywhere.

"Hey, listen," Peggy says over the screaming TV. "I'm going to be running late tomorrow. So you're going to have to get your own dinner. Okay?"

"Whatever—" I say, flipping through channels.

"—You take your meds today?" she says curiously. She squints her eyes, as if she's honing in on a lie, as if a lie is a tangible thing, something that can be seen or touched if one looks hard enough.

Either Peggy's been snooping around my room again or my pale mask is starting to slip away.

"Yeah," I say snappishly. Then, I reverse the soon-to-be interrogation and ask concernedly, "You okay?"

"Long day," she says with a half-smile on her face. "That's all."

She says goodnight and closes the door behind her.

6

After spending hours watching the same news coverage on Phantasy Worldz, I flip it the local news where I watch a breaking story about the storeowner of an antiques shop who turned down a customer based on his age. The customer is an elderly man in his late seventies, and he was rejected and forced to leave the antique shop because the store-owner, a woman in his early thirties, felt extremely uncomfortable in his presence. She claimed that she was having "a severe panic attack." The news reporter interviews the customer, who's bewildered by the incident and can't believe he received such treatment. He claims he did nothing wrong, but I must wonder if there's more to the story. Despite the increasing trend of mistreatment against elderly people around the country based on a concoction of issues, ranging from the new—and deadly—strain of whooping cough to the recent spike in verbal attacks and condemnation, even physical assaults, against a younger demographic to a basic way of life, like the other stories which often lack any quality video evidence, it's hard to believe the story to be true. The elderly man was looking for an anniversary gift for a close friend. According to his story, the storeowner refused his business. She called the cops after he failed to comply and said he started to "attack" her, which, according to the elderly man, is not true. He was only questioning why she wouldn't allow him to shop inside her establishment. He's incredibly distraught. At this point, I don't know what to think of the story. For now, it seems as though it's a story that can certainly pick up *steam* if it winds up on other news outlets—that is, depending on whether or not, how far he wants to run with the story.

I need more information.

7

I can't sleep.

All I can think about is fire.

I check the time. I've only been asleep for thirty minutes, and it feels as if it's been hours.

I decide to roll out of bed and get on my computer.

I pull up the Internet and gumshoe that recent story, which previously aired on WSS-3, ELDERLY MAN GETS TURNED DOWN AT ANTIQUES & THINGS. The shop is located about forty miles from here in Kernelson, a town similar to Spartacus, only much smaller in population. Elmira Brown is the name of the storeowner. She has a MyCircle page, which she rarely keeps up to date, and most of it, except for a couple of selfies taken at the shop or decorative and heavily filtered pics of "new antiques," has nothing to do with Antiques & Things. She frequently posts pics of leisurely activity, such as hanging out with her friends at sporting events or pounding fireball shots at bars or spending weekend getaways in the Appalachian Mountains. She's single and adventurous, from what I can tell, and spends the weekends with her girlfriends. After Elmira, I gumshoe the elderly man who was kicked out of the antique shop. His name: Ronnie "Road Runner" Shields. Before his retirement, he was once a distinguished photographer from Manhattan. Did a lot of work for fashion magazines. Also put out two self-published photography books: one, *Colorblind*, a black and white portrayal of America with various cityscapes throughout the county and all the different faces of the land, all shot in black and white, and then the other one, *Coloring Truth*, sort of a "what if" type of book where each photo is photoshopped with filters, creating a somewhat trippy experience. Both of the books did well on the market. He earned his nickname "Road Runner" from his participation in marathons. He runs frequently, even till this day, runs six miles every day. Apparently, Ronnie was passing through South Carolina. The latest PhotoBag post suggests that he was on the way to a friend's barbeque in Athens, passed through Kernelson, saw a lovely little antique shop, decided to stop, turned down, and then, according to Elmira, made a scene. Then, he called the Channel 3 news team and here I am, contemplating my next move.

I put my computer to sleep and grab a Tennessee license plate from the closet. I stare over the plates before finally making up my mind. I change into my night outfit and sneak out while Peggy's sleeping. I change the plates, grab a plastic tube for siphoning from the garage, as well as a 5-gallon gas can, and place them in the back of Maximus.

When I arrive in Kernelson, it's a little after two o'clock. The town is silent. Not too much activity, except for an occasional night owl, like myself, stumbling from a stinky bar. I make a pit stop in a sketchy neighborhood and siphon gasoline from several parked cars and fill up my gas can before I drive to the antique shop off Main Street.

I park the car a couple of blocks away from the shop and scope out the area.

I search for surveillance cameras, but I don't find any. Usually small towns like these don't have cameras because everybody knows one another, which, means everybody trusts one another—mostly.

I check the windows and peek inside.

Nobody's home.

I check the street, the parking lot.

No cars.

I'm ready.

I head back to my car, grab the gasoline, and then check my surroundings.

Once it's all clear, I kick off a loose brick from the corner of the building and toss it through the door window! No alarm, just as expected.

I clear away the shards of glass with my gloved hand, slip my arm through the glass without cutting myself, and unlock the door from the inside.

I call out a couple of hellos once I'm inside. Just as I thought, nobody's home.

I open the gas can and dowse the entire antique shop with gasoline, starting at the front where a miniature train set wraps around a table of antique clocks of all shapes and sizes. I take a moment to look over the train set. I used to own one when I was younger—actually, I used to own a similar one, if not the same. At the time, I was six or seven, I think. Bill didn't have a lot of money, except for an advance he received from the first book deal. I remember he worked at a store that specialized in stationery for a couple of months. I didn't know why he worked there until he came home on the night of my sixth—or seventh—birthday with a rectangular box underneath his arm. He lugged the box into the kitchen where Peggy finished placing six or seven candles into the birthday cake. I tore open the wrapping paper, as if I was a lion ripping through a fresh kill, fade to black. . . I work my way to the back of the antique store and dowse the vacant picture frames and mirrors along the walls.

Then, lastly, I leave a trail of gasoline along the floor as I make my way back outside.

I set the gasoline on fire with a match and watch the flames lick their way across the floor, like slow motion, then spread to each shelf and wall.

I admire the flames briefly, but only briefly, then I'm out, as if I was never even there.

3
.:.

POV – Destroyed beyond repair – Mad world – A Gaping Generational Divide – No more olives – Human error – *Peggy's Gotta Secret* – Missing a domino – Planning a fishing trip – Time bomb

THE next morning, I relish in the aftermath of my handiwork. The town of Kernelson burned to the ground. Throughout the middle of the night, the fires ended up spreading to the other neighboring businesses—which was never my intention. Firefighters didn't even show up until several hours after the initial fire. One half of downtown destroyed beyond repair. Reporters from various news outlets are interviewing locals, who stand at a safe distance and watch the towering flames. Their glossy eyes wrapped in tears. Storeowners, whose businesses were eaten up by the fire, are present as well, and they can hardly stand on their own two feet. Even Elmira Brown is on the scene, balling her eyes out. The reporter asks her if the fire had anything to do with the elderly man, Ronnie Shields, whom I can assume is being questioned by authorities right about now.

One journalist ends up tracking down Ronnie later that morning, and he's equally distressed about the whole ordeal. He claims he had "absolutely no involvement" in starting the fire, even states that he has already spoken with police. He has an alibi and publicly states, for the record, he was "not in Kernelson" when the fires were started nor, despite last night's story, bares any ill-will against Brown or her establishment. I hang around the house most of the day. Peggy leaves a twenty-dollar bill, as well as a note telling me to grab dinner on my own tonight because she has an important meeting with investors who are more than interested in expanding her Bitchin' Kitchen business.

The assistant manager of the Shoe Company, a guy in his early forties, gives me a call while I'm halfway through eating the rest of the pasta salad from last night. He wants to schedule an interview. With an upbeat voice, I tell him my schedule is wide open and I'm ready to work. He schedules an interview for Thursday at eleven o'clock AM. I've lost my appetite once I get through talking to the assistant manager, who, from the rigged tone of his voice, sounds as if he needs to get laid more. What's his name? I've already forgotten his name.

I lounge around for most of the day and spend the daylight inside burning my eyes with TV radiation. Nothing notable has surfaced over mainstream or social media. The local news runs a loop of the same coverage from earlier this morning.

I step outside for a breath of fresh air and rest my eyes and when I return, a BREAKING NEWS report flashes on the TV screen; however, the channel is stuck on YNN, not the local news.

Apparently, the story has spread to the cable news channels.

Another fire, *not* mine.

Most of the art district west of Downtown Kernelson is up in flames. The art district, which was gentrified four years ago, has a strip of modern day businesses, a Yoga studio, an art gallery, salon, and Yogurt bar to name a few, on South Dandie Street, known as "SODA." They even have a high-end clothing store called FAB+, which, according to locals, has drawn a lot of outsiders into Kernelson. New reports vary with each channel. One channel, Century I believe, claims the owner of FAB+ made a controversial post on social media last year along with the release of an edgy line of post-apocalyptic wear, which was made of leather, resulting in the anti-leather activists to infiltrate SODA, mainly targeting FAB+ and the surrounding businesses; however, whatever the cause of the fire, the images don't lie. The Yoga studio, art gallery, FAB+, all blanketed with flames. Over a dozen people transported to the hospital with life-threatening injuries. Pockets of violent riots have broken out all around Kernelson. Most rioters disguised themselves with hoodies and bandannas. Rocks and bricks and street paraphernalia seem to be the most effective weapons of their choice. On-the-ground journalists scramble around the chaotic scene, trying to prod interviews from what the reporters call peaceful protesters, who are cheering on FAB+'s inevitable demise, and civilians, who are caught in the madness. A body camera shows shaky footage of an unarmed black clad kid charging at a cop positioned behind a squad car. The cop tells the kid to freeze or he'll shoot. The kid, jacked-up by rage, rips off his shirt and doesn't break stride. The veteran cop, "fearful for his life," as he'll later reveal in a released statement, fires three gunshots, one bullet striking the kid's chest, instantly killing him, thus sparking more protests and outrage around the country. People are pointing fingers and blaming the other side, *not* their own. The tribes are beginning to take shape.

Can it really be this easy?

2

An hour passes, and I'm craving pizza, but I don't feel like leaving the house. Too much chaos is happening on all my devices.

As more ads with close-ups of stringy, melting, cheesy pizza flash across the TV screen, I decide to use the twenty Peggy gave me and order a large pizza with pepperoni, mushrooms, and extra black olives from Mario's.

As usual, the deliveryman is running twenty minutes late. The pizza costs $12^{50}. I hand him a twenty. In return, he hands me the greasy box of pizza. I check the pizza, and it's missing black olives. I voice the wrong order, but all I get in return is a harmless shrug. I want to say something to him and ask him why you or your fellow coworkers can't carry out the simple task of taking orders—the last two times I've ordered pizza from you and each time, the order was screwed up or missing a topping!

I bite my tongue. For one, I'm too hungry. Two, I'm not in the mood to waste my time arguing with this shaggy-hair stoner who'll probably forget our conversation by the time he drives back to the restaurant. Three, I'm in a hurry to get back to the news.

The deliveryman hands me a five, as if he's earned the extra two dollar and fifty cents for driving the two miles to get here. I tell him that the pizza cost twelve-fifty. He rolls his eyes and digs his hand into his pocket and fishes out two crinkled dollars and two quarters and slams the rest of the money in my palm.

I hand him a quarter and as I close the door behind me, I hear him mumble the word *asshole*. He's ten minutes late with the pizza. Not only that, he gives me the wrong change, which makes me believe that clearly, either he doesn't know how to count or he thinks driving around town delivering pizzas and dealing with the *real* assholes on the road, is worth the less than mediocre tip and he's entitled to the two dollars and fifty cents. I can relate to the latter part of what the job entails. I hate driving, not because of the driving part, but because of the other drivers on the road. Not only that, they left off the best topping: black olives! If the deliveryman gave me back the correct change, I would've gladly given him a tip that was greater than a quarter, which, I know, is insulting. If he didn't roll his eyes at me, I would've gladly given him a tip. If he sincerely apologized for leaving off black olives, I would've more than gladly given him a tip and taken the wrong order as a fault of miscommunication. If the deliveryman did even one of those things, like given me the correct change, or not show an attitude toward me, apologize for the order wrong, I would've let him keep the entire twenty. He's right. I'm the asshole.

3

Peggy's back to being her usual talkative self the moment she steps through the door. She's lying to me. Her cheeks are flushed. She's carrying a wide drunken smile; however, she doesn't appear intoxicated—at least, not from alcohol. She notices the greasy pizza box on the counter. I make sure to leave it where she can see it. That way she knows I've been using the money she's been giving me and not pocketing it for other items besides food. Peggy pours herself a glass of water from the pitcher of purified water and between sips, fires off a round of questions: How was your day? What'd you do today? You hear back from the Shoe place? I answer all the questions with short answers.

Fine.

Nothing.

Yeah.

Then, I hide my head in another room.

4

Firefighters, including ones from Shiloh, the town next to Kernelson, eventually gain control over the fires in the art district area.

As I'm about to close my eyes, another BREAKING NEWS flashes on TV. I rise from bed and turn up the volume. The news is covering a story about yet another fire at a rehabilitation center. I read the scroll below: REHAB BURNED IN WAKE OF PROTESTS.

Firefighters are trying to control the flames with fire hoses, but the flames are massive and they're chewing their way through the entire building. The patients, once housed inside, are standing outside, slouched and sickly-looking while others hooting and hollering and jumping around as if they're at a rock concert.

The camera pans to the right where a reporter comes back into frame and says the name of the rehab: "Fellowship For All."

They still don't know who's responsible for the fire. The arsonist—the copycat—is still at large. This is how it starts.

5

I wake up bright and early, more refreshed, knowing that soon the world will be mine. Soon, people will start eating one another, like in the Cannibal Games, and by the time they fall to extinction—at this rate, I'll give them a few months—I'll have the world all to myself. While scrolling through my feed on social media, I read that a church was set on fire last night. News outlets, however, never reported the story, at least not yet. Soon, the outrage will spread like the common cold. I can see trends like #BurnBabyBurn or #HellFreezesOver in the not-so distant future. The trend will spread to other countries. People will catch the firebug and burn down all remaining structures all around the world, consequently destroying all hope and humanity. I'll have to wait it out, of course, until the chaos finally ends. But it'll be worth the wait.

I go downstairs and pour a glass of orange juice before checking the news. I notice Peggy has slept in, which is unusual. She wakes up not too long after she hears me rummaging through the kitchen for a bite to eat. She's perky and hasn't even had her cup of coffee yet.

"You're not working today?" I ask Peggy, as she ambles toward the coffee machine, going through the motions of making her daily coffee.

"I've decided to take a half-day," Peggy says, yawning. "Nadia's going to be taking care of things today."

"Oh—okay."

"By the way, I talked to Bill yesterday."

That's the first time she's mentioned his name in weeks.

The first thing that comes to mind: *What happened?*

"You did?" I ask Peggy.

She proceeds to pour water into the coffee machine. Scoops a spoonful of coffee grounds into a filter.

"He was thinking about maybe moving up the fishing trip to this weekend instead of next."

"What do you mean 'this weekend'?"

"I mean *this* weekend—don't be a stinker."

"But I already have plans this weekend."

Peggy closes the lid to the coffee machine.

"You can cancel them, Josh," she says as she faces me. "What's more important? You know how much these fishing trips mean to him—"

"Yeah," I say. "I know. I just wish he'd give me a heads up before he readjusts his whole life around me."

"Then call him." She turns back around and programs the coffee machine. "I'm not going to get between the two of you." She leaves the kitchen and says over her shoulder, "Call him."

6

I call Bill, and we agree to bump up the fishing trip to this weekend. We don't talk that much over the phone, which I know kills Bill because he's eager to know what I've been up to since the last time we saw each other. I know he's saving the conversations for the fishing trip. After I get off the phone with Bill, I check the headlines. I expect to see more riots. I expect to see more chaos. I expect to see rivers of blood running down streets of each city across America. Straight-up carnage. Severed heads on spears. Cannibalistic tribes forming around the gallows in

front of a backdrop of burning buildings, landmarks, and toppling structures. Hordes of looters breaking into whatever stores that haven't been
touched by the flames. I don't see any of that. Instead, members of
three churches in Kernelson are holding peace rallies throughout the
town. The hospitals have made accommodations for those affected by
the fires, including patients at Fellowship. Several other surrounding
cities around the South and along the East Coast are having peace rallies, as well.

Now, I'm outraged.

What's going on?

4

Red shirt - Lost in translation - The job interview - The Enabler Part II - Bombshells - A town trying to recover - Raising the bar - Having self-doubts - #Joshua - Mostly clear now, mostly

---

I show up to the job interview wearing a red Polo shirt that my aunt Marlene—Peggy's older sister—gave me. The Polo looks way too big on me, two sizes too big, and the sleeves hang well over my elbows. The only thing Peggy and I have in common is that we both don't care much for Marlene. In others words, we don't get along with Marlene. I wouldn't go as far to say that Peggy hates her older sister. They just don't get along too well, and they're always fighting about trivial things, like Peggy not taking her shoes off when entering the house and tracking in mud all over the floors or leaving the back door open and letting bugs inside the house or forgetting to bring over the Crock pot that Peggy borrowed from Marlene. Everything is either a judging contest or a competition for them. They both try to outdo one another with everything they do, even when it comes down to their husbands. Peggy married a writer and then divorced a writer. A couple of months later after Peggy's marriage, Marlene outdid her little sis by marrying a man from Ohio named Lance Chadwick. Lance was an actor, mediocre one at best. Their marriage didn't last, though. Lance was a manipulative psychopath who once starred in the soap opera, *Times of Our Lives.* Years later, Lance wound up doing voice-overs for hokey TV commercials constantly running during the afternoons on the Family channel, like advertising a new drug on the market—his charming voice wheedling an old fart about all of the side effects of the drug. He also did toothpaste commercials. At least every time I see Liquidy Lance on TV, smiling with his perfect white teeth and his liquidy voice, I can say, "Hey, I know that guy. He's the piece of shit who tried to ruin my aunt's life." Mad props to Marlene for possessing the courage to leave that shit-stain. She dumped his ass and flushed him down the toilet, like the manipulative, egotistical turd he was. After Lance, Marlene married an interior designer. Not only did she outdo her little sis, but she also outdid herself. I remember the day she gave me the Polo. It was Christmas three years ago. Christian, who was currently attending his first year at State, drove back home to spend the winter break with Bill, since Bill and Peggy were still at odds. Peggy and I flew to upstate New York where we visited her sister and her "better" family with her "better" husband. I'll never forget what Marlene said to me that day. Any other day, those comments would've gone in one ear and out the other; however, since it was the holidays and I was feeling particularly ripe for confrontation or attention—depending how you want to look at it—Marlene and her comments stuck like splinters under my skin and the more and more I thought about them, the more I tried to pick at them or dig them out, the more they burrowed. I'll set the scene:

> Christmas night. Our plates are made, steam slithers upward from the food, and everybody's sitting around the table, waiting for the food to cool off as they sip from glasses of Pinot Noir and lather butter onto bread and stuff their faces and compliment Marlene on the wonderful spread; then, all of a sudden, the conversation turns to a topic, which I prefer to ignore, the one where you have to "explain" what you've been doing with your life for the past year. The year summary. Like all of the shit you've done throughout the year printed on the sleeve of a hardback. I would've been around fifteen, and usually, a couple of words were enough to summarize an entire year. School. Movies. Music. Girls. Injuries. Followed with a brief description. Marlene asks me what I've been up to, her tone one of deep concern. I keep my answer as short as possible, Peggy mostly doing the talking for me. Then, here comes Marlene with her comment launching like a stealth missile underneath her breath: *He's just like his father.* That was the first comment. Then, the second one came the day after Christmas.

I'll set the scene:

> I'm playing *Dreamcast*—a first-person shooter, I think—with my Cousin Gabriel—Gabe, for short. Marlene steps into Gabe's bedroom, wine glass in hand like a cigarette, her speech wet and loose with alcohol as she sways back and forth like a boat at the doorway. She's telling us to quit being so antisocial and hang out with us—*us*, meaning the rest of the fam.

I know exactly why they want Gabe and me to hang out downstairs from the constant thump of the low end of the stereo rattling the floors. At times, they treat Gabe and me like dancing monkeys. Eventually, Gabe caves in and does as Marlene tells him. Then, Marlene turns to me, wearing a strange expression on her face as she waits for me to respond to the question that she never asks. The expression, I know, is the question. She steps out of the room, mumbling the words *go figure*. During these times, I hate Marlene. Same with her stuck-up family. I hate every single one of them, except for Gabe, who, like Christian, acts as if he never wants to be at these family gatherings. Maybe it's a cultural thing, I tell myself, or the negative results of overbearing parents who smother and use their own children for entertainment, or maybe Marlene is frustrated by our lack of involvement and wants us to participate and show more effort in these family gatherings. I'd like to think that Gabe doesn't always enjoy my company because Marlene is embarrassing him in front of me. Next, I'm waiting at the very top of the landing, eavesdropping on the words being whispered about me, like a barbaric tribe discussing what they should do about the outsider upstairs. What's wrong with him? I hear Peggy defending me: he's going through a phase. We were once that age. Then, Marlene chimes in: That boy has issues. I go back to Gabe's room and think about what they're saying about me. I mainly think about those two comments, the one about my father and the other, *go figure*. What does that even mean? Go figure? Go fish?

Go to hell—*Excuse me.*
I turn to the manager sitting at the desk.
"I didn't say anything," I tell him
He guides me into a cramped office, which is located in the back of the store. He tells me to take a seat across from his cluttered desk. I sit down while he goes over my job application.
"I see you have a lot of experience in retail," he says as he reads off the many other jobs I've had.
"That's correct," I say.
He keeps reading off the other jobs. I've written down way too many. I thought that it might backfire on me, an eighteen year old who has already worked over six jobs in the past year. I had to be honest, though. Employers like honesty.
He scratches his goatee, tosses my job application on the desk, and asks, "How do I know you won't quit two weeks from now?"
I carefully think about the answer.

The manager waits on my answer.

My throat tightens. The saliva in my mouth becomes loose and watery and as I'm about to answer his question, the Swirly O's I ate before the interview start to climb up my throat. I try to hold them down, but the manager tightens his jaw, both muscles on the side of his face flex like tiny fists. I bolt from the chair and let it rip. . .

"What the—"

The manager bolts upright from his chair, his arms spread out in utter perplexity as more vomit projects from my mouth and onto his desk. He looks down at the clumps of vomit covering his shirt, then looks up. His face as red as a cherry. I can't help but laugh at how silly he looks right now.

The only word I can say as the manager glares at me is *oops.*

"Gee-zus," he seethes, "get the hell outta here!"

I leave, not embarrassed, not ashamed. It wasn't the right job for me, anyway.

2

When Peggy returns home from work, I tell her that the job interview went great and they'll call me whenever they've made up their mind. She holds her eyes on me for a moment too long, as if she's sifting through my lies. Then, she turns her shoulder and asks me, with her back facing me, if I was nervous going into the interview. Not missing a beat, I tell her, "Nah. I wasn't *that* nervous." Then, she goes on to ask me more questions about what I ate today. She moves from one spot of the kitchen to another, checking cabinets, then the pantry, searching for something to eat, first grabbing a nearly empty box of Swirly O's but there's not enough cereal to fill up a bowl. She notices certain items of food have been disappearing lately. I tell her that lately I've had the appetite of a pregnant woman but, obviously, I haven't put any meat on my bones. I'm still as skinny as a rail.

3

Friday is a complete wash. There's nothing much going on in the news. A guy—or girl, cops aren't sure at this point—dressed up in a Frankenstein's monster mask robbed a bank. He's—or she's—hit three banks in the past month. Each time, the person wears a different Halloween mask. Last week, the robber was Dracula.

Out of curiosity, I drive to Kernelson and first, cruise through the downtown area, which looks like a war zone. One side of Main Street is blocked off. Camera crews are stationed throughout the scene and filming a group of people with rollers painting over graffiti from the charred buildings in West End, as well as the art district, SODA, and scrubbing away conflicting slurs and slogans like *Babykillers* or *Angry Puppies* or *Hot Dawgs* or more intolerantly driven ones, like *Get the eff outta our way* or *da Pasture's callin' U* or *Click, Click, Boom* or *X-Out*, referring to Generation X, which I can only imagine will one day be replaced with the letter Z; also, another popular one that has been making rounds throughout Chatterzsphere is World War X, which, again, refers to the generation of the same letter.

Locals are holding a candlelight vigil for that one kid who was slain by the cop, now currently on administrative leave. I drive by the Fellowship. The rehabilitation center. Nothing remains of the building. I drive by a church, which was also destroyed in the wake of the fires, but all that remains is a pile of charred ruins.

4

When I return home, it's two o'clock in the morning and I'm exhausted from the mental strain of wondering why my whole master plan hasn't come to fruition. Do I need to kick it up a notch? Do I need to quit relying on people to do my bidding and start pushing the ball myself? First off: What do people love, and how can I turn them against one another? Food? Reality TV shows? Celebrities? Football? And dogs! What if I found a way to rid all of the dogs in the world? Or, even better, what if I found a way to turn the dogs against people or vice versa? An implant or collar that can rewire a dog's brain to kill? Or, a *doggy whistle that can turn that sweet Golden Retriever into a rabid beast?* People would no longer look at dogs as their friends or therapeutic companions. Yet, over time, because, really, it'd take a lot of time, they'd think of a once four-legged furry friend as a savage creature ready to dig into their flesh—same goes for all animals, except cats, of course—and perhaps, by changing this way of thinking, they'll convert back over to the most primitive instincts and eventually, everybody would start eating each other once all of the animals have gone extinct. Then, again, what about the actual vegans, not the ones pretending to be vegan? I could even start one of those "WE" challenges, like drinking poison or maybe something less conspicuous that results in death, and in return, proceeds supposedly go to a shady organization that raises awareness for a disease; however, once people start dropping like flies, people will raise awareness of the harmful effects of the challenge and the gig would be up before the shit hits the fan. If there's one thing this country is good at, it's raising awareness.

I turn on the news and search for the next hot-button issue. I flip through local news channels, one report claiming the cops have found the arsonist responsible for the fire before the segment cuts to commercial break. I rush to the windows, scan the neighborhood, and there, two houses down, a black Lincoln is parked on the street. I see subtle movements inside the car. I can't see the shadowy face of the driver; however, there is, in fact, a dark figure sitting behind the steering wheel. Before I left Kernelson on the night I set fire to the antique store, I made sure not to leave any evidence behind. I was extremely careful, as I always am. More than likely, cops have my license plate from a street camera—possibly, maybe—but that's not a problem because the plate wasn't mine, yet it was a plate that I pulled from a broken down Volvo.

I check the skies and listen closely for any approaching helicopters. I hear one, but it's trailing farther away. I glance down at my hands, and they're shaking. I can't help but stare at those pinkish scars running horizontally along the veins of my forearms.

My arms seem as if they don't belong to me, and for a moment, I forget about the scars.

I stop and think: What the hell am I doing here? What if they're all wrong? *What if* there is, in fact, a world beyond here? A world much better than this dreadful place? I didn't make anything of myself in this life, so why not try again in the next?

The fact: They don't care about me, and they never have. They don't care about me when I'm alive. Why in the hell will they remember me when I'm dead?

Here today.

Gone tomorrow.

I'm utterly irrelevant. What will become of my name when I'm gone? What mark will I leave behind? If so, what will it be? Just some unbalanced kid who disappeared from society? Another punk kid who couldn't find his way in life? Arsonist Number 2? I can't be known as an arsonist. Of all things, I can't be the kid who starts fires. Maybe the kid who played with fire. Sounds like the title of a book: *The Kid Who Played With Fire.* I wouldn't mind that. Not at all. But what if I don't make it before The Fall?

When I'm gone, will I be *trending* on the Internet? Even worse, will my name turn into a hashtag, only to be swept under the rug of social media?

Disturbed kid takes his own life after battling severe depression.

— #Joshua

They always have a name for something.

Your disease.

Your existence.

When did all of this start?

Hating the way I look?

My skin?

Often times I find myself being the most comfortable in my skin when it's at its palest, when the circles underneath my eyes are dark and everything around it is ghostly. Sometimes, I feel as if I could vanish into the ether where no would ever be able to see me. Imagine the freedom, being unseen like that, drifting around like the *Invisible Man*, messing with people, flipping off their hats, giving them wedgies.

No matter what, there'll always be someone out there, someone with a checkmark of approval, who wants to make an example out of something or someone.

Two-faced impostors who share the same idiosyncrasy as pedophiles posing as priests. As sneaking as car salesmen. Bending you over in order to complete the sale by using fancy words like *"radiant ember."*

Happy idiots who hand out bumper sticker-morals while, at the same time, steal the change from the dirty Styrofoam cup of someone who smells like the bottom of a shoe.

Grifters-in-disguise.

How about this one, Mr. Approval: *#Vulnerable*.

Another label for Mr. Approval to stick on your forehead, another brand, another hashtag for those who fail to pass His purity tests. Being upset—because that's what it really is, a severe case of the blues, me feeling down in the dumps, blah—it's like any other feeling, one of the plethora of emotions people deal with during the course of their lives. I took it too far—but how far is too far? How deep can the blade cut before hitting bone? The last I checked: I'm still here. Lost or simply prone to that awful feeling of blah? But there's always one prick in the Hashtag Generation who wants to benefit from your emotion—let alone, benefit from "your" story in general. The One who wants to, according to His point of view, "change" the world the way He sees fit without taking into account someone else's personal choice. Forcing impractical ideas on everybody. The One telling you how you should eat, think, what to eat, what to do. . . *How am I any different from* Mr. Approval?

Why didn't you see warning signs sooner, Mr. Approval, since you care so much about me? Why didn't you save me? He was too busy lubricating His nose and rubbing it in other people's cheeks—that's why. Chum swimming with the stream while gathering His flock, leeches who contribute nothing to society other than sucking away at the marrow of life. Mr. Approval, that half-idealist, half-opportunist, full-time narcissist. What a joke? Prancing along with His new shoes His vulnerable subscribers bought Him for keeping it real. Taking "selfies" of Himself throughout the day. Look at me, He posts. I'm at Revile Park, squeezing in a mile before the start of the day. *Selfie*. I'm at Golden Gate, yolo. *Selfie*. I'm having lunch with Craig the Benefactor, chilling at León Brioche. *Selfie*. I am, in fact, God's greatest creation, a unique and flawless collective. *Selfie!* And now, I'm worming my way into your house, into your computer, into your brain. Surprise!!! *Selfie.* Then here He goes with His campaign, as if Mr. Approval taking a million selfies of Himself wasn't enough: Let's be more informative about this deadly disease, He tells people as He steals all the credit and uses all the money he receives from all the clicks and views he gets to buy himself a brand new Hummer. Sometimes I want to seek out Mr. Approval in the broad daylight, catch Him off guard, and then, when he's not looking, bash His brains in. Sometimes, I just want to let loose the animal inside me. Sometimes, I just want to *feel* alive.

The news comes back on and snaps me from my trance. It's not me, but, of course, it's not me.

I check the windows once more, waiting for red and blue flashes of sirens to light up the house. A helicopter spotlight shining down on my face, then a Seagal-like voice behind the intercom: "Come out with your hands up! You're completely surrounded!"

I turn up the volume on the TV.

The kid's name is George Hollan. Twenty-three years of age. Native of Eastwood, Colorado. He's a college student at Creighton Community College. He doesn't live in Kernelson; he doesn't even live in the same state. Nonetheless, I'm in the clear for now.

I watch the news for the next two hours or so, searching for my salvation.

America wants to know: 'Who is George Hollan?' – Good karma – Men and their toys – The Highwayman – "On the road again" – Chattooga River – A fair fight – Women and their needs – Don't go in there! – The turning point – How to make a bomb?

I wake up with cold feet. My toes like ice cubes. I feel an unrest inside my gut, like a stirring of flesh, and a knot is growing in the base of my throat. All I can think about is George Hollan. I should feel proud about my loyal warrior, my minion, Georgie Boy, as well as his contribution to the end of the world, but I don't. In fact, I don't feel anything for him. Not even the least amount of sympathy for him; however, I feel like I could take George's place; my dumb face plastered all over the TV. My name like a wrenching echo. Each member of the media picking me apart, limb-by-limb, dissecting me like I was a fetal pig for a ninth grade lab experiment. TV people have already started their campaign on George, his family, friends, neighbors, anyone who knows, has spoken, or associated themselves with George. The media is trying to dig up all the dirt they can on Georgie Boy, but from what I've gathered so far, he seems as clean as a virgin. Family and friends say he's a good kid—quiet, though. I contemplate canceling the fishing trip while Peggy fixes me a typical Saturday morning breakfast: a fried egg with hash browns and slices of tomatoes. She's extra perky this morning, and she acts as if she's looking forward to having the house all to herself. I eat maybe half of the food on my plate and toss the rest of the breakfast in the trash behind Peggy's back. I head back to my room after breakfast and call Bill. The excitement in his voice changes my mind. He's like a kid ready to go on a field trip. Before I break the news, he asks me if I'm ready to fish. The answer volleys back and forth like a ping-pong ball inside my mind until I respond with a short *yeah*. I tell him I'm ready and suggest driving separate. It's a little over an hour and a half drive from Spartacus to the Ford Davie Campgrounds along the Chattooga River. Bill insists on riding together. He tells me that it'll save money, even though money's not an issue. I tell him that I'll drive, but he follows by saying that he'll drive. He always has to drive. *Always*. After the call, I exhaust the next forty-five minutes packing for the weekend: an extra set of fishing clothes and a pair of clothes for Sunday; toothbrush and toothpaste, since Bill never has any when I spend the night at his house. He picks me up at nine o'clock sharp. His face appears thinner and he looks like he's lost a lot of weight and I wonder if he's trying a new diet. After the car accident, he became a health nut, like Peggy. Hit the gym at least four times a week. Cut down on red meat and his salt intake. Limited the amount of sugar he put in his coffee. Starting drinking more protein shakes and eating foods that matched a rainbow. When I ask about his new appearance, he tells me that he's started a new diet, as I first thought. And biking, or "cycling," as he calls it, which he started to incorporate into his morning regimen a few months ago. He never was the "cyclist" type, more of the stationary sitter for most of the day, then the slow walker accompanied by long stares at sunsets, as if he was, in a way, pining away the day. When Bill used to be a runner, he'd use to pick me up from school after an early afternoon run, and he'd still be ticked off by a cyclist, one of those geared-up types with a skintight bodysuit, goggles, and aerodynamic helmet and a bike so fine tuned that it sounded like a gentle breeze, who clipped him while he was running at the greenway, which wasn't too far from the house. Bill hated cyclists, how most of them, especially the serious and deadly silent kind, not the cage-free, smiley-faced bell-honking Pee-wee Herman kind, who'd give former runners, like Bill, a merry warning of their sunny presence, had no respect for other pedestrians, especially runners. Now that Bill was a cyclist, of course, he hated drivers.

I'm somewhat impressed with his dedication to staying healthy. I can also tell from the smirk buried underneath his thin cheeks that he's been anxiously waiting all week to see me. He doesn't bother saying hello to Peggy as she stands like a proud pirate on the front porch. Yet, he gives her a wave as we drive off, as if she's a friendly stranger. It's part of the deal, I guess. Not even a second into the drive, Bill's drunk with excitement, so much he can't even sit still in his seat.

I decide to turn the conversation to the fly lure that I received in the mail before he can utter the question that's been on his mind all week: *What have you been up to all month?*

You know, the same ole same ole: defacing property, destroying historical monuments, burning down small local businesses in order to start The Whatever War, which will lead to the ultimate destruction of the world, thus allowing me to embrace my nomadic lifestyle without the disturbance of disgusting human beings. I pull out the fly lure from the small proposal ring-like box. We talk about the fly lure for about ten minutes, Bill mostly informing me about how he spent two Saturdays ago at a bait shop, the trouble he went through while purchasing the lure. He tells me a story about a fellow who came up short for a fishing rod while Bill was waiting behind him in line. Bill forked out the money to pay for the rod. Then, Bill and this fellow started talking and it turns out that the fellow's grandson goes to East Graham. His name is Dominic, and he happens to be the same Dominic whom Bill counsels. He tells me this side-story about Dominic, how troubled he is, how he's getting into fights during school, how many times he's been suspended, a "young man," he says, "without a moral compass." I don't give a rat's ass about Dominic and his lack of moral compass or how he's one fight away from being expelled from East Graham. I hate punks like Dominic, who wear their knuckles like rings, red and worn down and callused over from hammering away at bone and muscle, the branded alpha male types who walk around with a chip on their shoulders and try to start shit for the sake of starting shit; however, I need kids *just* like Dominic to help me destroy the rest of the world, even though they may be the last standing survivors who will still be lingering around like a bad jingle when society has consumed itself. I don't understand why Bill's telling me the story, but I know—because, after all, Bill is and always will be a storyteller—it has to do with me. So, Dominic's grandfather was trying to get Dominic into fishing like the way Bill was trying to get me into activities: music, sports, gaming, etc. The fishing rod was a gift for Dominic. Later that day, Bill stopped by Fitness City. So, Bill's working out, right. He gets done with his workout. Goes to the locker room. As Bill's changing shoes, he spots a folded twenty-dollar bill on the floor. Okay. So, what? Someone must've dropped the money while he was dressing, I tell Bill, but Bill didn't care about the money. He was more intrigued by the coincidence. Earlier that day, he gave Dominic's grandfather a twenty-dollar bill to buy a fishing rod. You already know this. Then, later that day, Bill found a twenty-dollar bill that nobody claimed. Bill says he was the only one working out, except for a couple of women. So, there is no way the money could've belonged to one of the women working out. Bill could've pocketed the money. Could've easily gotten away, hands clean, without anyone noticing. Lots of could haves. I ask Bill if he took the money. He tells me that he didn't.

"Why not?" I ask.

"Because it wasn't my money," he says, glancing at me through the corner of his eye.

I understand the significance of Bill's story. If you lose something— like a twenty-dollar bill or whatever—then, sometimes, the world gives something back. Or, if you give, then you will receive. Like good karma. I understand all of that mumbo-jumbo crap they teach you in literature books from ninth grade English, but I don't care about any of it. I just don't understand *why* Bill's telling me the story. I leave it at that. I don't push the subject anymore.

Then, Bill gets the upper hand in the conversation and starts his barrage of questions, first by asking me how the job interview went the other day. I guess he heard about the job interview from Peggy, but he never mentions her name. I tell him it went fine and expect, by giving him a short answer, he won't pursue with other questions. The tactic has no effect on him. He keeps asking me questions, like a detective does to a perp. I wonder if that's what he thinks of me, a perp, a thief, a spawn of the devil. Either way, he reminds me of the Bill I once knew as a child, that inspirational figure who'd venture out into a wilderness full of wild animals without a shred of fear in his bones. No weapon. No need. He'd make his own weapon, if need be. He was a man in charge. A man before he was a child. A father before a friend.

As I find comfort in the new, yet old Bill, I hear the guttural roar of a truck from behind.

I glance in the side-view mirror where a red souped-up truck is riding Bill's bumper.

Bill's eyes shoot toward the rear-view mirror, his face tightening, the sides of his jaw like two fists.

"What an asshole," I say to Bill.

Bill doesn't respond.

The driver behind us floors the truck around the double yellow lines along the two-lane road and passes us as we approach a curve. Unfortunately, there isn't an oncoming vehicle approaching in the other lane; otherwise, there would've been at least one less asshole in the world.

About a quarter of a mile down the road the truck hasn't gained much ground since it last passed us, and I can still see it at a distance. The truck approaches an intersection in front of a neighborhood. The light turns red right before the truck has a chance to speed through the intersection. The truck slows down, stops. We eventually catch up to the truck before the light turns green.

Once the light turns green, the truck speeds ahead of us.

Bill remains in a quiet, stewing state throughout the drive, as if, strangely, he's bothered by something, and it doesn't take me long to figure out his change in demeanor.

Ahead, once the driver in the truck, who's caught behind a cyclist on the side of the road and preventing him from passing due to the traffic in the other lane, finds an opening, he guns the truck past the cyclist, stops right next to him, only inches away from him, and then deliberately shoots a thick black cloud of smoke from the exhaust pipe in the cyclist's face. The cyclist is an older man, probably in his seventies, and he ends up falling from his bike as he tries to wave the smoke from his face.

"You gotta be kiddin' me," Bill seethes and suddenly speeds up to the truck.

"What are you doing?" I ask Bill.

He doesn't respond.

His face is clouded with red, and his entire body is pounding like a heart.

For a moment, I begin to worry about Bill, if he's okay, and why he's so triggered.

I glance over my shoulder at the older cyclist, and he's still lying on the ground. He appears badly injured; his face covered in pain. Another driver behind us stops and checks on him.

Bill suddenly accelerates, gaining on the truck. He's now driving ten miles over the speed limit, not fifteen, twenty. . .

As he catches up to the truck, Bill accelerates past the truck and cuts right in front of him.

The driver of the truck slams on the brakes and skids off the side of the road!

I yell for Bill to stop, but he's already storming out of the car.

The truck driver gets out as well, holding his hands up in the air. All I can hear is the rage in Bill's voice. He's dropping f-bombs left and right: *"Fuck you, you piece of fuckin' shit! For fuck's sake, you don't own the fuckin' road, you piece of fuckin' shit!"*

"Oh yeah," the driver says, backpedaling toward the truck.

He reaches inside the glove compartment and pulls out a handgun.

Bill doesn't even break stride. Yet, he continues to storm toward the truck driver, who's now aiming the gun directly at Bill's head.

"Big fuckin' man, huh? Does waving the thing around make you a fuckin' man, you fuckin' piece of shit?"

The truck driver warns Bill to back off.

Bill doesn't.

Instead, he keeps his hands down to his side and walks right up to the driver and then places his forehead directly to the barrel of the gun.

"Go ahead, Big Man," Bill screams. *"Shoot me!"*

My heart's pounding.

I actually think the man's going to shoot Bill.

I step out of the car and yell, "Dad!"

The man pulls the gun from Bill's head and backs off and stares at Bill in a state of horror. He gets back in his truck and drives off, as Bill stands there, in the middle of the road. If I don't know any better, he looks disappointed; and at that moment, I don't know whom I should be more scared of, a redneck truck driver who deliberately showcases his deteriorating masculinity by hiding behind a clichéd image of what a

man should look like while, at the same time, stereotyping his own inse-
curity, or my own flesh and blood.

You'd think Bill would want to cancel the fishing trip after that
whole ordeal with the truck driver. But he gets back in the car, as if
nothing ever happened, and we drive away from the scene.

We arrive at Okeenaw National Park north of the campgrounds, and
I'm still a little rattled from Bill's latest road rage; however, the sight of
the water washes away any intruding thoughts.

Before I ask Bill about the place, he tells me that he heard from a
teacher friend, also a fisherman, that trout are extremely "bountiful"
around here. He's also starting to use larger words, again. He used to
say strange words to me when I was younger, complicated words that,
at the time, were both hard to pronounce and over my head. He said
these words at a time in my life when he wanted me to expand my vocabulary. I can't help but wonder if Bill's trying to help me expand
something other than my vocabulary.

2

We dress the part of fishermen in our goofy-looking waterproof bibs and
locate a spot where it's shallow enough to wade. I try to stay as close to
the shore as possible because I can't swim too well. I'm like a pup when
it comes to swimming. Picture me: a teenager still doing the dog pad-
dle. It's pretty embarrassing, I know, but it's something that I could
never master. Bill tells me to stay close, Hot Dog. "Don't venture out
too far," he says. I do as Bill says and keep my feet firmly planted in the
soggy ground below. Fun fact: according to Bill, the Chattooga River
acts as a boundary line for South Carolina and Georgia, and we're both
literally standing on the border of South Carolina while casting our fly
lures in Georgia, which I think is worth the trip. I mean, not too many
people can say: "I was fishing in South Carolina, but I caught myself a
fish in Georgia." We fish for about twenty minutes until we start to get
bites from the infamous trout that Bill won't stop talking about. I end
up catching two rainbow trout. Nothing monster in size. Both ten-
inchers.

The little suckers put up quite a fight.

3

We break from fishing and take a load off on a log next to the river. Bill
grabs a cold beer from the other water cooler. Then, he offers me one.
Bill has *never* offered me a beer before.

"It's just a beer," he says and hands me a beer dripping with icy water.

I grab the cold beer, crack it open, and take a sip.

"How's your mother?" he asks, as he cracks open his beer.

He hasn't mentioned her name in forever, and I wonder why he is so interested in her when, only months ago, he acted as if she was a distant relative who died many years ago.

"She's fine, I guess. Working."

"I mean, how is she?" he asks.

"What do you mean?"

I think I should be the one who's asking Bill the same question. I'm tempted to bring up what recently happened on the road, with that truck driver. But I decide to let it die in the river.

"Is she happy?"

I don't know the answer to Bill's question. I don't know why he cares whether or not Peggy's happy.

"I guess," I tell Bill. "Yeah. She seems happy."

An almost sad and stoic expression washes over Bill's face, as if he has a lot of heavy thoughts weighing on his mind. He takes a bird-like sip from the beer, and then lets out a phlegmy cough. He waits till the cough resides before he finishes his thought.

"Lightweight," I say.

Bill doesn't care for the sarcasm, but he lets it slide.

"It's *cold*," he says as he flexes his throat. "Listen, Josh," he says heavily, "I just want to apologize."

For what happened on the road.

Finally.

I ask, "Apologize for what?"

"I want to apologize for what I put you two through," he says. I don't know why he's telling me this, but I listen anyway. "*You* two needed me, and I wasn't there." He turns to me. His eyes are watery, as if he's about to cry. "I was selfish, and I was only thinking about my-self."

"Why are telling me this now?" I ask bluntly.

"I just need you to know that I *did* try to make it work between your mother and me," he says clearly. "I didn't try hard enough. I gave up on the world. Most importantly, I gave up on you, Josh. But I'm not going to give up on you, Josh."

"Okay," I say.

Then he says, "Not everybody in the world is out to get you, you know that, right? There are people out there—good people—who do care about you."

Where does he get the nerve?

"Like you," I say, my voice trembling. "*You* care about me?"

"Of course, I care about you," he says.

I stand up from the log and loom over Bill.

"I don't get you," I tell him. "One minute, you nearly get yourself killed by some asshole on the road and the next, you're talking about how 'people care about me.' That's fucking bullshit—"

"—Watch your mouth," Bill says, standing up as well. "I'm *still* your father."

"No," I say. "You're just a guy pretending to be my father."

I storm back to the car. I hear the lid of the cooler being thrown to the ground. I glance over my shoulder and catch a glimpse of Bill tossing the trout back into the river. Eventually, Bill makes his way back to the car. He tells me he's driving me back to Spartacus. On the way home, we don't speak a word to one another.

4

When we arrive at the house, I can't get out quick enough. Bill's calling out my name as I grab my things from the back.

I struggle to look him in the eye.

Ignoring him is easier than facing him.

All I can think about is getting far away from his presence.

"I'm on your side, Josh," he says. "Don't forget that. . . ."

The only words I can muster: *Are you done?*

I regret the words as soon as they leave my mouth.

Bill slams the gear into drive.

He turns to me, and I know he wants to speed away and leave me in the dust. But he doesn't. He tightens his jaw and says to me, "Take care of Peggy, Josh."

Then, he drives away.

5

When I enter the house I see a light coming from Peggy's bedroom, and I'm seriously not in the mood to deal with her or her questions right now.

I close the door behind me, trying not to make any noise during Operation Don't-Wake-The-Bitch.

On the way upstairs, I shoot a glance in the living room and notice the pillows scattered on the floor. Same with a couple of magazines. A coaster. Two wine glasses perched on top of the bare coffee table. Both half-full. I hear Peggy in her bedroom; however, I can't tell if she's laughing or crying. I listen closer. Then, I hear it, that sound. If it had come from any other woman, I wouldn't have thought anything of it. *But* the sound came from Peggy. I inch my way back into the living room, and the sounds are more extreme. I check out the wine glasses, one with an imprint of lips and the other with greasy smudges. I get halfway to Peggy's bedroom before immediately stopping in my tracks.

She's yelling some guy's name. I can't tell what his name is—somewhere between a *Ralph* and an *Alf.* She's panting, and when Peggy says the name for the sixth time, it sounds like the word *ouch.* I want to check on Peggy, to make sure she's all right. I take a couple of steps to her bedroom. Then, she lets out another moan. I backpedal and quietly hurry to my room. Bill's words lift over the dead silence of my room, about him being sorry, about how he didn't try hard enough. The anger swells over me, causing every muscle in my body to tighten. I feel like ten Bill's wrapped in one body, like I'm harnessing the strength of ten men, and everything seems so vividly clear: Peggy's strange behavior over the past couple of days; the late meetings; the supposed "investors," who were investing in her company; constantly checking messages on her phone; the lies. I feel as if I've become the parent and my child is sneaking around with some rebellious boy behind my back.

I grab the door handle with a fistful of rage, and I slam the door shut, shaking the entire foundation of the house.

The impact is so violent the screws from the upper hinge spring loose from the doorway.

I wait in a deafening hum of silence. The moaning stops. The grunting. The rocking of Peggy's squeaky bed stops. The slapping stops. For a moment, the *entire* world stops.

Two minutes pass.

In those two minutes, two adults are scrambling around downstairs like two squirrels caught in the middle of traffic.

The front door opens and then closes. I walk to the window and watch *not* an adult but some guy in his twenties or thirties walking through the front lawn. He's adjusting his black dress shirt, mostly fiddling with the cuffs of his sleeves, and he walks with an arrogant gait. He stops at the white Beamer parked two houses down and as he's about to get inside, he looks toward the house. I think he sees me, but I don't care. I never pull my eyes from him. Yet, I keep them there until he finally gets into the car and drives away.

6

An hour later I hear a woodpecker *tapping* on my door.

"Josh," Peggy says from behind the door. Then, the door cracks open. Peggy pokes her head inside and asks, "Can we talk?"

I'm sitting in front of my computer, researching HOW TO MAKE A HOMEMADE BOMB.

I hide the page as Peggy steps inside my room.

"What you want?"

"I thought you were going to stay the night with your father."

I shoot an angry glance at Peggy, and she's examining the shattered frame of lures in the trashcan.

She crosses her arms and asks, "What happened?"

"I don't wanna talk about it," I say.

"Do I need to call your father?"

"No," I say, louder. "I said 'I don't want to talk about it!'"

"Listen, Josh," she says, as if she's about to start the speech that she's been reciting over and over in her room, "I wanted to tell you sooner—"

"—Who is he?"

"He's just a friend. . . "

"Just a friend," I repeat. "So what? You sleeping around with guys now?"

"Don't you dare talk to me like that," Peggy snaps. "What I do with my life on my personal time is no concern to you. Do you understand me, *Josh*?"

She waits for an answer.

I don't give her one.

"Don't you forget who pays the bills around here," she says.

We argue for a little while longer.

Peggy wins the fight.

Every time she brings up money, she always wins the fight.

7

Peggy storms back to her room. I go back to researching bombs. I write down all of the ingredients I need to make the bomb. Some of the ingredients I have in my own bathroom while others I can find in the garage.

I clear the search history and shut off my computer. I step into the bathroom with my list in hand and as I'm searching for the hydrogen peroxide, I stop and look at myself from the outside.

What's happening to me?

If I go through with this, then there's no turning back. They'll label me and put hashtags on me. They'll crucify me. Even worse, they'll call me a monster. They'll call me a lot of things, things that may or may not be true.

Who am I becoming?

What the hell am I turning into?

6
...

**Swinging for the fences – Celibacy in the City –
Murderous tendencies – Brainstorm – F'art – Hot 'Lana –
A police chase – Back against the wall – Saved by the
light – What is the Hate Train?**

THE idea suddenly crosses my mind while I'm staring at Sir Spur's swimmeret. I remember seeing a news article in the POP CULTURE section yesterday. The engines start running, each thought stringing together like a spool of yarn. I put aside the swimmeret, roll out of bed, and get on my computer. I first pull up the article from the website: Wanda Pak, a sculptor from Seattle, is unveiling this brand new sculpture next Friday night in downtown Atlanta. Wanda has also been posting teaser shots of the sculpture for all of her followers on PhotoBag. The theme, Wanda writes, revolves around a beautiful thing called love—or making love. The teaser shot of Wanda's new sculpture includes two subjects, both male and female, intertwined together like a pretzel. Cities will be the best place to start: for one, cities have the densest populations throughout the country; and two, most people tend to meet their significant other in the city. It's pretty evident that destroying the world is going to take longer than I expected. I can't just snap my fingers or wave a magic wand or say some spell and stand back and watch people evaporate into the air with a thunderous silence. If I can pull this off, and my lap dogs are down with the sickness, then people will think twice about "making love," Wanda Pak, or, worse, think about the very idea of spitting out another little snot into this world. And if they want to carry on a legacy, they can forget about artificial insemination. I'll disgust people so much they won't touch themselves anymore, even if they had a gun pointed at their domes.

It'll be like Celibacy in the City.

After I make up my mind on what I'm going to do next, I gumshoe graphic photographs of every STD (sexual transmitted disease) known to man.

I once saw a promotion for cigarettes when I was waiting in line to pay for gas. A guy in front of me who was buying smokes turned over the pack, as he was about to hand a ten-dollar bill to the clerk. I caught a glimpse of the picture of a guy missing a jaw on the back of the cigarette pack. I didn't believe it at first. I bought a pack for myself; however, the picture on the back of my pack was completely different: a lady with a gaping hole in her neck. Then another time there was a picture showing what a smoker's lungs look like after years of smoking: black and overcooked like one of Marlene's terrible Christmas roasts. Not sure if the tobacco industry or government agencies were responsible for sticking the horrowshow of side effects from smoking on the back of cigarette packs instead of using warning labels. Whoever was in charge, they clearly understood we are a visual country—considering the steady drop in cigarette sales over the past two years, which has forced the industry to promote "supposedly" healthier alternatives, like e-cigarettes, by advertising flavored cigarettes or whatever gimmicks these peddlers use to lure in the youth.

For sex, there are only two healthier alternatives: one, have sex with a condom; or two, refrain from having sex. The two options will help reduce any chance of women becoming pregnant, which will significantly reduce the population. If all goes according to plan, those options won't even be on the table. It won't destroy the world overnight, but it's a start. I gumshoe the most grotesque pictures—I mean, the most hideous exaggerations of each disease—starting in alphabetical order: BV (bacterial vaginosis); chancroid; Chlamydia; genital warts; gonorrhea; hepatitis; herpes; HIV/AIDS; HPV (human papillomavirus); LG (lymphogranuloma venereum); molluscum contagiosum; MPC (mucopurulent cervicitis); PID (pelvic inflammatory disease); pubic lice, "crabs"; scabies; syphilis; and finally, trichomoniasis. From what I gather, most of these diseases are curable—most, but not all of them. Most can be treated with a round of antibiotics. Maybe two. Then, back to the daily jerk-off routine.

I track down an online printing website. Stickers will cost me ten cents apiece.

I decide to go with the most graphic pictures. I gumshoe a few spicy chancroid pictures, which will cause the most courageous turtle to hide in its shell. I label the pictures in photoshop: the name of the disease, what it does to your equipment, how one gets the disease. Five diseases, I choose. I decide on a thousand stickers for each of the five diseases, which altogether will cost around five hundred dollars. I drive to the nearest grocery store after Peggy meets up with a friend to play tennis. Could be another lie. But at this point, I don't care anymore. I pur-

chase one of those VISA gift cards for five hundred and twenty-five dollars—the extra twenty-five for shipping and handling. I pay for the card
with cash. Then, I drive back home and place an order for the five
thousand stickers from the online printing website. I chose the fastest
shipment option. If all goes according to plan—cross my fingers—the
stickers will be here by Tuesday.

2

I break into Peggy's phone while she's taking a shower. Her four-digit
passcode: 1993. What's so significant about 1993? In the year 1993,
Duran Duran released their self-tilted album, better known as the *Wedding* album, which happens to be one of her favorite albums. Peggy has
the album on CD; and recently, she bought it on vinyl. I type in
Peggy's passcode and go through her recent text messages. I find a
lengthy back and forth conversation between her and perhaps *the* guy,
Raphael. They're texting about sex but not really using the word *sex*.
Yet, Peggy uses innuendoes and softcore flirtation to get her point
across—*eww!* I skim through texts until I find one from yesterday.
Peggy apologizes for yesterday. She tells him that he—which, I believe,
she's referring to "yours truly"—wasn't supposed to come home until
the next day. They plan on getting together again. I contemplate sending Raphael a text, asking him if he'd like to get together somewhere
private and then, once Raphael shows up, expecting to get lucky with
Peggy, Peggy will be nowhere around. Maybe she could meet him at a
fancy, five-star restaurant. Then, when he's waiting for Peggy to show
up, I can get to work on his car. Maybe tamper with it. Perhaps when
Raphael gets pissed off after Peggy stands him up, he'll storm back to his
white Beamer and find what was once a white BMW. Or, maybe I'll
tamper with his brakes. Maybe I'll arrange to meet the *Ninja Turtle* in a
back alley somewhere. It's been a while since I've used my blowtorch
and mallet. Maybe I could add another trophy to my collection. She'll
find out. She'll know it was yours truly. I'm the only one with her passcode. I can't do that to Peggy.

I close her phone and look up Raphael on the Internet. His full
name is Raphael Prescott, and he's a website designer from Trenton.
Moved to the South when he was a teenager. Went to an arts school
somewhere in North Carolina. More than likely, Raphael's helping
Peggy with her new website. She's been talking about it all week, how
it's going to look, the layout, how "original" it's going to be, how it's going to change the way we buy food.

I log off my computer and decide to leave Raphael alone.

At least for now.

3

When Tuesday arrives, I don't even leave the house. I spend most of the morning pacing back and forth from the front windows to the TV in the living room. Peggy stops by for lunch and asks me if I'd like to eat with her, but I tell her I already ate when, in fact, I have been nervously snacking all day. Peggy tends to her lunch and does so loudly and violently, like slamming the door after grabbing a cup and plate from the cabinet or dunking dishes in the sink and washing them as if she's competing in a competition with herself. After lunch, she piddles around the house for a while as if she's deliberately trying to annoy me. Vacuuming; doing the laundry; or taking out the trash: these are chores that normally get handed off to me at the end of the day; however, she does them as if the end of the day can't wait. The resentment from the other day shows on her blank face like a cold sore. Amazing how she can start mental arguments without even uttering a word. She may be a witch or maybe come from a bloodline of witches. She grabs her things and finally leaves, and I can't be more relieved. Yet, I'm still anxious.

As I head back to the windows to check for the mailman, the front door opens. Peggy sticks her head inside and says, "Josh, you have some packages out here." I hurry to the front where Peggy's waiting on the front steps. I grab the boxes from the porch and tell her that I ordered some clothes online. She tilts her head, as if she's approving from the initiative that I've made, and says, "About time. You could use some new clothes." Then, she glides to her car and heads back to work.

I lug each box to my room.

First, I peel off my address from each box. Then, grab my knife and open the boxes. The stickers came out better than I thought.

They came out greeeh-ate!

4

I check out the unveiling of Wanda's impressionistic style sculpture online. Hundreds and thousands of people have shown up to the event located in the fountain plaza in Five Points. One may think the sculpture depicts all humanity coming together, all walks of life, each limb and body part blown out of proportion. One may think the sepia sculpture is a depiction of our planet viewed from the past, like an aged monochrome photo. Or another may think it's just a bunch of aliens having a celestial orgy. The engines upstairs start to run again, and I think about another idea that will go hand-in-hand with my stickers.

I hit up several grocery stores in Liddell, and then several more in the town of Grispin Lakes. I try not to make it obvious by purchasing other things, like bread or milk and that sort of stuff. I toss away all of the other groceries in the trash and wait in my room until Peggy goes to sleep. Once she falls asleep, I dress like the night and drive to Atlanta.

5

It's a little after one o'clock when I approach downtown Atlanta. The nocturnal life thrives, but most of the action is centered at bars and clubs and whatnot. The night owls are too drunk to care about a guy wearing a mask. I find an opportunity as the night dies down and start applying deli meat. I end up going through nearly twenty packages of bologna to cover the entire sculpture. I move my way to the downtown area and start placing stickers on stop signs, road signs, business signs, billboards, small signs, big signs, sides of buildings, street posts, side-walks, as well as street tunnels. I place stickers over street art, flyers, and banners. Basically, I tag the entire city of Atlanta in sexual transmitted diseases. One box down. I work my way through my second box of stickers. I get about halfway done when all of a sudden I hear a siren *chirp* behind me!

I turn my shoulder where I find a spotlight shining on me.

I shield the blinding light with my hand; and through the cracks of my fingers, I witness the face of a cop. I pause for a second, waiting for the cop to make a move. The cruiser suddenly makes a left onto the street. I drop the box of stickers and take off down a side alleyway be-fore the cop can reach me. The sirens suddenly blare out with a pierc-ing wail, a sound that I've heard many times before but never expected to be directed at me.

As I run into another alleyway, the cruiser closes in on me; however, I manage to find a passage, too narrow for a car to fit, which leads to an intersection between buildings where I can choose from three different alleys. I instinctively choose the alley, which leads back to the same street where I was spotted.

I cut through three different alleys, the sirens fading farther from me. I stop and catch my breath behind a dumpster for a second. Stupid, stupid, stupid, I tell myself. My thoughts are racing, and all I can think about is being apprehended, then tossed in a smelly cage with a bunch of animals. My future nothing but an empty cell. A world surrounded by bars and the distant whispers of depraved men. I hear two more cruisers closing in. I take a deep breath, as if I'm about to dive under-water, and keep moving through the alleys. Can't get caught. *Never* get caught. Keep moving.

I find myself trapped in the middle of an alley.

The red and blue lights of sirens flashing at one end of the alley while lights flash at the other. At any second, I'll be spotted in the cops' range of vision.

I find an escape ladder, but it's too high to reach.

I'm frantic and completely disoriented and unaware of my surroundings. My vision narrows, like a straw, and my world starts to spin.

In my soon-to-be surrender, I spot a rock, which is wedged between a doorway. Smothered cigarette butts are scattered over the ground. I open the cracked door as soon as the cops pass the alley and immediately close it behind me. In the darkness, I listen closely to the sirens, and they're fading away.

I hear another noise, not sirens. Music. I turn my shoulder and find myself in a long, grungy hallway. The sides of the walls covered in graffiti. The floors as filthy as a bar bathroom. The air has a sweaty, humid stench to it, as well. I remove my mask and tuck it in my back pocket. A radiant red light beats like a tiny pulse at the end of the hallway. Not sirens but something else.

I proceed through the hallway until I come across a large room where the music is louder and heavy with bass. The music is unclear, however, glitchy, like an amplified scratch of a vinyl record pressed against a microphone. I follow the red light, which leads to another room tucked behind a feathery curtain.

Surrounded by a group of strange people stands some guy wearing an oversized visor attached to a bundle of wires, fed into a kind of gaming console. He's wearing a pair of white gloves, and he appears to be shadowboxing. I can't exactly tell how old the guy is. I can't tell much of anything, like the people, how old they are because they have their backs turned toward me and they're staring in a trance-like state at a massive projection screen, which curves like a horseshoe around the wall.

On the wide screen plays a first-person-like shooter: the POV of two hands pulverizing a guy inside a subway car. Each and every punch booms throughout the speakers overhead, and the cringing *crunches* and *cracks* of bones breaking ring out. Each punch thrown in the game mimics the guy shadowboxing. Then, the screen goes smoky, as if steam is pouring from every orifice of the character on the screen. Droplets of water fall down the screen like a stream of tears. I inch closer to the group, wondering if I've walked in on a strange cult. A secret club or gang or something. Whatever it is, it most definitely intrigues me.

As I'm about to get a closer look at the projection screen, I feel a rocky hand grab me by the shoulder.

A gravelly voice follows: "You're not supposed to be here."

I turn my shoulder.

A burly security guard with the word *security* written in white over his skintight black shirt is towering over me.

I apologize, I think.

I don't even know what I say.

I, too, am left in a trance from the game.

Not only that, the security guard is twice the size of me, and his hands are so massive that they look as if they can easily fold me into a lawn chair.

He crosses his arms over his chest and waits for me to leave.

He doesn't toss me out.

He easily could, but he doesn't.

I throw my head in a nod at those dark, mysterious silhouettes standing in front of the screen and ask the security guard, "What is this place?"

He follows my nod, then turns to me, and says without missing a beat, "This is the Hate Train. Now get the fuck out."

7.

**Polka-Dotted Cooties - Dream of trains - Desperato -
Saturday Night Wrist - They call him 'Needles' - Well,
meet d@ m@wwwb - Like UR, but not UR - Welcome to the
Hate Train - IRL - Side efx of unplugging - New friends -
"live" spelled backwards?**

THE angry eye in the sky is already out when I reach Spartacus.

The entire trip back home goes by so fast. I can't stop thinking about the Hate Train. What is it? Is it a group? A gang? Or, is it a game? Whatever game that guy—or girl—was playing last night, he—or she—seemed like the person in control. The game reminds me of a virtual reality game, only this one appeared way, *way* more intense and—not to mention—more real. The graphics were next level stuff.

I make it back home and I don't even think about the sculpture or what condition it may be in until I step inside my room. Peggy's downstairs going through her morning ritual of making coffee and probably—more than likely—preparing questions about where I was last night. I turn on the TV, flip the channel to the local news, and watch a ten-minute loop of news. Sure enough, the bologna prank made it on the local news, not mainstream but local. There's a chance that the mainstream will get a hold of the story, and when it does, the idea will spread like an infection. A reporter is standing in front of Wanda's sculpture. Crowds have gathered in the street. All sorts of people, including Wanda, are peeling away slices of bologna and at the same time, stripping away the paint. The sculpture now is covered in polka dots. The reporter also mentions the stickers. She warns that the next images are not suited for younger viewers. Discretion is advised. The only thing the cops have is surveillance footage of the "vandal" running through the streets. They show the vandal running away from the cops like an idiot. I'm sure the cops look more like idiots than I do. I don't spend a second of my time worrying about the footage. I was wearing a mask, as well as gloves. They don't have my face or fingerprints. I didn't leave any trace that would lead cops back to me. And, last but not least, I was driving a car with stolen tags.

In other words: the cops have nothing.

2

I dream about a dark forest. I'm wandering through the fog. From a distance, the red light of a scanner is descending through the fog, like at a rave. The red beam runs across my face and eyes, as if I'm a product with a UPC. The red beam suddenly vanishes, and dark objects start to move around me in the forest, ducking and weaving through the grayish slits of skeletal trees. I look down at the ground below, watching my every step through the heavy foliage, watching for creatures stalking in the shadows, the snakes.

The devils.

I leave the forest and find myself walking along a set of old railroad tracks. I watch my feet step over each weathered plank until I pass a bridge, then make my way back into the dense forest. Those tracks spread out like veins in every single direction. I stay on the same tracks and never venture from my initial course, even though the idea of changing tracks is at the forefront of my mind.

But where would I go?

I stop for a moment. So many directions to choose from. I can only see a few feet in front of me. Only one path remains clear: the one straight ahead.

The horn of a train echoes throughout the dense fog, and the planks below my feet start to shake. Each rusty nail trembles, softly at first, then violently. Two headlights appear in the fog before me. The rumble of an engine causes my body to shake now, hands especially, both curling into tightly coiled fists. The light brightens, the fog glowing all around me. A beast of a train emerges from the fog, a ferocious thing made of blood and metal. The train charges at me, but I stand my ground.

The train closes in; and as we're about to ram heads, I bolt upright from the bed. I'm cold and sweating, feverish. I roll out of bed and check the window. Peggy's car is gone. I check the time on the nightstand. It's noon. She's doesn't work today. Maybe she's picking up lunch. Maybe she's with her new douche-bag boyfriend, Raphael. I throw on clothes and go downstairs where I find a ten-dollar bill on the counter. No note. She usually leaves a note, but this time all I find is money. I turn on the TV; the local news is playing the same loop from earlier. Nothing breaks. Same funny polka-dotted sculpture. Blistered, pus-filled penises and inflamed, infected vaginas plastered all over the streets of Atlanta. I check the other networks. The story hasn't made

69

headlines yet. But it *probably* will. For some reason, I'm not too worried about the story, especially if it doesn't break. I make myself a fried bologna sandwich with the leftover bologna as I search through the news for the next thing to destroy.

3

I search through the news all day but can't find anything. I end up wasting two hours watching TV, mindlessly flipping through channels. I come across a story about the scarcity of eggs and how the cost of eggs will start to rise in the next couple of weeks. Americans love eggs. I'd admit: I do too. But I could probably wing myself off eggs, if I needed to. I come across a story, one of those cautionary pieces about the power grid and how vulnerable the country is without a robust security surrounding our most valuable source of energy. It wouldn't work. Let's face it: When the power goes off, people will start paying attention to their surroundings, including other people. They'll come together, talk, and be friendlier to one another, which doesn't help me at all. I turn off the TV and stare at my own lazy reflection on that black screen. That's when the engines start running again: What do people need to survive? I go through the everyday necessities of survival. Food, of course. People need to eat in order to survive. There's no way one person can contaminate the entire food supply. How about water? People need water. Again, it'd be impossible to contaminate America's water supply. Even so, then people will go to bottled water where the water comes from natural springs. There'll always be an alternative, healthier or not. Plus, I'm *not* a murderer. I can't kill people. I'd rather have others do my bidding for me. However, if it came down to me pushing a red button that would wipe out the human race from the face of the earth, I'd probably push it. What am I talking about? Of course, I'd push it in a heartbeat while I hunker down and remain at a safe distance. I start to grow frustrated with my options—and I have so many options to chose from, whether it be doing things on my own terms, which haven't worked out as favorably as I had planned, or the other, Plan B, the one where I gather a team. The truth is, as much as I hate people, I need them. I need people—copycats and whoever or whatever—to help me destroy the world. I can't do it alone. That's a fact of reality.

4

It's Saturday night, and I can feel myself climbing out of my own skin. Anxious, bored, and slightly curious, I decide to pay a visit to Kernelson, a town hanging on the edge of ruins.

As I'm about to cross the railroad tracks that separate Piedmont Springs and Kernelson, the barricades start to lower. The constant *ding-ing* of the bell causes me to drift off in a trance as those red lights flash above like a flying saucer. I stop before the crossing and turn to my right where a train's approaching. I watch the train pass by. That's when the engines start running again. *The chugga-chugga-choo-choo* building momentum, fueling each thought and clouding my vision. As soon as the train passes and the barricades ascend back to their upright, erected position, I slam the gear in reverse and make a U-turn and plot a new course.

5

I make it to Atlanta in good time. I drive by Wanda's statue, which is roped off with yellow CAUTION tape. Some of the stickers have been removed from signs and buildings; even the stickers that were removed have left behind a white, sticky residue along surfaces, and if you're looking in the right place, it's obvious to point out where I left my mark. But to be fair, it's not worth bragging about? On the contrary, it's somewhat embarrassing after spending all that money on the stickers, only to be left with the image one would commonly find from a poorly attempted removal of a price tag on the back of a product.

I park not too far away from the location where that mysterious club was playing the VR game. I reach the same door from before, the one, the one in the alleyway, with the rock wedged between the doorway. The rock is missing. I give a tug on the door handle. It's locked. Okay. Now, what? I walk around the building and keep searching for a way inside. A couple of shops line the other side of the old building: one being a bank, which is closed; the other one, a boutique specializing in urban attire, closed; then, lastly, a sandwich shop called Meme's. I stop in front of Meme's, which is lit up with flickering fluorescent lights. Only two people eating, both of them hunched over the tables like linebackers. I walk inside the restaurant and check out the menu, which mostly consists of gyros and grilled steak or chicken sandwiches. In the kitchen, a slab of sweaty meat is spinning on a metal pole.

Not too far away a robotic Asian lady wearing heavy shades of purple eyeliner motionlessly stands behind the front counter.

"Good evening, sir," she greets me in this tranquil, almost hypnotic state. "May I take your order?"

I look over the menu once more. I'm not hungry, but I feel as if I should order something instead of standing here like a dick. I turn to the soda machine, and then face the strange Asian lady.

"Large coke, please," I say and hand her two dollars for the cup.

I take the cup, then the change, and fill up the cup with water.

On my way out of the restaurant, I can't help but notice one of the customers. One bite after another, he's shoveling food into his mouth. His right leg is bouncing up and down underneath the table, as if he's about to explode from his body. I take a sip of water and leave the restaurant.

I walk back to the door in the alley and check once more but the door is still locked. I set the cup aside and search for other doors. Check each one. They're all locked. I start to question whether or not I'm in the right alley. I check for objects or structural flaws that I witnessed while I was running from the cops. I recall a dumpster with a crushed wheel. I find the dumpster and sure enough, it has a crushed wheel. Okay. I remember a pink garish sign above one of the doors. Tattoos? Tailor? Totem?

I search around the alley and spot a sign: TELLER.

The sign is hidden underneath a broken canned light. The first part of the sign is burned out. Shards of glass lie scattered over the ground below. I read the blacked out word *Fortune*. Fortune-teller. Okay. Right alley.

I check the windows above. One is glowing with a familiar faint red hazy light.

Next to the fire escape ladder hangs a sign with the glowing word LIVE.

Below: *The Loft*, spacious apartments available for rent.

And below that: a phone number.

I type the number into my phone.

Save the number.

Then leave the alleyway and search for other ways to get inside by standing on the quiet street and listening to my surroundings.

In the silence, the answer comes to me in the sound of steel-toed boots tapping along the sidewalk like the claps of a horse's shoes. I pinpoint the sound to my right where a man with a spiky Mohawk struts toward me. He's wearing a black leather jacket with sharp metal studs on his shoulders, and he sashays in a signature walk: both hands firmly planted in his pockets and his eyes are facing the ground and yet, for some reason, he appears as if he can see *everything* around him. He cuts through clouds of steam oozing from the manholes below.

Before he passes me, I ask him for a smoke. He pulls out a cigarette pack from his pocket, and I bum a smoke from him.

"You seem lost," he says as he hands me the cigarette.

"Ah—I'm not sure," I tell him.

He takes a step back and looks over my body. "Hey, man," he says over a breathy chuckle, "I don't mind pointing you in the right direction. . . ."

"I'm looking for a train—" I say, "—you know where I can find one?"

"You must be talking about the Peachtree Center Station—"

"—Not that kind of train," I correct myself.

He looks me over once more.

Then, he flicks his head at me.

"You a nark?"

"Nark?" I say, flexing my brow. "No."

"You sure?"

"Yeah," I say. "I'm sure."

Again, he gives me a once over as he runs his fingerless gloved fingers along the side of his chin and almost imitating my previous gesture, cocks one of his eyebrows into his forehead.

Finally, he says, "*Follow me.*"

I follow Mohawk to the same restaurant as before—Meme's—and strangely, a part of me always knew I was in the right place by the feeling I got whenever I ordered a cup of water. He holds open the door for me, flicks his head at the lady behind the counter, who, in return, responds with a nod as well, a slow and steady bow of the head. Next, she acknowledges me, not with the same nod, but with a cold, empty stare.

We walk past the soda machine through a dark, narrow hallway, which leads to the restrooms. We make our way past the restrooms and hook a right at the end of the hallway.

Mohawk asks me for my name.

"Josh," I tell him. "Josh Lamb."

"Josh Lamb, huh?" He smirks. "Well, Josh Lamb, they call me Needles."

"Needles?" I say, tagging along. "Why they call you that?"

This man, Needles, smirks again.

"I like needles," he says.

Before entering the kitchen, Needles has me stand in front of a surveillance camera mounted on the ceiling.

"What is this?" I ask.

"We're just being cautious."

"Why?"

"Well, we want to know if you're really who you say you are."

"You don't believe me—"

Needles points at the camera.

"—Just look at the camera."

I do as Needles says and look at the camera above.

Needles receives a text on his phone; he looks at it, reads it, and then he enters the kitchen.

"Right this way."

Still confused by his behavior, I follow but do so more vigilantly. We walk past a pair of tired-looking cooks chopping away at meat with butcher knives, and head toward a set of secured doors in the back of the kitchen. We enter the door next to the freezer. Again, he holds the door open for me, then walks me down a steep flight of stairs. At the bottom is that same flashing red light from before. I hear music playing, similar music from the last night, however, with a low hum underneath a glittery and yet minimalist beat.

At the end of the dark hallway: the glowing red words *The Basement* above the doorway.

"The Basement," I read out loud.

Below stands the same security guard. He slaps hands with the guard.

He points at me and says, "He's with me."

The security guard lets me through.

We walk through the large, rundown room, which looks as if it used to be a club. We walk past a sleepy bar where two dolled-up Goth chicks sip on iced drinks with green leafy stuff in them. One of them checks me out. One of them calls me cute, I think.

"By the way, Josh," Needles says, "how old are you?"

"Nineteen," I say, "well, technically eighteen going on nineteen. But you already know that, right?"

"You got a birthday coming up."

"Yeah," I say. "Soon, I guess."

"You strike me as someone who hates birthdays."

"That obvious, huh?"

"You'll fit right in."

"Fit in?"

"Normally," Needles says over a sigh, "we don't allow underage kids into our little merry circle of awesome, *but* I guess there can be exceptions."

We arrive at a room that branches off from the bar, which is the same room I snuck into last night. About a dozen or so people are hanging around a blank projection screen. I notice other people hanging around in the shadows, but they look, more or less, like observers. Needles says that the area used to be an old music venue during prohibition. He calls it their "secret" gem.

"Yo," he hollers out to the group, "this here is Josh Lamb. Apparently, Josh has taken an interest in what we do."

"How'd he hear about us?" an upset guy says from the crowd, as if I'm not standing in the same room as him.

"I found out about this place by mistake," I say before Needles can open his mouth to speak.

I hear someone say from the back: "Thought we were done taking in strays."

"Did Glass check him?"

"Yup," Needles says, as he glances over at me. "He's cool." He grabs me by the shoulder and introduces me to the others. Some of whom around my age while others a few years older. "The mouthy one is Hammer." Needles points at Hammer, the mouthy one with a long and thin European-like face, gelled back hair. Then, points at a husky, expressionless guy dressed in an all black getup sipping from a slender beaker of what looks like mimosa at another lounging area. "The loner over there, that's Wage." Wage gives me the smooth cat nod. "Next," he motions at a starry-eyed blonde with pigtails throwing up the peace sign, "Lexis Lox. Don't let the name fool you, though. She don't mess around." Next to Lexis stands a rather short darker-skinned girl with tight cornrows, "Lil' Express," he says. Next to Lil' Express slouches a pale-looking kid with a silver grill and a thin patchy brown beard, two zigzags trimmed in the side of his head. "White China," Needles says. Then, White China chimes in, "Sup, Playa." Needles moves to the two Asian girls, who are both dressed in holey cardigans and skintight blue jeans. "The Meme twins, Me-One and Me-Two." They both throw their hands up in a subtle wave. 'Meme's," I repeat. "They run the joint upstairs," Needles tells me and points at others. "There's Respawn," he says. Then another: "That's New Jack." New Jack doesn't acknowledge me. Instead, he gives me a sour expression on his face, then continues talking to a girl around my age who appears smitten by his presence. He wears lots of jewelry, very showy cat, yet he comes across as a hipster. "Then," Needles says, "there's the Arabian Assassin, better known as Double-A." Double-A wears a lot of animal on his body, leather and a scarf made from a rodent's tail. "Last but not least," Needles points at a shy-looking but incredibly cute redhead standing all by herself, "Mayhem."

"Mayhem," I utter.

Needles turns to me and holds out his hands.

"We are the Mob," I think he says.

"The Mob?"

"No," he corrects, "The *Mawb*. M-A-W-B. Mawb—"

"—So," Hammer calls out, "we gonna start or what?"

"Why don't you wait till your nuts drop before you start barking orders, Hammy," Needles teases. "First, I'm gonna get his feet wet before we start a campaign."

"This noob better not be trash," White China says arrogantly, as if I'm not in the same room.

"Hey, we were all noobs once, brah. . . "

"Bite me, *Respawn*."

"Tell it to the Train, WC—"

"—Chill you two," Needles says, acting as mediator. "I'm just gonna show him the ropes." He walks me to the projection screen behind the group and grabs two headsets with ear buds, as well as two sets of gloves from the holder. Then, before he hands me the headset and gloves, he turns to me and says, "*First*, you need a username."

"I've never played virtual reality before. . . "

The others laugh behind me.

"This isn't exactly like that commercial VR bullshit you're used to seeing advertised all over the place," Needles says.

"How so?"

"Let's just say this makes virtual reality look like child's play."

I look over the strange console: VR-XS.

"What's the XS stand for?"

Needles smirks.

"You'll find out soon enough," he says and switches on the projector. On the screen displays a menu with the pulsing words PLAY and OP-TIONS behind a shot of the front of a train bursting through a concrete wall. I turn back to Needles, who's waiting for my username. Then, I turn around and see the others impatiently waiting, as well.

"Just Josh, I guess."

"Come on," Needles says with a strange glint in his eye. "You can do better than that. Think about it, Josh. You can be anybody you want. . . "

I think about a username. I'm guessing all of these people who Needles just introduced to me are all going by their usernames. It'd be hard to upstage a name like Mayhem.

I call out the first and only word that comes to me. I can't tell if Needles is impressed or taken back by the name. Either way he's totally cool with the username.

As Needles did with me speaking "Mawb" the wrong way, I correct him with both the pronunciation and spelling of my username.

"A'ight," he says and hands me the headset and the gloves. He helps me with one of the gloves first. Then, I pulled down the visor until it's covering my entire face, like a pair of oversized glasses.

Once I'm plugged in, I first need to take a snapshot of my face, or personal selfie, which, according to Needles, is taken by a microscopic camera along the top of the visor. Needles doesn't give me any warning. As soon as my picture is taken, an image of my face flashes on the screen, then appears beside my username.

"Now, the game has synced your username with your face," he says, "so whenever you put on the headset, the game will recognize you."

"This is insane," I say, still in awe.

"You haven't seen nothing yet," Needles says and pauses. "You ready?"

I take a deep breath.

"I think so."

Needles turns on TRAINING MODE and the screen displays a set of hands hovering in blackness. He shows me the sensors surrounding the gloves, as well as the room. Then, puts on the other glove. Whatever movement he makes with his hand, the hand on screen replicates his every movement. He balls his gloved hand into a fist. On screen, the hand balls into a fist. He does other movements like giving me a thumbs or even flicking me a middle finger to prove, as way of example of the extreme sensitivity of the gloves. Any movement, he emphasizes, you make will correlate with your avatar in the virtual world. He helps me with the other glove. My hands are now fitted with two gloves. Lastly, he runs me through the headset.

He says, "Like the gloves, the sensors inside the headset will pick up every move you make."

He puts on his headset. I follow suit and put on the headset and then slip the ear buds into my ears.

The world suddenly before me goes black. I look down at my hands, both open palms lost in a forever blackness.

A voice says over my shoulder: "Got the hang of it so far?"

"Yeah," I say. "I think so."

I turn to my right and see a staticky man standing in the blackness. He suddenly stretches farther away from me into a wash of blinding light. A grid of neon lights pulls across my eyes like a hot net of wires. Then, I find myself standing in a desolate subway. I look around the gritty subway. I'm disoriented. It feels as if I'm in a subway. Literally. I can't tell whether or not I'm in a game. It feels *that* real.

"It takes a while to get used to," I hear Needles say from afar. His voice gets closer: *But when you do, I swear, it's like a drug.*

Needles approaches me, and he's dressed differently: he's wearing a pressed suit with a black tie. His greasy black hair now slicked back.

"You look different," I say.

"This here is my avatar."

Needles walks me over to a poster, similar to the main menu, of a train speeding out of control. Hanging on the wall is a poster for the film, *The Hate Train.* Below are the credits and whatnot, and the poster could pass as one you'd find hanging outside a movie theatre. He pushes a button on the bottom right corner of the poster. The poster dissolves, revealing a touch screen with the two users: Needles and myself. My image is blacked out while Needles' image looks like a celebrity mug shot.

"Stand still," he says. "Smile, if you want. Doesn't matter."

"What are you doing?"

"Say cheese."

He pushes another button on the touch screen.

A bright flash momentarily blinds me.

Then, I hear a *clicking* sound of a camera.

"Just verifying your avatar," he says, as he pulls up a still of me standing before the poster. Looking like a complete idiot. He widens his fingers over the touch screen and my image pulls back, revealing my entire body.

Stark naked.

Then, I look down at my body below.

I'm naked.

However, I'm missing the one thing that makes me. . . me.

"What the. . . where did, you know, it go?"

Naturally, I quickly cover myself with my hands. But then I realize what's the point since there's nothing down there.

Without Needles looking I spread my legs and make sure it's not tucked between my legs.

"Don't worry," he says, grinning. "You're *not* really naked." He turns to me and smirks. "It's time to choose."

"Choose what?"

"Male or female or other."

"Other?"

"Fill in the blank, if you want. Nobody's judging."

"Male," I say without hesitation.

Needles has me press on the male option.

All of a sudden, I'm showing.

I cover up myself, for real this time.

"You can make you bigger, if you want."

"Bigger?"

I look down at my shriveled little penis, a turtle's head.

"Let's just get this over with," I say, embarrassed.

He clicks on a pair of pants on the touch screen.

"There you go," he says, as he takes a step back and leaves it up to me to dress myself. "Dress yourself to your liking. It has over a thousand stock outfits, or skins, or you can custom fit yourself." He scrolls through a list of various skins, all in alphabetical order, starting with the letter A's, for instance, a couple of skins catch my eye, like *Acid Attacker*, *Agent Orange*, *Agitator*—which, oddly enough, consists of a similar costume as me, black jeans, black hoody, black ski mask, black gloves—*A.I.A.* (Artificial Intelligent Assassin), *Airhead*, *Alien*—which, when clicked on, opens up a bullet of at least two pages of alternate versions of the slouched, gray-skinned being, like *Alien Cook*, *Alien Deliveryman*, *Alien Resident*, or my favorite, *Alien Cat*—then, finally, *Anon*, which I recognize. "Whatever you want," he says.

He doesn't bother scrolling through the B's.

"What do I do?"

"It's no different than, say, a phone," he says. "Use your finger to scroll. Then when you find your look press the FIT button on the touch screen."

I scroll through the hundreds of outfits, or "skins" on the touch screen. I decide to dress myself in a black kimono.

"Don't forget," he says lastly. "Your weapon."

Next, I scroll through a list of weapons; and while I'm scrolling through weapons, I can feel each one gripped in my hand.

Of all the weapons, I come across a favorite of mine.

"A katana?"

With confidence, I *confirm* my weapon of choice; and then, all of a sudden, it appears in my hand. I glance down at the katana gripped in my hand. Even my hands, as well as my arms are, not bigger, but thicker and hairier and strangely, manlier, like Bill's before he turned into a health nut.

"Suits you," he says.

I hear talking behind me, not in the game, but outside. People are making wages, placing bets. I hear someone say the word *hurl*. I don't think anything of it, at first.

Suddenly, the horn of a train echoes throughout the dark tunnel and ceases my attention.

"That's our ride," he says and walks to the edge of the platform.

"This feels so real," I say.

"Just remember," he says closely, "Two rules. First rule: Never turn on another user. Like don't go overboard and mistakenly kill me. I'm on your side. Got it?"

"And the other rule?"

"Second rule: Whatever happens in the Hate Train stays in the Hate Train."

"Easy enough," I say with a shrug.

The train approaches us. Stops. The doors slide open.

Anticipation builds, as I wait to step into the train.

Needles holds out his hand, letting me inside first.

"All aboard," he says, wearing a thin smirk.

I step inside. The doors close behind us. The train starts moving forward.

"These people part of the game?" I ask, looking over other passengers sitting in the seats, as well as clinging to the handrails.

"This is the game," Needles says. "There are different modes in the game: campaign, side-ops, or free-for-all (melee)."

"What are we playing?"

Needles pulls out a hypodermic needle from his coat pocket and jabs it into the neck of a smelly elderly homeless man, who is lying across two seats. He pulls the needle from his neck. Then, his body flops over the floor, and the homeless man passes out.

"Free-for-all."

"What did you just do to that man?"

"It's free-for-all," he says. "You can do *whatever* you want."

"They don't fight back?"

"Some do." Needles looks ahead at some guy with wide shoulders standing at the end of the train. His eyes are wide and bloodshot, and crazier than crazy. Fuck me crazy. He's on another level of crazy. He's wearing a black 80's retro *Lightning Vision* shirt underneath a fashionably ripped jean jacket. Meaty sideburns the size of pork chops. A greasy hairdo. Tight jeans and black leather boots with spurs. I see an object glaring in his hand, but I can't tell what he's holding. I get a closer look and realize it's a hunter's knife—however, a switchblade would be more appropriate, considering his 80's getup. I acknowledge Needles. He points at the 80's freak and says, "He'll fight back."

Suddenly, the 80's man charges at me. He weaves around each passenger. Needles asks me if I'm going to use "that thing" or what and I don't even realize what Needles is talking about until I glance down at the thing in my hand. The katana.

The 80's man strikes at me, and at the very last second, I raise the katana and block the blade. I block each strike, but he's more powerful. I try to swing at him, but the katana hits the pole behind me and prevents me from making a decent strike.

"Katana on a train," Needles says to me while shaking his head. "Poor choice, if you ask me."

"Now, you're telling me this," I say, backpedaling.

"Hey," Needles says casually, as he stands back and watches me getting my ass kicked, "you wanted to be a samurai."

"Can I change my weapon?"

"Too late," he says, "however, it's free-for-all. With that said, whatever weapon you find it's all yours."

The 80's man forces me to the floor. I crawl away as he stabs a passenger who gets in his way. His eyes, even more intense. Penetrating. He looms over me, his eyes wide with a madness that could only be seen in an over-the-top anime.

Meanwhile, Needles stands against a pole with his arms crossed. Watching in fascination.

The 80's man suddenly rears back the knife and just as he strikes down at me, like he's about to sacrifice a virgin, his head jolts to the side. Blood sprays all over my face. His red eyes roll in the back of his head, and he drops the knife, falls to the floor, and dies. Hammer reveals himself behind the 80's man, a bloody hammer gripped in his hand.

"Look who decided to join the party," Needles says.

"I was getting sick and tired of watching you two dick around," Hammer says.

"So," I say, out of breath, "that's why they call you Hammer."

"I forgot to mention," Needles says, "up to four people can play at once."

I stand up, and I see Mayhem walking through the door at the other end of the car. In her hand, she's holding a Molotov cocktail.

"You might wanna duck, *Gaud*," she says.

The 80's man suddenly springs to his feet. Now he's charging at me again. Mayhem flings the Molotov at my direction. I duck, as she commands, and the bottle shatters over the 80's man body.

He ignites in flames, punching and kicking and scrambling around the train. I grab the fire extinguisher from the wall. I turn it the other way around, bottom facing up, and hit the flaming asshole with the butt end of the extinguisher, smashing his face. The 80's man falls to the floor and dies, for real this time.

I hear a *dinging* noise, like coins are being flushed from a slot machine.

A hologram pops up in the corner of my eye: "Gaud," it reads. "1000 points."

"A thousand points," Needles says casually. "Not bad for a first time. I 'member I struggled to get a hundy when I first popped my cherry."

The blood rushes through my veins. A wash of red light flashes over my range of vision.

"What was that?" I ask.

Hammer says, "Turn around, genius."

The homeless man, the one who Needles jabbed, is standing behind me, positioned in a fighting stance. He throws a couple of karate chops at me, but I dodge them while next to me other players are starting fights of their own on the train. Behind me, Needles is repeatedly stabbing some guy with his needle. Hammer is racking up points by bludgeoning random passengers—one by one—as if their heads were nail heads. Then, Mayhem is doing what she does best, which is causing mayhem.

The homeless man lands a couple of blows. Flashes of red wash over me, revealing a weakening health bar. . .

"You're almost dead, Gaud," Needles says. "*Fight back!*"

The homeless man throws another wild punch, but I catch his hand and pull back on his arm. He lets out what sounds like a hiccup as he staggers toward me. Now, my face is nearly pressed with his, and his body odor reeks of a sewer that had been extracted into cologne and even one sniff alone of the fecal stench burns my nose hairs. His crusty, chapped lips split apart like an old wound, exposing his tiny yellow teeth scattered like crooked tombstones along the pale gums of his mouth.

With my left arm I uppercut the bottom of his elbow. The bone in his forearm breaks and part of it projects through his sleeve. He stumbles backward, clutching his stringy, dead arm in agony. He's screaming out: What'd you do? What you do? I return the assault and throw a punch of my own, which sends him against the handrail. I loom over his body as he holds onto the handrail for dear life and start pounding on his face until he's choking on his own blood. I keep punching, despite his immediate surrender. A sudden force comes over me. I can't stop swinging. I'm like a machine without an off-switch. In that split second of losing control, I'm not inside the Hate Train. Instead, I'm watching the world being infected by madness behind the window of my golden-laced penthouse. Below me people are scrambling around in a state of frenzy on the moss-covered streets of Times Square and eating one another like cannibals. Then, fast-forward to months later, the feast is over, and I'm looming over the last remnants of mangled bodies clinging to their last dying breaths and telling them in their last moments of life how pathetic they are. Then, fast-forward years later, I'm watching the Tongass Forest burn to the ground. There's nothing left of the polar ice cap, and New York City is flooded and the skyscrapers look like the nails of giants barely inching above the surface of the water and from my penthouse suite, the view is better than paradise. Rewind, I'm breathing in the smoke from the millions of crematories burning the inhabitants of a lost world. Then, rewind farther back, I'm standing on top of a dune as the blood of the earth oozes from the floors of the Atlantic and smothers the perfectly sculpted bodies on South Beach in black gold. In the split second, I'm flicking over black manikins like army men toy soldiers along the ashen ruins of a modern world. In that split second, I'm looming above the heavens and pulling on the billions of strings attached to the limbs of my cursed children.

In that second, that moment, that flicker, that flash, I'm playing God.

I hear a voice over my shoulder: I think he's dead.

More points tally up in the corner of my eye. Doubled. I stand up from my kneeled position, and my hands are throbbing.

The train comes to a stop.

Then, doors open.

"This is us," Needles says, and I follow him outside while Hammer and Mayhem stay on the train.

The doors close and the train proceeds down the tunnel. Mayhem walks to the window and watches me, and I watch her as she drifts farther away into the glittery blackness of the train tunnel. I turn to Needles, who, again, is wearing a thin smirk on his face. He places his hands on the sides of his face and removes his head from his neck. His body scrambles like an old VHS tape. Then, he disappears without a trace.

I'm left standing alone in the subway.

Panic creeps up into my shoulders, my chest. A tingly strangeness replaces my body, a similar feeling that I've experienced twice before in my life: once while spending the weekend with my cousin, Gabe, at Lake Cynosor, me tubing while Gabe was pulling me with a jet ski. I remember he accelerated over a steep wake. I fell off the tube, but Gabe kept riding and I was left alone, treading water in the deepest of ends, unaware of the devilish creatures swimming below in that murky water. The world started to spin and shrink all around me. It was, by far, the scariest feelings I have ever felt, being all, in the deep. I hated that feeling. And for a while, I hated Gabe for leaving me behind in the water. Eventually, he realized I had fallen off the tube. But that feeling, I'll never forget it. Then, the next time, just a few years later, the same feeling was upon me like an awful stench. After I botched my first attempt, I tried once more. The last time, I think it was more or less a cry for help than me wanting to die. I filled the water in the bathtub up to my bellybutton and waited for the inevitable to happen. As blood started to paint the water red, that same feeling was upon me. Frightened of the creatures waiting below me. My world shrunk into the palm of my hand; and for a moment, I felt as if I could squeeze my fist and crush the very life that I held—*tap, tap, tap.* . . The footsteps increase in speed and deepen in volume, like something microscopic walking along the threshold of my eardrum.

I grow panicked.

My hands start to shake, and my body tightens up. High-pitch whispers move like silky phantoms throughout the dark tunnels and the lost corridors of a subway which, strangely, holds an eerie similarity to Lake Cynosor like a divinely grand emptiness engulfing me and making feel so little; whereas below me, an entire world unseen by human eyes—those dubbed devils.

A sharp, stabbing pain shoots through the back of my neck. A hazy blackness washes over my vision. A blurry head hanging from a wire manifests before me. The face consists of a spectrum of all colors in front of a lit backdrop.

I rub the blur from my eyes, and Needles is revealed standing in front of me with my headset in his hands. My head starts to spin as my eyes try to readjust themselves to the other world.

Needles is telling me to take *deep* breaths *slowly*, he emphasizes, like a nurse talking to an incoherent patient. I do as Needles tells me, then focus on one object inside the room. The object happens to be not an object but a person: Mayhem. She's plugged in next to Hammer. Both of them are going to town on each passenger inside the Hate Train.

The dizziness stops as I focus on the projection screen. On one side of the split-screen, a fire is spreading inside the train. Like an action film, Mayhem leaps through the back window of the train. The shattered glass rains down all around her like snow. Then, she rolls onto the tracks and firmly plants herself in an action pose. She stands up and casually walks through a side access door; and inside the amber-lit room, she finds a duffel bag of money on top of a table. More points tally up over her side of the split screen. Needles is saying something to me, but his words sound so distant. He taps me on the shoulder—*Gaud.*

"*GG*," Needles says, as he leans over into my vision.

GG?

After he tells me again, "GG" or "Good Game," which is like universal language for gamers or a sign of respect for the fellow player, the buzz finally wears off.

"It takes a while to get used to," he says, inching closer. "How you feel?"

I direct my attention back to Mayhem. She pulls back the headset over her forehead first, then slips one of the ear buds from her ear. Carrying that same vacant expression on her face, she turns to me.

Behind me, Wage is slapping a wad of the cash in his hand. He takes the cash, runs it like a cigar underneath his nostrils, and takes a whiff of it. That's when the nausea comes back with a vengeance, like a stinger in the gut.

I suddenly rush through the hallway as my stomach starts to do pull-ups against my esophagus. I make it to the alleyway before I can make a mess of myself and let loose behind a dumpster.

"Everybody *hurls* the first time," so I've heard.

In the corner of my eye, I catch a glowing orange sign in the reflection of a murky puddle next to the stomach bile. I see the wavy word *evil* rippling in the water.

PART TWO
THE ENGINEER

**The Lie: Understanding the Ins and Outs of the Hate Train
– Double Standards – Less than zero – There's something
↑ with Mayhem – Bummer – Very strange attraction –
Other drugs – Not the same**

SAM the Shrink asks me what it felt like playing the Hate Train for the very first time. I look around the stale, sleepy room, and then glance at my reflection in the mirror on the wall. Before I draw my attention back to Sam, who patiently waits for my response, I think carefully about my next answer.

"It felt like. . . " I start, ". . . like a rush."

"Is it fair to say you wanted to continue playing this game?"

"It took awhile for me to find my bearings after I unplugged, but once the disorientation subsided, I couldn't wait to go back in."

"What did you think about Mayhem after she came to your aide during your first initiation into the Hate Train?"

I pause, and again, think carefully about my answer.

"Obviously, I was impressed by her skills," I say. "She was definitely next level. I dunno," I say, trying to find the right words, "it felt. . . *comforting*, knowing that someone had my back."

Sam peeks down at his notes on the table.

"Rule Number One: Never turn on another user."

I say, "I knew that rule was going to come back to haunt me."

Sam asks, "Why did you struggle with rule number one?"

I take my time and think more carefully about my next answer because I know that, whatever I say, my words may be used against me.

#

After two games of free-for-all, I'm dying of thirst. I tag along with Needles back upstairs to the restaurant. I grab a booth near a window while Needles grabs two medium-sized cups from the icy-faced server. He flirts with her for a minute—at least, I think he's flirting from the way he plays with her jet-black hair. I can't tell whether the server is smitten or extremely terrified by his presence. Needles whispers in her ear, causing the server to take a step back and clear her throat. Needles leaves the counter; however, the server's demeanor is less icy and more fidgety and strangely, insecure. She struggles to keep her once stern, guard-like posture. I focus my attention back on Needles, who's making a drink with each sample of soda from the soda machine. He turns his shoulder and waves me over. I walk to the soda machine and fix myself an orange soda.

"Suicide, baby," he says.

"Suicide?" I repeat.

"Yeah," he says and takes a sip of his concoction of soda. "The drink."

"Why you call it that?"

He hands me the drink.

"Try it," he says.

I hesitate at first.

"Don't worry, man," he says. "I don't have cooties."

I take a sip of the drink, a nasty brew of corn syrup and artificial flavors.

"It's an acquired taste," he says and takes another gulp.

We head back to the booth and sit across from one another.

"I'm gonna be straight up with you, Gaud," Needles says over a drawn-out sigh. "How'd you really find out about this place? You hear about it from one of the guys? Hearsay—"

"—Nah," I tell him. "Like I said, I got lost last night. Saw y'all playing that game. I guess—I dunno—I was just curious to find out what it was. That's all."

"That's your story? For real?"

"Yeah," I say over a forced laugh. "That's my story. Don't you believe me?"

He looks me over.

"This place is special," he says seriously. "I've seen lots of people come through here. People without homes. People with absolutely nothing. No family, friends. People who went through their share of shit. Some people who want to find a release at the end of their day. People who just want to 'fantasize' what they can't do in real life, you dig?" I don't know whether or not Needles wants me to respond. I just give him a nod of the head. "For example there's this one dude, Wolfgang, comes in on Wednesdays, as straight as an arrow, business type. Think he works in accounting or whatever—something that involves wearing a suit and tie. Dude is straight up legend in the HT. I never ask him why he comes here. To him, it's a release, I suppose. All that animosity that's built up inside him all day, taking orders for The Man, being a slave to The System. In a way, HT is his salvation. His great escape. And believe it or not," he leans in closer, "the one thing that's keeping him from the box."

"Box?" I say. "You mean death?"

"Nah," Needles says. "Jail. Not like there's a difference, right?"

What do I know about jail?

"Tell me," Needles says after a tense pause, "what are you looking to get out of all of this?"

"What'd you mean?"

"You said you were lost, right?"

"Yeah."

"So, what are looking for?"

I think carefully about my next words.

"Ah—I dunno," I tell him.

"You don't know?"

"I wasn't looking for anything," I say honestly. "I was just walking around the city."

"You do that a lot, huh?"

I give Needles a shrug.

"Sometimes," I say. "Yeah."

"That's dangerous." He takes a sip of his drink. "Lots of *dangerous* people out there."

"Y'all don't seem dangerous," I tell him.

"Oh yeah," he says, surprised by my comment. "So you've already figured us out, huh?"

"Nah," I say, "*but* I think I'm pretty good at reading people."

"How about May?" he asks. "Can you read her?"

I don't respond as quickly as I should.

"Mayhem?"

"What'd you mean?"

"What do I mean?" he repeats. "She likes you, fool."

"Really?"

"Shit yeah."

"I never picked up that vibe from her."

"I've been playing with May for about four months now," Needles says. "She's boss. I mean, if the Hate Train ever went mainstream, she'd be like a rock star. Queen *May*hem, the queen of all lords. Players like May don't rescue other players, only players who she knows will be beneficial to her."

I can't see myself being beneficial to Mayhem. If I am and I've given her some kind of false impression, I wonder how I can benefit her or vice versa.

I ask Needles a question that's been weighing heavily on my mind: "How'd *you* find the game?"

Needles doesn't answer at first.

The question comes off as one a nark would say.

"Respawn knows a guy who knows a guy who works in the gaming industry," he says, studying me closely. "He said his guy recalibrated the XS prototype because it'd overheat over time, *but* all of that's beside the point. The *point*:" he says, "just follow the second rule and everything will be just peachy. You dig?"

Not really the answer I was looking for, but whatever.

"Whatever happens in the Hate Train stays in the Hate Train," I say. "Easy enough."

"There you go," Needles says and makes a *clicking* noise with his mouth. So, where you from, Gaud?"

"Mount Olympus," I tease.

"Seriously."

"I thought y'all didn't like talking about the 'outside' world."

"Noobs are exceptions," he says, taking another sip of his drink. "Don't be shy. . . "

He waits for an answer.

I tell him, "Spartacus."

"No shit," Needles says, his voice climbing a couple of notches. "New Jack lives not too far from there. Bellamoore, I think."

"I know Bellamoore." I try to think of something else to say before the subject turns to recent events that transpired right outside Bellamoore not too long ago. "So most of y'all live in Atlanta?"

Needles bobs his head.

"Most of us," he says, "except for Wage and a couple of others."

"So Needles," I say. Just the sound of his name on my tongue sounds foreign. "That's not really your name," I say, "is it?"

"You kiddin' me?" he says, laughs a little. "What kind of parent would name their kid Needles? Of course, it's not my real name."

"But you do have a real name, though," I say. "Don't you?"

He puts aside his drink, reaches his arm across the table, and holds out his hand.

"Travis Slake," he says with that same untrustworthy smirk on his face.

I finally shake his hand. The handshake is firm, business-like.

"Between you and me," he says closely, "I wouldn't be so—how do I say—eager to get to know the others. You know, personally."

"Why not?"

"Normally, except for a few chatter birds, we don't speak about our other lives," he says. "Most of the time we leave that nonsense at the door. *But* you remind me of myself when I was your age."

"How so?"

"A guy *always* looking for something else," Needles says in the same serious tone as before. "When I. . . stumbled across the Hate Train, I stopped looking for something else. This here was my new thing. My New Drug." He removes the glove from his left hand and shows me a tattoo of a hashtag on top of his hand. "Four hundred and twenty-three days sober now. Believe it or not, the HT actually helped me kick the dope. Like every drug, though, it must be done in moderation. Otherwise, that's when it starts to control you, as it once did me. That's why we only meet up three times a week. Fridays. Saturdays. Then, Wednesdays. Wednesday nights usually have smaller crowds because most people have to work the next day."

I ask, "Why the hashtag?"

He looks over the hashtag, runs his fingertip along the lines of the tattoo as if it's precious, like a birthmark or a scar, a flawed feature so unique that it's hard to erase.

"Not a hashtag," Needles says, smirking. "Number sign." He extends his hand over the table, gives me a closer look at the tattoo. "When you're an addict, everyday turns into the first day of your life, like you die the night before and you're reborn the morning after. You're constantly throwing away all of the crap from your previous life and starting over from scratch. I hate four hundred and twenty-three. Yet I need the number as much as the number needs me. It reminds me of how far I've come; yet, it reminds me how small I am in this big-ass universe. The number keeps me humble. Balanced. Most importantly," Needles holds up his drink, "it keeps me sober."

Needles laughs at his own comment; and somehow, I find myself laughing, not like a snicker or chuckle but a heady laugh that carries throughout Meme's. I've always laughed at my own jokes. I've always laughed at other people and how ridiculously stupid they are or how they find humor in the dumbest shit. I've always laughed at mimicking or mocking other people. I can't remember the last time I actually laughed because someone else had made me laugh, even though Needles wasn't really telling a joke. But to me, it felt like a joke. It feels good to laugh again, the way it was intended.

I hear a couple of people talking over Needles' shoulder. Mayhem and the Me twins enter from the kitchen. Double-A isn't too far behind.

I stop laughing as soon as Mayhem makes eye contact with me. The twins grab food from the kitchen while Mayhem and Double-A walk outside. Mayhem lights up a cigarette while Double-A pulls out a necklace holding an e-cig.

I turn to Needles, who's shooting glances at Mayhem, as if he's encouraging me to talk to her. I stay in my seat. Needles lets out a sigh and stands up.

"Gotta use the head," he says, then once more holds his gaze on Mayhem outside.

I grab Needles before he walks away.

"Are they, you know, together?"

Like a couple, I want to say.

Needles nods at the two standing outside.

"Them?"

"Yeah."

"Nah," Needles says. "May, she's really not his type if you know what I mean."

"Oh," I say, recognizing Double-A's mannerisms, especially his overtly dramatic gestures while he drags from his e-cig. "I see."

Relieved, I turn back around and Needles is shooing me away.

I get the hint and go outside where Mayhem is swiping her finger across the screen of her phone.

"You got another one of those?"

She reaches her hand in her breast pocket and pulls out a smoke for me. It's a menthol. I hate menthols, but I don't want to come off as a pussy. She hands me her already lit cigarette. I light up my cigarette with the lit end of her cigarette, and then hand the cigarette back to her.

"You're welcome," she says teasingly.

"Thanks," I reply and take a drag from my cigarette.

We both share a smile, not so much a smile, but more or less an involuntary twitch of the lip.

"I'm actually trying to quit," I say. "More of a social smoker."

"Why don't you quit then?"

"Yeah," I say. "That's probably a good idea."

"Honestly, the best way to quit," she says, "is to surround yourself with other people who smoke. Sounds unorthodox, I know, but it worked for a friend of mine."

"It's so true," Double-A says, blowing out a massive vape cloud. "Builds up your tolley."

"Tolley?"

"Tolerance," Mayhem says.

"Really?" I say. "I didn't know that—"

"—The more you can resist the urge to smoke," Mayhem says, "the easier it is not to crave a cigarette. Seriously, you're *never* going to not be around smokers. It's part of life. People smoke. They've been smoking since, like, forever. You can't go cold turkey. Trust me. Tried once. It was hell."

"I know exactly what you mean."

"You have to slowly wing yourself off—"

We both speak at the same time: me uttering *where*, then Mayhem uttering the word *how*. The two words combined sound like the word *wow*.

"You first," I say, allowing Mayhem to ask the question.

"*How* do you like the game so far?" she asks me.

"It's different," I reply. "How do you like it?"

"I wouldn't be here if I didn't like it."

"Okay." I ask her, "So what got you into VR?"

She shrugs, then smiles.

"Guess it beats going to a bar and getting hit on by a bunch of fuck boys," she replies, the comment stirring a laugh from Double-A. "Everybody I know goes to bars. I'm not into that anymore."

"You in college?"

She shakes her head.

"Went to Central for two years, then dropped out," she says. "I haven't quite figured out what I want to do yet."

"Same here."

"How about you?"

"College?"

"Yeah."

"Nah." I take a drag. "I'm currently looking, but I don't know. College is too expensive."

"Not to be brutality honest, but it's pointless," she says. "Big fat waste of time. I've been thinking about going to a technical school instead, somewhere that specializes in one particular field."

"What kind of field?"

"Graphic design, mostly. I dabble on the side, but I'd like to get better at it." She points inside. "You see the menu?"

I hesitate.

"Ah—yeah," I say. "You did that?"

She bobs her head.

"That's cool."

"How about you?"

"What about me?"

"What are your interests?"

I think long and hard about my next answer.

I decide to tell her what she wants to hear.

One white lie won't hurt.

2

The Mawb calls it a night.

Mayhem disappears for a while, and before I can say my goodbyes, she's nowhere to be found. Double-A tells me she had to run.

Needles and I exchange phone numbers. He tells me the next time I decide to show up out of the blue I need a password. Otherwise, he says, I won't be let inside the Basement. He says they, a mysterious character named Glass, who apparently is in charge of maintaining the property, switches up the password every week.

He'll text it to me, if I'm interested in playing.

I tell him I'm extremely interested.

And that's the other rule—the third one—which isn't much of a rule but rather a cover charge without the charge: If you don't have a password, you don't play.

In other words:

No password. No play.

Easy enough.

3

A red glow washes over one half of the sky, and I can't even believe where the time has gone once I check the time on the dashboard. I leave Atlanta and drive back to Spartacus. I don't listen to any music on the way home. The idea of switching on the stereo doesn't cross my mind. Instead, I just drive in a car filled with silence and think about the game, the Hate Train, and how—even though, it's just a game—how great it felt to play. I also think about all of the new friends I've made. Most importantly, I think about Mayhem.

4

When I return home, the TV in the living room is still on and most of the lights downstairs are turned on as well.

I quietly close the door behind me and check my phone. I have five missed calls, one from Needles, then the rest from Peggy. She's even texted me, which is something she rarely does. The text reads: WHERE ARE YOU?

I head straight to the stairs. I hear Peggy from behind as I reach the second stair. She's back to her old pissy-self again; and before she can speak the inevitable words *Where have you been*, I tell her that I was at a friend's house. I never talk about my friends with Peggy, mainly because I don't have any friends—at least none whom I can call "friends." She's been worried all night. I can tell from the dark bags underneath her eyes.

"This is going to stop," she says. "The next time you decide to spend the night out would you—at least—let me know?"

"I don't want to do this right now," I say and proceed upstairs.

"Joshua!"

"What!" I yell back, even louder, as I make it up another stair.

Blood creeps into the sides of Peggy's face. Her eyes swell, then go black like a cat's eyes right before it's about to pounce.

"Have you been drinking?" she asks.

"No," I say. "I haven't been drinking—"

"—Drugs?"

I smack my gums, which can come across as an amplified "No" or me simply avoiding the conversation or me not wanting to admit that I am on drugs, which I'm not. But it's the only thing that naturally comes out of my mouth. I've never been the type to smack my gums. I know very little about drugs. I've tried them once or twice, but I don't care much for them. Like smoking pot which I did with the neighborhood stoner, but I didn't like the way it made me feel.

"Josh," Peggy says, her voice calmer, "would you just please let me know next time? That's all I'm asking for. . . I respect your privacy, Josh, but you have to let me know next time. Are we clear?"

I'm not in the mood to argue with Peggy. I compromise.

"Okay," I say and head straight to bed.

5

I manage to catch a few hours of good restful sleep until I'm woken up by the sound of a vacuum running downstairs.

I vacuumed yesterday when she was at work. The downstairs is clean. The downstairs is always clean, all thanks to me. I know it's Peggy's unspeakable way of telling me it's time for me to wake up.

I grab a bite to eat downstairs and Peggy, the curious cat, wants to know what I did last night.

"Were you with a girl?" she asks, as if she's waiting for me to say yes. "Well," she says, "you can tell me. What's her name?"

"Mayhem."

"Mayhem?" She's looking at me, as if I'm crazy. "What kind of name is Mayhem?"

"I dunno."

"What's her last name?"

I don't think she told me her last name.

"I don't wanna talk about it."

"Okay." She makes an attempt to leave the kitchen, but before leaving, says, "Well, did you at least have fun?"

"Yeah," I tell Peggy. "I did."

One side of me likes the way the truth rolls off my tongue.

Another side hates it.

6

I gumshoe "VR-XS" but can't find any information on the system, which, according to the Internet, doesn't even exist. I check gaming community websites, streaming channels, and forums and find a couple of unreliable sources mentioning a replica of VR-XS in the works but as I dig further, I end up running into a dead end.

Finally, I research the game, *The Hate Train*.

Again, I find nothing related to the virtual reality game.

Which is weird.

7

Later that afternoon, after spending hours staring at my computer screen, I make a charge for a new OPTIC headset, which connects to my computer.

I waste my entire Sunday playing a post-apocalyptic game called *Annexation: The Fall of Helm*. I'm a lost nomad trapped in the same over-used environment where everything is ashy, gray, and gloomy, and the entire world is suffering from the fallout of a nuclear war, which has given rise to machines and the fate of *all* humanity lies in my hands. It's all the same rehashed bullshit, only with a different title. Although the graphics are fairly decent, they're not as realistic as the Hate Train. Not even close.

8

By Tuesday, I get sick and tired of playing *Annexation*.

Wednesday can't come soon enough.

9

At noon, I receive a text from Needles: *TOUCHSMART.

I text Needles back: WHAT TIME YOU GOING?

He texts me back: 9:00.

I text: I'LL BE THERE.

9.

Atlantageddon – The Fix – Exploring the Hate Train – Skins– Just a game – Kill or Be Killed – A dynamic duo – A Perfect Shot – Saved by Mayhem – Not Ronnie – What am I? – His name is Bryan – Tree hugger

"GOING to the movies" is what I tell Peggy before heading out the door. She's thrilled that I've opened up more dialogue between us. She asks if I'm going out with the same person from the other night, this so-called "Mayhem" girl. I say yes, and tell her that I'll be back around midnight, maybe a little bit after midnight, but if I decide to stay out, I'll let her know via text. She likes knowing that she's now in the loop. She likes seeing me do things with other people. If she only knew the truth.

I arrive in Atlanta, and the traffic is a mindfuck. There's been a major wreck. I get off at the exit before downtown and try to make my way around the congestion but end up running into more traffic. Every turn I make, there's traffic everywhere, like everybody's trying to get somewhere fast, resulting in one colossal clusterfuck. I start getting anxious. If my hands grip any tighter around the steering wheel, I feel as though I'll crush it between my fingers. I'm trying to do everything in my power not to rip off the goddamn thing and chuck it at the slow-ass car ahead of me. Left and right, people are driving like glorified assholes. I'm screaming at them, too. The drivers. I'm watching *every* rule they break either from not signaling to making illegal turns along the median to cutting in front of me. One driver pulls out in front of me and doesn't bother to give me a "thank you" wave. I scream at him. He screams back at me. Next thing I know, we're both screaming at one another, me through the window, him, through his rear view mirror. Other drivers cut me off. One of them comes inches away from hitting me. I'm starting to feel cornered. I take the ramp and get back on the highway.

The traffic is moving again.

After about a half-mile of moving at a steadier and manageable pace, the traffic bottlenecks again, leaving me at a complete standstill. I'm starting to feel ultra-violent, a step beyond violent, like the makings of some sort of supernatural monster in a movie. The prequel, back-story, origin story, or whatever the hell Hollywood seems to be shitting out these days. I'm tempted to ram Maximus through each and every one of them and even take out innocent bystanders for extra points. I turn my thoughts away from the violence—all of the blood and guts stained over the red highway—then direct my thoughts to more pleas-ant, fantastical ones, like the notion of hover cars in the science fiction movies. There, I envision my car farting out a pillow-like cloud of smoke from the exhaust before launching into the sky above and hover-ing over the traffic as the pedestrians—now size of ants—slowly slip from their obsolete vehicles and gawk above at my fancy hover car. The thought alone comforts me. My hands loosen. Then, suddenly, my thoughts go awry again. I think about these hover cars and how they'll never be around in my lifetime. Most of the dates in these futur-istic movies weren't so futuristic after all. Yet, they were like a couple of years from now, or even worse, several years ago. What the hell hap-pened? Did filmmakers and the writers who created these stories have such high hopes for us? What went wrong?

The thought alone tempts me to rip off the car door like a band-aid, wield like a weapon, and hammer away at the POS in front of me until there's nothing left of it but a pile of crushed metal.

Traffic starts to move, slowly at first, then steadily. Then, I'm gain-ing speed. I'm driving again.

The traffic eventually clears, and I find open road before me. I breathe a sigh of relief.

I pull out a smoke from the new pack and start smoking again.

2

I burn about an hour driving through the downtown. I stop by the Peachtree Center Station and hang around there for a little bit before making my way back to Meme's.

A different security guard is standing outside the Basement.

He asks for the password.

"TouchSmart," I tell him, and he steps aside and lets me inside the club where I see Wage sitting at the bar. Only a few people are here. Most of them I haven't met before.

Must be the Wednesday crowd.

I approach Wage—The Man in Black—since he's the only one from Saturday night whom I recognize.

"Sup, Gaud," he says smoothly, as we pound knuckles.

"Seems kind of dead."

"Yeah," he says. "Wednesday nights are usually slow."

I spot that guy who Needles was talking to, Wolfgang, playing the Hate Train. In the game, he's beating the shit out of a man dressed in a business suit and Wage informs me that Wolfgang's username, "The Wolf," is taking out his weekly aggression on the Boss Man, as usual.

We spend the next five minutes talking about Atlanta traffic.

I learn that Wage is from the city of Charlotte, which he refers to as a melting pot. He talks about the traffic there as well, and the roads, and how Charlotte's transportation is years behind and according to him, he believes those who developed the city never expected it to be as populated as it is today.

A couple of more show up: Double-A and a skinny-looking guy with a skeletal face whom I've never met before.

Double-A says sup, and introduces us to a new friend of his who goes by the name Jason, who, in return, immediately corrects Double-A by calling himself by a shorter and more appropriate version, which is "Jay." I ask Jay if he's playing the Train tonight, but Jay tells me that he's only here to watch and then he slaps Double-A on the backside. It's not until I notice the two being extremely handsy with each other, like Jay giving Double-A a titty-twister or Double-A reciprocating by ticking the tender and most vulnerable spots under Jay's ribs, resulting in Jay to smack Double-A's hand away and shout, "Cut it out!" that I realize they're on a date.

I hear girls giggling behind me. I pinpoint the giggling near the club's entrance. Lexis Lox enters the club via the alleyway. Mayhem is not too far behind her. She smells the back of her fingers. I don't know why she'd be sniffing her fingers. I don't think much of it. I check the time on my phone, which reads ten minutes till nine. I don't see Needles anywhere. I ask Wage if Needles has shown up yet. He says he hasn't seen him; and then, before I can track down Mayhem in the club, I feel two cold hands cover my eyes. The air behind me reeks like an ashtray.

A deep, croaky voice from behind: "Guess who?"

"I dunno," I say. "The Cookie Monster?"

I hear Lexis Lox laughing from behind.

The hands are removed from my face.

I turn my shoulder and see Mayhem standing with a cute smile on her face.

"Hey, Gaud," she says.

"Mayhem."

She leans into me, but it's not a typical hug nor a hand or arm shake, but more or less, a pressing of our bodies.

Lexis Lox lifts her hand to her chest and gives me a wave.

"Lexis Lox," I say.

"Sup, cutie," she says.

"You've seen Needles?"

"He couldn't make it tonight," Mayhem says, more upbeat than the other night. "He has to get up early for work tomorrow."

Wage cuts in: "Pah-lease. I get my ass up every morning at five o'clock. You don't see me complaining 'bout work."

"Well, some people actually go to a job to work."

"Whatever."

Mayhem pinches me on the arm.

"I got first dibs," she says, as she holds out her hand. "What do you say?"

3

After the Wolf is finished fantasy-murdering his boss, Mayhem and I put on our headsets, and she plugs us into the Hate Train.

First off, Mayhem walks me to the same movie-style poster from before, the one where a subway car is bursting through the wall like the Kool-aid Guy. Mayhem, I notice, is wearing the same outfit, or "skin," as before: a black and glossy dominatrix-type outfit underneath a cutoff red blazer, like something you'd see in a BDSM porn flick only without the blazer. Her red hair appears much brighter, though, like the color of fire. Me: I'm dressed in the same samurai outfit, which has been saved under my username.

At the poster, Mayhem pulls up the menu where a list of items are available: Campaign, Side-Ops, then two symbols (✔☞), which Mayhem explains is a check mark and a hand pointing a index finger to the right direction—basically, a "Checkpoint."

I don't bother asking her what checkpoint means. I've certainly played enough video games in my lifetime to understand the importance of the crucial checkpoint and how both relieving and rewarding it can be when saving your progress at a checkpoint, especially whenever playing a hard campaign. The absolute worse is playing a game, stopping halfway toward the end after hours of burning her eyeballs out from staring at the screen, then having to stop playing for whatever reason, like giving your eyes a rest or Peggy calling out dinner—then when coming back to the game at a later time, having to start over from the beginning because you forgot to save your progress. I can't tell you how many times I forgot to save my progress, then had to start over from the beginning, which resulted in me smashing the controller to bits out of a bloodthirsty rage, then days later, after the rage wore off, me scrounging up money around the house like a junkie to buy another controller.

Lastly, below Checkpoint is "Options," then, finally, "Archives," which speaks for itself.

Before I further inquire about the rest of the main menu, Mayhem touches SIDE-OPS on the touch screen, resulting in yet another screen to pop up.

"I've never played side-ops before," I tell Mayhem.

"There's always a *first* time for everything." In a flirty way, the corner of her lips curl into a smirk. Her squinty eyes heavy with seduction, as they cut right through me. I want to know what's going through her mind and what she thinks of me when she looks at me? "Don't worry," she says playfully. "I got your back."

"Uh—thanks," I tell her.

"Thank me later," she says.

She asks me what kind of game I'd like to play while she scrolls through various storylines within the side-ops mode: *No 1 Left, Stop the Train, Sniff Out the Terrorist, eXtinction, The Hijack, Bringin' Home the Goods,* and then lastly, a LOCK symbol over a blacked out picture of the sign, *The Warriors,* which I'm guessing is a bonus level of some kind.

"What's 'Stop the Train' all about?"

She touches the tab for Stop the Train and reads the description to me:

> "The train is speeding out of control! You have exactly three minutes to stop the train before it reaches The City. The catch: every passenger on board is infected with a new disease called *mysteria,* and if the train reaches The City, the sickness will result in worldwide pandemic. The symptoms of mysteria range from irritability to uncontrollable rage. The most common symptom is cannibalism. However, all hope is not lost! Teams of scientists are eagerly waiting with a cure close by. All you have to do is stop the train. . . "

"Sounds interesting," I say. "So, how do you 'stop' the train?"

"The only way to stop the Hate Train is to derail the train," she says. I ask, "And how do we do that?"

"Well, several ways," she tells me, "slam on the brakes. Clearly, that option doesn't apply to us. The other: place an obstruction on the tracks, which will force the train off the tracks."

"But how do you place an obstruction on the tracks when you're already riding the train?"

"And so, the question emerges," Mayhem says sarcastically. "I can't give you an answer, Gaud. You're going have to figure it out for yourself."

"How about 'eXtinction?'"

"You basically pick a target (a skin)—" which Mayhem says is a gamer term for referring to the outfit of a character, who wears certain clothes, as well as cosmetics, or uses certain weapons, like for instance, after scrolling to the letter P's, "PKN," Pocket-Keyboard Ninjas, whose weapons are phones that transform into shurikens or *throwing stars*, "— and you don't win the game till every single NPC with that skin on that team is dead. In other words, extinct."

"NPC?"

"Non-player character."

"You mean, like a bot?"

"Sort of, more like AI—"

"—*Artificial intelligence.*"

"Exactly." She smiles nods me closer. "Check this out. . . "

Mayhem touches a tab, revealing random groups of NPCs, not in alphabetical order: Square-faced Mascots; -imps; Group Latte; The Minimalist Party; *Brakemen*; Walking Preps.

"Right," I say, pointing at zombies with the Ivory League haircuts. I read the description: "Zombie frat boys."

Mayhem corrects: "Zombie frat boys with an enormous appetite for brains."

"Nice."

She continues to scroll through the various groups on the screen: Toler-tyrants; HillChillies; Red Collars; Uber Urbanites; Know-it-Alls In Overalls; Mr. Approval—

"—Mr. Approval," I pointed out. "I know the type."

"Lol," Mayhem says.

More groups: Slumlord Carnivores; Hats; Long Arms; Star Techies; Gonzo Gurus; Pledgers; Cankers; Spankers; Tankers; Pencil Pushers; Thrash Metal Larkers; Mobs of Finger-Waggers; Three-Eyed Trolls; Dummies; Chummies; Agitators—which I've already seen—Insti-Instigators; Nay-nayers; Raskulls.

Then she clicks on a sub-genre of 90's rock: Pale and Powdered; Soft Batch; Neverminders; Pearl Butter; Sponge Cakes.

Then, another yet category: White Lightning; Reich Bros.

Another: Hemp Hoppers; Gobby Goobers From the Fifth Circle of Hell; River Things; Snow-Its; Blueberries—no joke, human-sized blue-berries with these cute little smiley faces and tiny stem-like arms project-ing from the sides of their round, bloated bodies—Brownie Sniffers; Professors who overuse the word "*quite*" a lot in a sentence in order to sound educated; Chrome Junkies—or your typical hog enthusiasts decked out in black leather—WWWitches; Tappers. . .

When Mayhem stops on Tappers, the screen displays police officer characters tapping batons in their palms as if they're ready to use it.

"Cops, really?"

"You should see New Jack play this one," she says. "Believe it or not, he holds the highest score."

According to Mayhem, New Jack is one of the better players in the Hate Train and has the highest kill ratio and uses up very little stamina when he plays.

"Yeah," I say, thinking it over. "Dunno 'bout that one."

"What?" Mayhem says innocently. "It's just a game, Gaud."

"Yeah?" I look around. "Then, why does it feel so real?"

I move my eyes back to the screen and finish skimming through the other groups: Jockstraps; Pro-Tip Prophets; Ketchuppers. . .

She scrolls through at least thirty more groups, or skins. The list goes on and on. All of who are over-the-top characters, all ridiculous and exaggerated and oddly, not to be taken at all seriously. I mean, "Ketchuppers?"

"I don't know if I'd feel right playing that one," I say, pointing at the group from the letter B's.

"Beat-A-Nick?"

"It's just random guys named Nick."

It's obviously a poke at beatniks.

"Gaud, it's just a game," Mayhem emphasizes. "Remember the rules, right?"

"I know, but still. . . "

"So, pick one," she says.

"What the heck," I say, eyeing another game other than eXtinction. "No 1 Left."

"Good choice," she says. "Now, pick your level."

Mayhem scrolls through a list of various levels on the screen and each time she comes across a different city, the environment around us abruptly changes. She lands on Los Angeles, which she says is a hard level; and in awe, I gaze around and find myself standing on a platform overlooking the hazy city of LA, a sky drenched with pinks and purples under the silhouette of the cityscape. She scrolls past Chicago, the noisy L-Train weaving around skyscrapers like a dirt-stained gray serpent. The sky above changes from day to night and now, the skyline is a cityscape of Chicago, not Los Angeles.

She scrolls through other places with trains, including, not cities, but countries, like, for instance, Japan, where the sleek bullet train, or the "*Shinkansen*," runs through the entire island, or the rickety locomotives barrel their way across the hazy countrysides in India, or a yellow beast of a train full of tourists grazes the snowcapped Alaskan mountains. She pulls up familiar places like, for example, Washington D.C. or New York—

"—New York City," I say, as I look around and find myself inside a gritty subway station.

Idling on the tracks is "Train **8**."

All doors are open, and the train is waiting for us to board.

"You sure?" Mayhem says. "It's one of the trickiest levels in the game."

"What's the saying: If you can make it in New York City, then you can make it anywhere."

"The hell if I know," Mayhem says.

"As long as we have each other's back," I say, "then it should be a piece of cake. Right?"

I turn back to the train, and the dim lights are flickering and on the verge of burning out.

There's something about the train that doesn't seem right.

As if I'm about to walk into a trap.

4

After the third stop, I'm taking back my words.

Each and every one of them.

I routinely check my health bar in the top corner of my vision, and it's drained and continuing to drain. Mayhem's health doesn't look too good either. She only has a couple of bars left before she's toast.

"Told you it was a tricky level," she says, as she looms over the dead bodies of city-dwelling lowlifes lying on the floor. The flickering of shoddy overhead lights pulses through the darkness of tunnels and high-lights splatter of blood covering Mayhem's face—I swear, she looks and acts like a movie in these moments of tension.

Mayhem helps me to my feet. Another gang storms closer to us, and they mean business: thin, greasy hair, black sport coats without anything underneath, no shirts or ties, only sinister-looking dragons, beasts, and an assortment of mythological monsters tattooed over each one of their finely carved chests; and their biceps are about the size of both my thighs combined, and they look like the spawn of a Wall Street psycho.

The head member—a sickly, Euro-type villain with an extreme re-ceding hairline standing like a placeholder—waits in the other car while his three tattoo-faced stooges march through the sliding doors from the other car. They're all carrying aluminum baseball bats in their hands.

Two other gang members file in behind him like protectors.

"More of them," I say, out of breath. "They keep coming. . . "

"And they'll keep coming if we don't take out the leader."

"Got any plans?"

"I'm five hundred points away from getting the detonator," she says. "If I can get a clear shot at the leader, we still might have a chance."

"Will that give you enough points?"

"Should," she says.

"Then, what?"

"Then, we blow up the train," she says. "The point of the game is to kill everyone on the train, remember? My energy is low, and you're almost dead. . . "

I spot a crossbow on the floor, then a broken pole. I peel open the curled spider-like fingers wrapped around a bean burrito inside the dead hand of some stockbroker on the floor and scarf down the burrito as quickly as I can, which helps raise my health three bars.

"How good is your shot?"

I pick up the crossbow. One arrow left.

"Better than yours," Mayhem says.

I hand Mayhem the crossbow and then pick up the broken pole from the floor.

"Hang onto something," I tell her and hit the emergency brake.

The train jolts forward, causing each approaching gang member to fall to the floor. I rear back my arm and using all of my strength, fling the pole through the door's window. The pole pierces through the glass windows of both car doors, coming inches away from hitting the Euro-trash.

"I'm afraid you missed me, Gaud," he says in his phlegmy German accent.

But that was the whole point.

"Now," he says and pulls out a Luger pistol from his sport coat, "it's time to end you once and for all. . . "

"Thread the needle," I yell at Mayhem, who, in return, carefully aims through the hollow pole stuck between the two doors and fires the arrow into one end of the pole. The arrow finds its way into the hole, *clinking* and rattling all the way through. Then, it shoots from the other end of the pole and strikes the movie-like villain directly in the jugular. His eyes swell, and he's eating his own words as the blood streams from his mouth. He falls to the floor, knees first, and dies.

The other gang members rise to their feet and prowl closer. My points go up a little for the assist. Mayhem scores over three thousand points for the remarkable shot!

However, we're still *not* in the clear.

I try to hold off the other gangsters while Mayhem rushes to the telephone box and removes the detonator from inside.

"Got it," she shouts. "Let's go. . . "

I throw a couple of strikes at one of the gangsters; however, the blows don't seem to have any impact on him. I'm outmanned, and my strength doesn't even match the strength of the gangsters. I pull back and hurry toward Mayhem, who's waiting for me at the other end of the car. I tell her to push the detonator; then I use my remaining bars to turbo my way through the car. She waits. Times the jump. Then, as I zoom toward her, she pushes it. I grab her hand. We jump hand-in-hand from the back of the train as a ball of flames erupts behind us.

Each bomb dominoes from the front of the train to the very back and sets off a massive explosion throughout the tunnel. We land onto the tracks. I shield Mayhem with my body. Streaks of red flicker all around me like bolts of lightning cutting through a night sky. I hold onto Mayhem as tightly as I can as the flames rise above us. I open my eyes and look into those soft, glossy eyes. A wall of red suddenly slides across my eyes. My pulse is slowing. I'm dying.

Over the hazy redness, I hear several grunts and groans coming from Mayhem. She's moving my body, but I can't move. My body is a couple of faint pulses away from dying. I'm blinded by red.

She drags me to safety and seats me on the side of the tracks. I hear a *squeak* of a heavy metal door opening; then I feel a tug on my arm. The red starts to soften. The tracks come to light before me. To my left is the train engulfed in flames. All of the red fades completely now as Mayhem wraps a bandage around my right arm. The clothes covering my arm have been singed away and all that's left is this blackened limb.

"That's twice you've saved my life," I say, out of breath.

"Yeah, well," she says, "don't get any ideas."

She finishes wrapping the rest of my arm. I grab her hand and tell her thanks. We share a long gaze before her head snaps to the left from the sound of a *crackle* and a *pop*.

"Sounds like someone's cooking," I say.

"No," she says gravelly. "The game's not over yet. There's still one left."

"I thought we killed 'em all."

"Apparently not."

She stands to her feet and helps me up and we walk back over to the flaming train.

Along the way, she hands me a Beretta and I use one of the two clips I earned during the bonus round and load the handgun. We make it back to the wreckage, but the rear of the train is too hot to enter. I help Mayhem onto the platform of the subway and we find a car that's not as damaged. We make our way through all of the black smoke, debris, dead bodies, and twisted metal until we reach the first passenger car.

"There," Mayhem says and nods at the body movement coming from the end of the car.

I turn off the safety as I approach the last passenger who's crawling his way to the cab where the operator has been thrown through the front window. His legs are broken, smashed—both of them—and they drag behind like dead tentacles leaving long trails of blood along the floor. He manages to prop his body against the wall. He turns around and reveals himself to me. Ronnie Shields, the photographer from Manhattan—Ronnie the Road Runner. One half of his old, blemished, wrinkled face covered in blood and soot. His clothes frayed from the explosion. He's shaking, and he's scared. So I am.

I hear Mayhem saying something over my shoulder, but I can't make out the words.

"—*Gaud*," she says and pulls at whatever's left of my sleeve.

I turn to Mayhem, and she's worried.

"What are waiting for?" she asks me.

I fall into a trance: I'm standing inside Antiques and Things. It's night. I don't know why I'm here or what I'm doing. Displayed around me are all kinds of antiques and other things, lost, forgotten, or tossed aside. At that moment, I feel no different than one of the antiques inside the store. I feel lost, forgotten, and tossed aside, like Mayhem, like Needles, like every single member of the Mawb.

Ronnie's crying out for help. He's confused but still scared, and it shows all over his face.

My hands steady, and I feel myself growing a couple of inches. I'm peeling a match from the pack of matches and then lighting the match, then holding the tiny flame between my fingertips.

Gaud?

I snap from my trance, aim the Beretta at Ronnie's head, and right before I pull the trigger, I see Ronnie as me but older, much older. My face is wrinkled and covered in spots. My eyes look so innocent, like those of a child.

I shake away the hallucination and then shoot Ronnie directly between the eyes.

Our score tallies over a broken piece of glass; both of our usernames climb to the top of the leader board.

I turn to Mayhem, but she's already gone.

I remove my headset, still left in shock from the sight of Ronnie inside the Hate Train.

Mayhem walks over to me.

"GG," she says.

"Thanks," I say, as I drift off and think about Ronnie.

"What's wrong?" she asks.

"Ah—nothing."

"Did you see something in there?"

"Nah," I lie.

"Just a game, remember?"

"Yeah," I say. "I know."

I look around at the other members of the Mawb watching us, and they appear as equally shocked as me.

5

In an awkward silence, while we wait for Mayhem's return from the restroom, I ask Lexis if she's in school and her hesitant response is "out of school," as in she recently graduated. "Recently," I learn, is like four years ago. She has a business degree in Marketing, but she can't find work in her particular field, which I have a hard time believing, and yet, she's working the graveyard shift at the Daily Depot, stocking goods to pay back all of her student loans. Other than that, she tells me in a passive-aggressive tone, she can't complain. I suggest that she could market the Hate Train, since it'd be in such high demand, especially now with all of the chaos going on. People jacking themselves into first-class VR to expel all of their bottled-up aggressions toward the world. I can't be living proof that it actually works, that the game has somewhat softened and dare I say, delayed my plan to destroy the world. But there's no denying the feeling I get whenever I unplug. That feeling, like a high, my mind calm and my limbs loose and not wrung tight like a towel. It's like all of my troubles with the world don't exist. Some believe it's cathartic and even compare it to sex. Lexis hates the suggestion, but she doesn't actually say it with words, rather with her facial gestures. She prefers to keep the game, as she puts it, "exclusive."

Lexis switches subjects and brings up Phantasy Worldz—which is random, but I internalize and tell myself it's not as random as me asking her about school. We start talking about what's been going on lately, like the protests or boycotts and how people are getting more and more unhinged and easily *"triggered,"* which is a word Lexis has often heard. I feel as though the conversation is about to shift to a topic in politics— which I hate and really, have no interest in talking about. I anticipate her next move and immediately reel her back to the subject of Phantasy Worldz. She brings up Raymond Chancellor and the statue that had been vandalized by yours truly. She tells me how much the statue meant to her little brother, who's confined to a wheelchair. He has a "traumatic brain injury," Lexis tells me. I ask her how he ended up with this injury, and she doesn't want to tell me at first. It's personal. Yet, she brought it up. Maybe she wants me to feel sympathy for her. I don't know. So, I don't push the subject. Then, she tells me that he fell off a deck one night. He and a couple of friends were partying when the parents were gone on vacation. He landed on his head. Changed his life.

She tells me his name is Bryan.

6

After hours, Mayhem and I decide to take a walk around an eerily quiet downtown Atlanta. We spend most of the time walking in silence and admiring the quietude around us. Mayhem doesn't mind the silence; however, I feel as if she's ready to know more about me, as I am ready to know more about her.

She breaks the silence by asking me if she can ask me a question. I agree. Then, she asks: "Why do you play?"

Why do I play?

I never really thought about why I started playing.

Then, I turn the question back to Mayhem.

"Why do you play?"

"I asked first."

I think about the question. I think back to the first time I was plugged in with Needles. I think about the feeling, first being left in a state of wonder and then before unplugging, being scared shitless.

"It makes me feel alive," I tell Mayhem.

"That's it?"

"That's all I got."

"Okay."

"Now, your turn," I say. "Why do you like the Hate Train? Be honest."

"Me?" she says. "I guess—I don't know—it's better than going to a gun range—"

"—Or a bar?"

"Or that," Mayhem says, sighing. "It's a place where I can, you know, relieve stress. When I'm plugged in, it's like all of that stress from the day seems to just—I don't know—melt away, I guess."

"Do you ever think about leaving?"

"Leaving?" she repeats. "You mean, like taking a vacation?"

"No," I say. "I mean, like going somewhere else."

"Where would I go?"

"I don't know," I say. "Like somewhere away from here, away from people."

"You mean. . . like the mountains?"

"No," I say. "Not the mountains. Like somewhere less remote. A place with structures and stuff but like—you know—*less* people."

Mayhem turns to me and she's wearing a strange expression on her face.

"You don't like being around a lot of people, do you?"

I give her a simple shrug, and I'm tempted to tell her the truth about people and how much I hate them.

"This place isn't so bad, especially at night."

I look around at the tall skyscrapers that stretch into the black sky. A couple of late-night stragglers occasionally move past us like insects scuttling into a dark nook.

Mayhem leans closer to me: "Sometimes, late at night, it almost feels as if you have the entire city to yourself. Face it, Gaud—"

"—Call me, Josh."

"Okay, Josh."

She pauses.

"Face what?"

Mayhem loses her train of thought for a second, then remembers: "Everywhere you go, no matter how *far* you travel, there'll always be people. People aren't so bad. You know, I spend most of my day surrounded by people and you know the one thing that I've learned about people?"

"What's that?"

"They just want to be loved," she says. "That's all."

We share another intimate gaze. The blood rushes through my veins, and I find myself growing in size, not in height or anything, but in other places of my body. My throat tightens. My palms become sweaty. Then, my stomach flexes and everything inside it is prepared to launch directly at Mayhem's face. I don't know what would be more humiliating: me hurling my guts all over Mayhem's face or me trying to hide the bulge in my pants.

We stopped walking, and now, we're standing inches away from each other.

Before leaning in closer for a kiss, I hear Lexis calling out from across the street: "Time to jam!"

Mayhem turns to Lexis, then faces me again with that same serious expression on her face.

"I gotta go," she says. "Work. You understand, right?"

"Of course," I say.

She gives me a hug, not like the one before, but a kind of boyfriend-girlfriend hug. Then, she leaves.

As she crosses the street, she turns her shoulder and says, "I had fun tonight."

I wave goodbye to her.

Me too, I tell myself.

Early Bird – Yet another tragedy – Peggy shares what's on her mind – Elephant in the room – Numb – Back to zero – You're messing with the wrong dude, dude – Revenge is anything but sweet – 'Express' Round – Sup, Mayhem? – The ultimate diss

---

I'M up at the crack of dawn, despite only getting maybe an hour of shuteye. Peggy's downstairs eating breakfast, one of those low-calorie cereal bars that tastes like a chunk of cardboard.

"You're up early," she says, her brows raised in surprise as she chases down the bite of food with a sip of coffee.

I've been getting a lot of that lately, these surprised reactions or the "Do I know you?" type of facial gestures. I tell her I couldn't sleep, and she insists on making me breakfast.

I give her a shrug, which Peggy mistakes for a yes.

I fix myself a glass of orange juice while she gets to work on slicing through an avocado. I find two bruises about the size of blackberries on the inside of my elbow as I'm placing the OJ back in the fridge. I must've gotten them while playing the Hate Train. Sometimes, I really get into the game despite the sensitivity of the motion sensors.

Ignoring the bruises, I head into the living room and notice the TV is still on in Peggy's room. I overhear the news—or better yet, a morning show—with a shrill-voiced anchor talking about another shooter on the loose. She's even going off-script and putting in her own opinion about the shooter: *What has gotten into people these days?*

I turn on the TV in the living room and watch the report while Peggy continues to make my breakfast. Over fifteen protesters have been killed. Shot dead. The murder count, the TV people are saying, will continue to rise as the day goes on. Dozens, children included, currently in critical condition; most with life-threatening injuries. There was a protest against age-discrimination last night in front of a courthouse in the small town of Rover, Texas. Two days ago, like the whole Ronnie Shields incident, only this one caught on camera, a sweet old woman was the victim of a discriminatory act moments after letting out a beast of a cough prior to entering a beauty saloon that, apparently, she had been going to for the past twelve-plus years. Then, yesterday, even crazier, an elderly man was brutally attacked outside a laundromat and now fights for his life in the ICU. According to the report, he was beaten within an inch of his life. Suffered severe brain damage. Doctors stated in the news conference that he's facing a long road to recovery. The individual— who goes by the name, James Pharos—was minding his own business when he was blindsided from behind, and all of this went down just feet outside the range of a surveillance camera and only a couple witnesses spotted what they thought to be the assailants leaving the scene in a hurry. The cops still haven't found the person—or persons—responsible for the attack. They have a couple of suspects wanted for questioning, but the investigation is ongoing.

I flip through the other news channels, YNN, Century, The PC, and stay on the channel with the best coverage.

"You hear what happened?" Peggy says from the kitchen.

"No," I say. "What?"

"Some maniac shot all those poor people while they were protesting," she says with despair. "They say whoever did it pulled up next to the crowd and just started shooting. It's awful."

"They know who did it?"

"They're not saying," Peggy says. "They said the shooter is still on the loose."

I turn my attention back to the news and the reporter is talking to witnesses who were present at the scene when bullets started flying. One footage shows a cell phone video of the shooter unloading an assault rifle on the crowd. The shooter, who looks male, is covered in black from head to toe and wearing a bulletproof vest. The video goes shaky before the screen scrambles and cuts to black.

"Here's the thing," Peggy says mindfully, as she grabs the carton of eggs from the fridge. "Why are these people out there causing all this trouble to begin with? They said they were blocking traffic and throwing rocks at police officers."

"Who? Protestors?"

"*Yes!*" She suddenly pauses and corrects herself, "Well, let me take that back. According to locals, most of the people weren't protestors but outside agitators, who were there only to cause trouble. You think all these agitators really care about people, especially the vulnerable? I tell you, Josh, they're nothing but mean to the bone." She paces around the kitchen. "I just don't understand it anymore. I *really* don't. Sometimes, it's best not to watch television. Watch enough of it, it'll make you hate the world we live in." She's pacing around the kitchen and she's distraught and doesn't know where she's going. She opens the fridge and closes it, as if she's forgotten what she's doing. "Whatever happened people showing respect to one another? Instead, people want to go out of their way to destroy you if they don't agree with you! Things aren't so simple anymore, I guess," she says. "Not like they used to be. When I was your age, Josh, I didn't have time to go to protests. I was too busy working or trying to get an education to better myself—"

"—Yeah, well," I say, "the economy sucks. A lot of people are out of work. It's hard to find work—"

"—Don't give me that baloncy," she says, her voice more bitter than before. "When it comes to rolling up their sleeves and getting to work, they bitch about how they can't find a job. I swear it's like they're *always* looking for something to complain about."

I know her comments are indirect insults toward me.

I know, if I push the subject anymore, we're going to start arguing again, and I'm not in the mood.

She stops what she's doing and I don't even know what she's doing, except pacing around the kitchen.

Then, she squares herself to me.

And says, "People who go around looking for trouble and try to make it harder for others to live their lives have nothing else better to do. They're not doing it for a cause. You know why they're doing it?"

I don't answer.

"They're selfish," she says bluntly, "and they're powerless and they're looking for someone else to blame but themselves and their own misfortunes. That's no way to obtain power. What about the single mother out there, busting her butt, trying to keep food on the table, or the college student toiling away at two jobs in order to pay for school. You see them out there burning down the same grocery stores where they buy food? No," Peggy answers her own question. "You don't. You know why? Because they have a life, Josh." She places down the knife with a clanking *thud*, places her hand over the bridge of her nose, and breathes carefully. "Sorry," she says, holding her head downward. "I shouldn't have said that," she says quietly. She cracks open the egg on the side of the counter, pours the egg white into the pan by passing the yolk back and forth from one half of the egg shell to the other until the egg white is in the pan.

She watches the egg cook in the pan; however, I know that's not the only thing she's watching.

2

I notice an empty bottle of Chardonnay in the bottom of the trashcan as I'm clearing my plate. I check the dishes in the dishwasher and find a wine glass with a red imprint of a bottom lip along the brim. I look for any other wine glasses, but I can't find one, except the one with the smudge of lipstick.

3

While Peggy's showering, I go through her phone. I skim through her messages and find a text from Raphael. I'm guessing they had an argument either on the phone or face-to-face. Peggy wasn't the type of person to carry on text conversations. She's what I call "old fashioned," a person who likes to talk on the phone. I read Peggy's first text, and she's saying that she's sorry for what she said and that it wasn't her intention to hurt Raphael's feelings. Raphael replies by telling Peggy to never text him again. And his text is in all caps. So, I know he means business. I don't know what she said to him that made him so upset.

A part of me simply doesn't even care.

4

Before heading out, Peggy tells me that she left some money on the kitchen counter. I stop her as she opens the front door and ask her if everything is okay.

"Why wouldn't it be?" asks Peggy.

She's lying.

"You seem upset," I say.

"I'm not upset." Yet another lie. "I just have a busy day today. What are you going to do?"

"I was thinking about picking up more applications," I tell her.

"That's good," she says, then, as she attempts to close the door, she turns back around. "Josh," she says, "you know I didn't mean what I said earlier."

"I know," I say.

"It just makes me frustrated, seeing people treat each other that way."

I feel like she's about to go on another tangent.

"I understand," I say abruptly.

She walks back inside and gives me a hug.

"Everything's gonna be okay," she says.

I stand there, baffled as to why Peggy's acting so strange. Peggy hasn't hugged me in years. It feels like a stranger hugging me.

"Have a good day," she says and closes the door behind her.

I watch Peggy start up her car from my window. She's crying. She grabs a tissue from the glove box and wipes away her tears and then re-applies makeup on her face while looking through the visor's mirror.

Then, once she puts on her face, she drives away.

5

That afternoon I go on a website called Tracker and find out where Raphael lives.

I gather everything I need for Raphael and hide them inside my trunk while Peggy's at work.

When she returns from work I act nice and don't draw any suspicion. I wait until she's asleep and then sneak out of the house and drive to Raphael's home address in Mellview. He lives in a ranch-style house, a well-kept place in a more decent part of town where the only crimes committed happen in the safety of one's house. His Beamer is parked in the driveway, which slightly changes the original plan.

After parking at a safe distance, I grab the can of gasoline from the trunk and walk to Raphael's house where I pour gasoline over his Beamer. I pour gasoline underneath his car as well, and mainly concentrate most of the gasoline near the gas tank.

Next, I break the driver's side window and pour gasoline inside.

Finally, I leave a trail of gasoline along the driveway and strike a match and then toss the flame on the gasoline before it dries.

I stand back and watch Raphael's beautiful white Beamer shoot up in flames. I watch the flames. I admire the flames. I marvel at the flames.

One of the neighbors' bedroom lights switches on.

I rush back to my car, which is parked on the street adjacent to Raphael's street.

The Beamer suddenly explodes, a ball of flames mushrooms into the black night sky. The porch lights come on. Raphael races from his house wearing nothing but his tighty-whities. He tries to put out the fire with the hose but the fire is too great for him.

6

I'm up early again Friday morning. Peggy's downstairs making coffee while creating her own website on her laptop.

Curious, I peek over her shoulder and check out the website: i-Expanse, a new website that allows entrepreneurs, such as Peggy, to create their own websites from various templates without having to learn code, which, to Peggy, is gibberish. Very user-friendly to people, like Peggy, who aren't the least ashamed to admit that they're dumb when it comes to technology. She's surprised to see me again at this time of the day. She acts as if the day before didn't exist. I wonder if she heard about what happened to Raphael and his sweet ride. I don't ask her, though. Not my place.

"Do you want me to make you breakfast?" she asks.

"Nah," I say. "I'm good."

"I bought more eggs."

"I'm good," I tell her.

"You sure?"

"Yeah," I say. "Sure."

I make my own breakfast while Peggy gets back to work on creating her new website.

7

It's Friday night.

I'm back in the Basement again.

The security guard asks for the password.

I use the one Needles texted me earlier today: *Swingline.*

He steps aside, letting me pass without a problem. I first search for Mayhem, but I can't find her anywhere. I figure she's probably smoking a cigarette or killing time with Lexis.

I spot Hammer, White China, New Jack, Respawn, and finally, some dude named Skin Job, a member of the Mawb or friend of a member. I haven't met the guy before; however, he comes off as a rather shy guy who keeps to himself, unlike the others who are acting rowdier than usual and amped off shots of hatorade.

They're playing a round robin type game where the members of the Mawb state things that they hate, like the things that really get their blood boiling. Hammer calls it the "Express Round," which is like a ritual these guys do before they play the actual game. Like an appetizer before the main course.

I hang back for a while and wait for Mayhem to show, but she's a no-show. I don't really mind the sausage fest, even though, in the back of my mind, a part of me hates being in a room surrounded by a bunch of dudes. On a more positive note, I think of it as a moment where I can get to know them better.

I ask White China if he's seen Mayhem anywhere. He tells me in his thick Southern drawl, "They say she still thinkin' 'bout stayin' in, man. You know how she is."

Staying in on Friday night?

The news bums me out, but I try not to let it get to me.

Hammer overhears me talking to White China. He asks me to join in on the "Express." So, I decide to join since there's nothing else to do.

Respawn, who drives a POS hatchback that's one pothole away from shattering to pieces, voices his hatred for guys who drive nice cars.

Which I can relate to, for sure.

Well, maybe not the car itself, but, more or less, a preconceived notion of the guy behind the car.

Well-off.

Entitled.

Conceited.

Born in swimming pools of money.

Looks down at others, like me.

When the world finally comes to an end, I'd like to round up all of those nice cars out there and drive them off cliffs as a sport, like shot put or javelin, only instead of heavy balls or spears, high-performance sports cars.

"How about you, New Jack?" White China says.

New Jack thinks for a moment, then says: "I hate how we keep renaming things. Like I was talking to this girl the other day, right? And she pulled me aside and she was like 'Hey, you wanna take a *live photo* with me?' I was like," New Jack places his hand over his chin like the Thinking Man, tilting his head to the side with an otherwise perplexed expression, "Mmm'k. Mean like a video? 'Nah,' she said. 'I mean live photo, NJ.' She shows me what a 'live photo' is, right, on her phone, right? What she calls a 'live photo' is a goddamn v-i-d-e-o."

"Hey, New Jack," Hammer hollers, holding out his phone, "you wanna take a live photo with me?"

New Jack smacks his gums and waves at Hammer.

"Get outta here!"

"I hate the word *epic*," White China says.

"Know, right?" Hammer replies.

Next is Skin Job, who says in a monotone voice, "I hate my dad, for real."

The Mawb laughs.

Hammer says over the others, "Care to elaborate why you hate your dad, Skin Job?"

Skin Job sighs.

"I hate my dad," he says. "What else is there to explain?"

White China nods at me: "How 'bout you, Gaud? What do you hate?"

My stomach drops for a moment from being put on the spot. I hate people who put me on the spot.

I ignore my own hatred for those who put me on the spot, even though it's not White China's intention to put me on the spot, but I know it's only his way of encouraging me to participate in the Express game. I pause and think about the question and as I'm thinking, my mind is racing from one thought to another.

I tell them, "I hate a lot of things."

"Name some, man," White China says.

I swallow my guilt and name some of the things I hate. I don't tell them everything that I hate, but still, I tell just enough.

Skin Job and I end up tying the record on Sniff Out the Terrorist.
I'll set the scene:

> I'm patrolling the Hate Train when all of a sudden Skin Job
> flags the so-called terrorist by eavesdropping over an eighty-
> something man's grumblings. The old man is sitting with a
> beagle and watching a girl obnoxiously chewing bubblegum,
> blowing and popping big pink bubbles in other people's faces.
> His eyes moving from one person to the next. Each person—
> mostly younger people—starts to get under his skin from the
> girl smacking gum to the punk letting expletives fly through-
> out the train without any regard for the other people to the
> smelly kid with the cheese steak sandwich crop-dusting the old
> man. Then, all of a sudden, the old man pulls out what looks
> like this remote control from his coat pocket. The beagle's
> eyes turn red and electronic. The dog turns out *not* being a
> dog but an animatronic dog packed with Semtex. He stands
> from his seat with the little robot and holds up the detonator.
> "All of you inbreeds can go straight to hell!" he screams to the
> top of his lungs. I snatch the dog-bomb from his hands and
> fling it out the window while Skin Job uses the TaZer gun, an
> electroshock weapon that fires two barbs attached to wires,
> striking the so-called terrorist, and then using the battery to
> shock him into paralysis. We save the train and for a mo-
> ment, it feels as if we did something good.

We unplug from the game.

Respawn has called dibs on the next game. Mayhem has made it
out tonight, which catches me off guard. She's chatting with New Jack
near the bar. I shake away the dizzy spell and take a moment to gather
myself.

I play it cool and walk over to Mayhem and when we make eye contact, she acts distant at first, as if our conversation Wednesday night
didn't mean anything to her. New Jack's flirting with her, doing that
thing where he touches his chin like the Thinking Man as he moistens
his lips, like all Mayhem is to him is a piece of ripe and succulent fruit.
He touches Mayhem along the thigh, which causes her to giggle and
curl and bat her eyelashes.

I butt into the conversation before New Jack can move his hand further up her leg: "Mayhem, you came. . . "

New Jack bursts out laughing, a booming *ha!*

"She *came* all right," he emphasizes and gives me this look like he
wants to hurt me.

"I didn't have much going on," she says, both cheeks like roses. "Lexis was talking about going to Flynn's later, but you know how it can be on Friday nights."

I act as if I know how Flynn's can be on Fridays even though I don't have a clue about Flynn's.

"Know what you mean—"

New Jack interrupts me, "—We should hit up Flynn's."

"I don't know," Mayhem says. "We'll see."

New Jack turns his back on me and starts talking to Mayhem as if I'm not even there. Like I'm a ghost. It makes me feel as though I don't exist anymore. Is he that scared of me?

I leave the bar and join the others watching the game, but in the back of my head, I can't stop thinking about Mayhem and why she would be interested in a stuck-up rich kid from Bellamoore.

I'm tempted to come up with some bullshit excuse why I have to leave, but I don't want to make a scene, especially when I'm starting to make friends. So I stay and watch the chaos unfold in front of me. Mayhem and New Jack talk for about thirty more minutes. Then, before I know it, both of them leave without saying goodbye to the rest of the Mawb.

11

A red and violent dawn – Bloggin' a dead site – Not some collector's item – Standing on the edge of a blade – The text – A desperate cry for help – Kiss of a spider – Walls never stopped a flood – Fingerless – "They smile in your face. . ." – Breaking the #1 rule

SATURDAY morning is a complete and utter wash. I spend most of the morning treating fresh cuts along my arms and wondering how random markings ended up on my body.

Have I been sleepwalking, again? What the hell have I been doing while I'm asleep?

I take a hot shower, which helps ease the soreness in my hands, as well as my feet. Afterwards, I spend a few hours blogging. Most of it consists of me venting to people of the Internet World. A couple of trolls hit up the comment board, but I put them in their place and leave the scraps for my minions. I'm burned out by lunchtime, so I take a walk at a nearby park late afternoon, then sit by the edge of Lake Rama and watch the animal life all around me, mainly the birds. The calmness of the water helps clear my thoughts, as well. It helps rid a lot of things, especially the violence.

When the sun finally sets, I'm still left without any plans for tonight. I pace around my room for what feels like several hours and contemplate whether or not I should drive to Atlanta. If New Jack is there, he'll be all over Mayhem. He'll also be hogging the game like he did before Skin Job and I started playing. I know he's been a part of the Mawb longer than I have and I'm in no position to call him out, but sometimes New Jack acts like he owns the Hate Train. I certainly don't want to wear out my welcome.

I turn on the TV.

Nothing new: a shooting in Chicago—three dead, one of them was a kid no older than nine years old—a building fire in St. Louis; protests at nursing homes around the country, advocating for peace and fair treatment; several protesters in Baltimore were injured during a scuffle.

I decide to drive to Atlanta anyway after about an hour of pacing around my room while chewing the skin from my fingers. The Basement is crowded tonight, packed with both new and old faces. I don't see Mayhem or New Jack anywhere in sight; however, I spot Needles, who's talking to a four-eyed, sweaty-haired hipster dressed in raggedy flannel and blue jeans that appear as if they're two sizes too small. Needles acknowledges me. Waves me over. He's glad I came out tonight. We slap hands and he asks me how I've been.

"Good," I say and look around at all the people who showed up tonight. Then, I ask Needles, "Is Mayhem here?"

"Why you ask?"

"Just wondering."

"You gotta thing for her." He gives me a tap. "Don't you?"

Instead of giving Needles a straight answer, I give him a shrug.

"She caught the bug," he says. "Something going around."

"Maybe the whoop?" says the hipster.

"She said she wasn't coming tonight."

Once more, I look around.

I don't see New Jack here, either. Maybe he's around.

Now that I know Mayhem isn't going to be here, I sort of hope New Jack is.

2

Turns out New Jack is a no-show.

Hammer says that he wasn't feeling the hate tonight, which is a shame because I wanted to play the Hate Train with him, especially after learning that Mayhem wasn't going to show up.

Needles and I play Bring the Goods, and it's thus far one of the trickier games in the Hate Train.

The objective: We have to deliver "twenty cars full of merchandise from point A to point B."

The catch (of course, there's always a "catch" while playing the side-ops in the Hate Train): part of the track is missing and the part that's missing happens to be on a derelict bridge crossing a canyon. The problem is the bridge has been obliterated and all that remains is a hundred and fifty foot gap separating one cliff from the other with a river running through the canyon. A hundred and fifty feet! That's roughly half of a football field. Needles informs me there's something in the cargo we're carrying that may come in handy.

3

Long night.

I'm feeling depressed when I make it back to Spartacus. I had a blast playing the Hate Train with Needles, but, as he warned me, at the beginning, like trying a drug for a second time, you look for an equal—if not—better rush or high from the previous time you were jacked in. The catch is to maintain a balanced level of playing and not overdo it, he stressed. Take sips, I remember him saying. My clothes are smelly and soggy, and I'm ready to ooze underneath the blankets when I step into my room. I lie in my bed and stare at the full moon from my bedroom window. I think about Mayhem lying beside me, both our hands interlocked as we fall asleep underneath the pale moonlit sky.

4

I receive a call from Bill early Tuesday evening while I'm scrounging for food in the pantry. I don't answer the call. Instead, I let the call go to voice message. I hear the phone ring again, but this time it's not coming from my phone. It's coming from Peggy's.

I step from the kitchen and see Peggy talking on her phone. She steps from her bedroom and motions to the phone, mouthing those words, "It's your father."

I shake my head and give her the cutthroat sign. Then, she slips back into her room and it's like she's pulling teeth while she's talking to Bill. She finally slips from the room after she hangs up with Bill and says, "Your father's been trying to get a hold of you."

"I already know what he's gonna say," I say. "He's gonna want to go fishing this weekend."

"Well." Peggy waits for my answer before even asking the question: "Aren't you going to go?"

"I don't feel like it."

"Please go, Josh," Peggy says. "You *know* how much these fishing trips mean to him."

"I know," I tell her, "but I don't wanna go. You can't force me to go."

Peggy sighs and walks back to her room.

"You call him and tell him yourself," she says over her shoulder.

5

I receive a text from Bill: DO YOU WANT TO FISH THIS WEEKEND?

I text him back: I HAVE PLANS. MAAYBE NEXT WEK.

Maybe is the same thing as saying no. I know this will go on for the next couple of weeks. I'll keep texting him maybe. Then, after a while, he'll get the picture. He always does.

6

Both Mayhem and New Jack show up on a Wednesday night. New Jack's not acting as flirtatious as he was the last time I saw him with Mayhem; in fact, they seem at odds with one another.

Mayhem and I play a campaign together.

The first level starts off at the beginning of the first passenger car where we take out various gangs. After each car that we empty, we move onto the next; however, the gangsters become tougher along the way—and as big as heavyweight wrestlers! We end up making it to the last car where we face off against the Boss: a faceless, wizard-like cat who's dressed like an old, reclusive Jedi. His weapon of choice are these ancient-looking cast iron explosives, which, when exploded, give off a cloud of poison, which causes severe hallucinations.

Mayhem and I end up defeating the boss and moving onto the next level.

We leave the train and make our way through the subway tunnels for food and supplies when all of a sudden Mayhem removes her head-set. Wage's avatar appears next to me. Pump-action shotgun gripped in hand. I ask Wage, "Where'd Mayhem go?"

"Sup, Gaud," he says. "She split. Wasn't feeling so hot. . . "

Wage and I proceed to the next level.

I decide to quit halfway through the level.

Respawn takes my place.

I look around the club, but Mayhem's nowhere in sight. I can't find New Jack, either. I head upstairs, acting as if I'm going outside for a smoke.

As I reach the hallway leading to Meme's, I spot Mayhem and New Jack standing outside on a sidewalk. They're both making out as if it's the end of the world. I start to feel sick from the sight of the two kissing.

I rush to the bathroom. Along the way, I bump shoulders with one of the Meme twins who's exiting from the kitchen; however, I can't tell which twin it is—Me-One or Me-Two? She looks as if she has morphed into her sister, and for the life of me I can't distinguish one from the other. I excuse myself and hurry to the sink where I hurl in the sink. I wipe my mouth with spicket water, take a couple of deep breaths—three, actually, inhaling through my nose and exhaling through my mouth—then, I go back downstairs and play the Hate Train with Wage and Respawn.

I ask them if they want to play a side-op. Respawn isn't really in the mood to play, but Wage is down, as always.

Eventually, I talk Respawn into playing. We play the game, eXtinction. I pick the group, which rank "Hard as Fuck" in the level meter: Kleptoparasites, mutant-like ogres with eight limbs who consume and absorb the abilities of its attackers, and are, by far, one of the toughest skins to beat in the game.

We paint the entire train red with blood.

Carnage everywhere.

We destroy everything that crosses our paths.

We play as if, for a moment, we're gods.

7

I make it back to Spartacus and my voice is gone from screaming throughout the entire drive home. I storm out of the car and pull out my phone and look over Bill's text, asking me if I want to go fishing. The sight of the text makes my entire body cringe.

I take the phone and smash it over the street until there's nothing left of it but bits and pieces. I stomp over the broken pieces of the phone, breaking the already broken pieces on the street. I don't care if I wake the neighbors, like they'd care anyway. I don't care if I make a scene nor do I care what they think of me.

I don't care about anything anymore.

I know it's not the phone's fault nor is it New Jack's fault as to why I feel so much hate inside my bones.

Only one thing to blame.

But. . . I'm out of fingers.

8

Before Peggy wakes, I sneak outside and clear away all of the debris from last night with a broom and a dustpan. I toss the remains in the bottom of the trashcan. Peggy's going through her daily rituals, like stretching away night-stiffness, as I carefully sneak back inside the cool house.

"You just now getting home?" Peggy asks sternly and studies my face, mainly the swollen bags underneath my eyes.

Soon, she'll start nagging, and I'm not in the mood to deal with her.

"No," I tell her, my voice hoarse. "Left something in my car."

"Oh." Her facial expression changes from surprise to more surprise. "Okay," she says, wide-eyed. "Have you eaten breakfast?"

"Yeah," I lie. "I ate earlier."

I tell Peggy about my phone and how I lost it last night.

"Did you check your car?" she asks.

"Just did," I tell her.

"Any luck?"

None.

Then, she asks me about my voice.

I tell her it's from allergies.

9

By lunchtime, Peggy returns home with a newer, much nicer phone for me. She's says that "they," as in the phone service, canceled the signal on my phone and if anyone tries to use it, they won't pick up a signal. I still have the same phone number, though. I somewhat wish they would've given me a new number.

10

I skip Friday night and decide, after hours of pacing in my room, to hit up the Basement on Saturday night.

The crowd has doubled from the week before. I see more new faces among the crowd. I see some old faces, too. New Jack heard about how good I did while playing "eXtinction" that he wants to team up with me and try to beat the record together. Not sure why he chooses me. He could've easily chosen Wage or Respawn, who are both as good as me. I think maybe he wants to prove in front of Mayhem he's not only the better "player," but also the better "person" for Mayhem. I feel like I'm now stuck in a love triangle, and I now have to square off against my competitor in a dome covered in spikes where only one survivor makes it out alive. I feel like the fool fighting over a girl. *That* guy who deserves to be put out of his misery.

I play along anyway and New Jack picks the skin: Tappers.

He targets badges while I take out as many slimy attorneys as I can, but I make sure to stay away from the cops—even if I get close to one and he attempts to whack me over the head with a baton, New Jack takes out the NPC. I don't eliminate the Tappers, yet I incapacitate them for good measure. Knock them out with the butt of my katana or when need to, hack off a foot or a hand. New Jack's not a team player at all, not like Mayhem and me. He's reckless inside the Hate Train. Greedy and bloodthirsty. He plays as if he's showing off. All dick, no brain. His weapon of choice: a crowbar. He uses it on one cop, straddles the cop after he gets hit in the back of the head, and falls down to the floor.

There, in New Jack's wild rampage, I find an opportunity, sneak up behind New Jack as he's beating the cop to a pulp, and brandish my katana.

I don't realize what I've done until I'm jerked backward.

My head suddenly stretches away from me as if my body's made of goo. My headset is ripped from my head, causing a bolt of pain to streak across my eyes. New Jack's now on top of me, like he was with the cop before me, punching me in the face. I don't shield the blows. Yet, I kiss each one of his knuckles. Needles and Hammer rush to my defense and pull New Jack off of me. New Jack's yelling at me: "Who keeps inviting this muthafucka to begin with? Get this piece of shit outta here!" I run my hand underneath my nose and pull away a handful of blood. I turn to Mayhem, and she's not the only one who's shaking her head in disgust. They're all staring at me. They're all disgusted by my actions. I'm the one who has broken the number one rule of the Hate Train. I'm the bad guy.

12

Not so bad – The Victim – Checkpoint(zzz) – Minutes to midnight – A death in the family – Step #1: Learning how to grieve – B and E – What is Bill hiding from Peggy?

THAT same feeling floods my body, the feeling where I'm left floating all by myself. I'm terrified from all the emptiness around me. I don't know what's going to happen, whether I'm going to be torn to shreds or swallowed by the emptiness.

The feeling alone squeezes the air from my lungs, and I'm having trouble breathing.

I concentrate on the breathing, taking in each breath through my nose and out through my mouth. My left nostril is clotted with blood. I take in a deep breath and blow out hard and a dark ball of blood shoots out of my nostril, and I can breath way more clearly, so much that it stings my nose. I do a routine for about a minute or so (in through the nose, out through the mouth) until the thoughts of doom fade into an afterthought.

For the third time in my life, I see myself from the outside: the pathetic waste of flesh that I am, a *thing* taking up space, an undeserving individual who doesn't deserve what the world has to offer. For the third time in my life, I feel like a product. Like I'm utterly replaceable.

I check my face in the window of my car. I look like a horror movie. One side of my face is covered in dark strings of blood. My left eye is nearly swollen shut and blood is caked over my eyelashes like clumpy mascara. I don't recognize myself anymore. All I can see is leftovers of what used to be the son of a Decent Man. I hear my name being called out from behind. Mayhem is rushing toward me. I don't want to see her face. So, I open the door. She closes the door before I can step in-

side my car and my hand comes inches away from being jammed in the
door.

"What the hell are you doing?" I yell at her.

"Josh," she says, trying to calm me, "stop. . . "

She touches me on the arm, but I thrust my shoulder backward and
push away her hand.

"What the hell do you want from me?"

"What do I want?" She turns the question back at me, her voice
much louder.

I can hardly look Mayhem in the eye.

"What's gotten into you?"

I don't answer.

Then, Mayhem shouts, "I asked you a question!"

I hate questions.

I hate my answers.

I struggle to look Mayhem in the eye, not because I'm afraid of her
but because I'm afraid of the reflection in her eyes.

"I don't know what's happening to me," I tell the ground.

"This is about New Jack," she says. "You're threatened by him.
Aren't you—"

"—I don't care about New Jack," I say over Mayhem.

"Then, what was *that* back there?"

I have trouble trying to answer the question.

"Do you like him?"

"Who?"

"New Jack," I tell her. "D'you like him? Or, are you doing this all
for show?"

"For show?" she says, a deep furrow creasing between her eyes.
"What the hell is that supposed to mean?"

My eyes go all twitchy and something comes over me. My muscles
tighten in my jaw and neck. I can see myself from the outside again.
The watcher. I look like a cartoon character with the veins and muscles
blown out of proportion in my neck, like I have electronic cords pulling
down at my face, and my right eye—the good one—is the color of a
radish.

Then, the creature seethes, "You know *exactly* what I mean!"

Mayhem holds her hands in the air and cautiously takes a step back.

"You need help, Josh," she says, as if now she's concerned for my
well-being, as if she truly cares about me.

I hate sympathy.

Like she's in any position to give advice.

I don't want it or her sympathy.

"Me?" I say, stepping closer to her. "I need help?"

Mayhem starts to backpedal. She's scared of me. *I'm* scared of me.
I witness that warped reflection of myself in her glossy eyes. I want to

yank the snarling creature from the inside of both her eyeballs and strangle it until it no longer carries any breath in its lungs. Then, as I step closer to Mayhem, she backpedals toward Meme's, keeps a close eye on me, as if she's making sure I don't follow her. I stand my ground. It's better this way.

"Good," I say, as Mayhem finally turns her back on me. "Go! Walk away! I don't need you people anyway!"

#

SAM is puzzled by why I didn't accept Mayhem's help.

"That's *not* what I said," I say, growing upset with Sam. "Aren't you listening to me? She was using me."

"Using you for what, Josh?" asks Sam.

"I dunno."

"Did you at least give Mayhem a chance to explain herself?"

"She didn't have to," I say and pause. "I know Mayhem's type. I've spent years being rejected by those same girls who would rather follow the crowd than their own feelings."

"And you believe Mayhem had feelings for you—"

"—If she didn't have feelings for me, then I'd say she's probably the greatest actor to live on this planet. Of course, she had feelings for me. Something changed, though. Ever since she started hanging out with New Jack, she's been avoiding me."

"Well," Sam says, "sometimes people have a hard time trying to express their feelings, Josh. Relationships take time and effort and if you truly cared about Mayhem and let's say that she did like New Jack and felt attracted to him not only physically, but also emotionally, then you wouldn't have run away. You would've been happy for her—"

"—I didn't run away."

Sam looks down at the file of papers before him on the table.

"According to witness statements, you got back into your car and sped away."

"Stop it!"

I slam my fist on the table, causing the glass of water to tremble.

Sam leans back in the chair and tells me he'd like to change the subject.

He wants me to explain exactly what happened after I left the Basement.

In my own words.

The images come back to me.

Mayhem's face, then seeing the pale expression on her face, her eyes swollen and zapped with shock.

She lifts up both her hands from her abdomen and they're covered with blood.

2

I get inside my car, slam the door shut, and scream until my throat burns. The insides of my head, around my eardrums, crackle like a distorted speaker, and in the wake of that deafening roar, I can hear sounds and disturbances from miles away and those sounds closest to me, the constant hum of the streetlight, the *clicking* noise the traffic light makes when it flashes yellow, or even rubber soles of a late-night loner tapping the concrete when strolling on the sidewalk. I roll up the windows, cancel out the manmade sounds around me, and listen to the blood rushing throughout my body. It sounds like an old river. I lose myself in the old sounds, and in that moment, I find peace.

3

I have a tail when I drive back to Spartacus.

It's not until I finally reach the house that I start to worry about the suspicious car creeping into the neighborhood.

I pull into the driveway, turn off the ignition, and as I make my way toward the house, keep the car in the corner of my eye but not once do I fully turn toward the driver. The lights inside the house are turned off, and I soon realize Peggy's car is not parked inside the garage. She never gave me any indication or even left a message saying that she had plans tonight.

To the right of me, I hear chattering and laughing and hollering over Top 40 music playing in the neighbor's backyard. The neighbors next door have visitors, I can tell, and as always, they're being loud and obnoxious. It's not exactly a party per se—I count at least four cars in the driveway—but more like a small gathering of noise-polluting ass-holes.

I ignore the noise next door, and as I shut the door behind me, I check the front windows of the living room and watch the car creep by the house. The white car slows down, comes to a crawling stop, then keeps on driving farther down the street before making a right-hand turn down yet another road. I witness two dark bodies inside the car; however, I can't make out their faces.

My heart beats faster, and after calling out to Peggy throughout the unlit house but receiving no answer from her and then checking the kitchen and not finding a note on the fridge or kitchen counter, I'm left in a greater state of panic. *What if* she's in trouble?

I head upstairs and go straight to my bedroom, which happens to be on the side of the house closest to the neighbor's house. From the darkness of my bedroom, I hear them hooting, hollering, yelling, and howling like wild animals and even the words they speak are wet, slurred, muffled, intelligible, and riddled with laughter.

As I sit in bed and plug my ears with buds to block out the noise coming from next door, I pull out the phone from my pocket and search for the right playlist, a soothing one with a lot of Sade or 70's R&B, and let the ashes clear from my eyes. I don't even make it to the first song.

I have "12 missed calls."

Apparently, Peggy has been blowing up my phone. Ten of the calls are from Peggy. Two from a number I haven't seen before.

As I check the messages in my voice mail, I hear the sound of a car door shutting outside.

I check the window; however, I can only make out the rear of a car and the dimming of red brake lights washed over the driveway.

I grab the closest weapon that I can find, which happens to be one of my trophies, the swimmeret from the Raymond Chancellor and Sir Spur statue.

With weapon in hand, I rush downstairs and peek out the front living room window for a better look outside. Parked on the side of the street in front of the house is the same white Beamer I recently torched.

Raphael's Beamer.

The front door opens, and surprisingly, I'm somewhat relieved.

I conceal the swimmeret behind my back, as the door closes.

Two dark figures step into the house.

But based on their size and shape, they're not Peggy or Raphael.

As the dark figures robotically approach, their eyes softly flicker like that of cat's eyes.

"Who goes there?" I ask, holding swimmeret in front of me.

I locate the nearest lamp and switch it on.

There, at the edge of the foyer, stands Mayhem and New Jack.

"Josh, we don't mean to scare you," Mayhem says.

"What the fuck are you doing in my house?"

"I know how it looks—"

"—You can't just walk into somebody's house."

New Jack turns to Mayhem.

"Told you this was a bad idea."

"And why is he here?" I ask, pointing at New Jack.

"*We*," Mayhem says, referring to New Jack and herself, "we felt bad for what happened tonight."

"So you followed me home?" I ask. "You could've called me."

"We wanted to see you face-to-face."

The missed calls?

Twelve of them, two from a number that I didn't recognize.

"I want you to leave."

"But Josh, we need to talk—"

"—I don't want to talk!" I shout over Mayhem. "I said 'I want you to leave!' Right now!"

The two stand their ground, and I'm more angry by the idea of them barging into my private space, unannounced, like two criminals. If they mean well, then why would they sneak into my house?

I give them an ultimatum: "If you don't leave right now, I'm going to call the cops. . . "

New Jack says, "Serious?" He turns to Mayhem. "You two can have each other. I'm outta here."

New Jack leaves.

Mayhem is hesitant to leave.

A part of me wants her to stay.

But I stand my ground.

"Just leave," I tell her and eventually, she does.

A few moments after Mayhem closes the door, I hear commotion outside, and it's not coming from New Jack or Mayhem. The sounds, those voices, are familiar, ones I heard when I first arrived at the house. One of the voices is whistling, then another barking like a dog.

Curious, I poke my head outside and see New Jack talking shit to one of the neighbor's friends.

He says, "Mind your own fuckin' business."

"Wha'da fuck you jus say to me?" the neighbor's friend, an inebriated man in a dirty tank top and bagging pants barely hanging off his ass, says, as he struts toward New Jack, who steps in front of Mayhem, as if he's protecting her from the three approaching instigators—four now, I count, then five and growing.

New Jack is outnumbered, clearly.

Six against one.

I don't expect Mayhem to step in and help.

I wouldn't want to put her in that position.

So, I take action and tell them to leave, to get off the lawn.

They don't; in fact, they keep pursuing New Jack.

As much as I can't stand to see New Jack's face right now, I'm not going to stand back and watch him get beat up.

With the swimmeret still gripped in my hand, I storm through the lawn and scream at the six drunks, who are looking for a fight.

New Jack isn't helping at all, either, as he continues to fling one insult after another at the six drunks.

As the head-drunk shoves New Jack, I step in between the two and shove the drunk off New Jack, resulting in yet another drunk to step in and shove me. I brandish the metal swimmeret and tell him if he or any of his trash-friends take another step closer that I'll beat them to death. They laugh, as my words have no effect on them.

As New Jack and another drunk start throwing punches, one of the drunks blindsides New Jack by cracking a beer bottle over the backside of his head. I start swinging away, making contact with, I think, the neighbor, who falls to the ground, his head busted open, bleeding profusely. Others rush to his defense and pile up on me. I snap and I swing the swimmeret like a madman. Mayhem steps in and tries to break it up.

In a blind rage, I suddenly lose control of myself and when all of the fighting stops, Mayhem stands before me. Her pallid face covered in shock. She slowly moves her head downward, only to find the swimmeret protruding from her chest.

Shocked as well, I stumbled backward.

New Jack screams, "What in the fuck, Gaud!"

He stops picking the pieces of broken glass from the back of his bloody head and tends to Mayhem, who's now lying on the ground.

The rest of the drunks, including the neighbor, split and make a run for it back to the house next door while New Jack holds Mayhem in his arms.

"I didn't mean to. . . " I mumble, ". . . it was an accident."

"Accident my ass!"

"Whaaahh. . . what happened?" Mayhem asks, still in a state of shock.

"Be quiet and just relax," New Jack says and comforts her.

I backpedal to my car, get in, then do the one thing I'm good at.

#

"THREE days later, a police officer discovered you sleeping inside your car in an abandoned parking lot," Sam says.

"Yeah," I say defeatedly, as bits and pieces of the night start to fit together, like a puzzle. "So much for my getaway to Mexico."

"Where did you go after you left the house?" Sam asks.

"I just drove around." I recall that awful day I heard about her death on a small 12-inch TV mounted behind the convenient store clerk while I was buying dinner, which consisted of a bag of potato chips and trail mix, and two chocolate candy bars, one with peanut butter and another with nougat, as well as a 22-ounce bottle of orange soda and a handful of bottled water. As I hid my face underneath the hoody of my jacket, I witnessed my face—which looked a lot different, as in ghostly and frail—plastered all over the TV. All the talking heads, the news people, the crime analysts, the wannabe Nancy Drews, or those who'd say anything, even as absurd as calling me "evil," all to receive attention, had their five minutes of fame under the bright spotlight. Not like I made it hard for them. I was an easy target, not because of what I did but because I fitted into their on-going tale of violence where key parts of the story, like supporting actors who were not only involved, but also contributed to Mayhem's death, as well as details, including witness statements or critical timelines, were shrugged off, cast aside, or simply taken at face value. "I didn't find out until the next day on the news," I say to Sam. "All the things they were saying about me, like calling me a murderer. . . "

I shake my head in disgust.

"Well, as you said, it was an accident, right?"

Sam waits for a response.

A confession.

I know those jagged dicks behind the one-way mirror are bouncing on their toes in anticipation, ready to put a wrap on their case.

They don't call Sam "The Closer" for nothing.

As I stare into Sam's eyes, I realize where I've seen him before. It suddenly dawns on me that this isn't the first time I've seen him.

On TV, I remember.

The night that Fellowship For All burnt down to the ground.

The man in the crowd.

His worn face.

I remember that face.

Sam?

I stand up and walk to the one-way mirror and press my forehead against the glass and peek inside. I can't see them, those detectives, but they can see me. One characteristic jumps out at me: their cat-like eyes, hovering like fireflies in the night.

I pull my forehead away, leaving behind a greasy imprint on the glass.

"This isn't real," I say, ambling back to the table.

"Excuse me?" Sam asks, as he shuffles papers in a folder.

"*This*," I say, pointing around the room, "this isn't real."

"What is real?" asks Sam.

"You," I say, nodding at Sam, "you're *not* real. Neither is this place."

Sam leans forward in his chair.

"If this place isn't real, then where exactly do you think you are, Joshua?"

Then, I say it without any hesitation or doubt, "I'm *still* inside the Hate Train."

Sam smirks and organizes the folders in his briefcase before closing it. He stands to his feet, ready to exit the interrogation room.

All of a sudden, the floor starts to tremble, the table, the chairs, the fluorescent lights above, the ceiling, then the walls, as well as the one-way mirror.

The entire room is now shaking, violently. . .

"What's happening?" I ask Sam, who braces himself against the table.

"I'm afraid my job here is done," he says and rushes to the door.

Before I can chase after him, he closes the door behind him.

The shaking intensifies.

From a distance, I hear the familiar roars of an engine.

The roars get louder and louder.

I pinpoint the sounds coming from behind the one-way mirror. I attempt to break the glass with a chair, but it has no effect whatsoever.

As the sounds become deafening, I seek cover in the corner of the room and brace myself.

The glass shatters!

A subway train comes barreling through the entire wall, shooting debris and filling the room with clouds of dust. The front of the train comes inches away from hitting me, as it comes to rest. As the dust clears, I witness two figures emerging from the ruins.

Mayhem, who's wearing a look of disappointment on her face, reveals herself to me. She walks over to me, kneels down; and before I can ask Mayhem what's going on, she places both her hands inches away from the sides of my head and removes the invisible headset from my head. . .

I find myself on the cold floor inside the Basement, members of the Mawb looming over me, staring. They all look at me as though I'm a criminal, an outcast, a freak.

I glance up at the screen above, and in that moment, I recognize the game ✔☞ ("Checkpoint").

Mayhem says we started playing the game right after I broke the number one rule of the Hate Train, which was "Never turn on another user."

On the screen is Sam Glasser, "Glass" for short, as Mayhem explains, a program, nothing more than a "feature" in Archives.

"You mean," I say, trying to wrap my head around what Mayhem is telling me, "he's not a shrink."

"No," she says expressionlessly.

"I don't know what happened back there," I say. "I lost control over myself. But I get it. I screwed up. And I'm sorry—"

"—And that's what makes this so difficult, Josh," Mayhem says, struggling to hold back the emotion.

"May," I say and then turn to New Jack and the other members of the Mawb, "I'm sorry."

"You're a liability, Josh. . . "

"What?"

"You're out."

"What?"

"I said, 'I'm sorry.' What else do you want from me?"

Mayhem doesn't respond.

Needles pulls me aside and tells me that maybe this isn't for me. As in the Hate Train.

The pocket suddenly vibrates first, then starts to ring. I pull out the flashing phone from my pocket. It's Peggy.

I let the call go to voicemail.

After I receive a message in my voicemail, Peggy sends me a text on my phone: CALL ME PLEASE!!!! ASAP!!! IT'S BILL!!!!

I excuse myself from Needles and check my voicemail.

I have two messages. The first one is from Peggy, and she's telling me I need to call her as soon as I get this message. She sounds angry. The second, the most recent. It's Peggy, again. She sounds upset. She tells me Bill's in the hospital. Her voice is cracking over the phone and she's sniffling a lot, as if she has the flu.

I know it's serious.

4

I'm breaking every law on the road on the way to Aire Memorial. I crookedly park in two lanes. I don't care about my poor parking job; in fact, I don't give a shit about anyone around me. I rush through the emergency room and frantically search for Peggy. She calls out my name from behind. The expression on her face cuts through me like a blade being spun around my belly, like that old game we used to play as kids. Spin the bottle.

I approach Peggy, my legs heavy. Parts of Peggy's mascara are clumped together below her bloodshot eyes while other parts are smeared along the upper corners of her cheeks from where she has been constantly wiping tears from her face. Her mouth opens in a gaping yawn as soon as she witnesses the cuts and bruises painted over my face. She places a hand over her gaping mouth.

Then examines my face: "What happened to your face?"

"I got into a fight," I tell her, my voice cracking.

Her jawline tightens, her face goes hollow, her eyes darken.

"Who did this to you?"

"Doesn't matter," I say faintly.

Peggy pulls me close and hugs me. I lose control and start crying. She helps relieve some of the pain, but the pain is still there. What if it's *always* going to be there? I ask about Bill. She tells me that he's not doing so good.

"What happened?" I ask her.

"One of his neighbors," she says, "Charles, he found Bill unconscious." She's doing all she can to tell me what happened, but her words come out in various bursts. "Your father went in for check up a couple months ago," she says to me. "Doctors found a tumor near his pancreas. It's bad. They said he only had a few months to live. He kept it secret from us, Josh. Why would he do that?"

I don't know why Bill didn't tell us about the cancer.

"So," I say, "they can remove the tumor. Right?"

"The cancer's already spread," she says. "Right now, they're making sure he's comfortable."

"Comfortable?" I say. "What do you mean 'comfortable'?"

"He doesn't have long, Josh."

My father, she says, doesn't have long to live.

How do I even respond to that news?

5

One after another, I smoke three cigarettes outside while Peggy's waiting to have a word with the doctor in the waiting room. I look up at the glowing windows of the hospital above me, and each window is like the empty box of a crossword puzzle. At any moment, a letter is ready to appear inside the box, a story with a beginning and an ending.

6

The doctors let me see Bill after they move him to a room on the fifth level. My hands are shaking as I approach his room. I'm thinking about what to say to my father before he dies. Just the other day he was talking about fishing and now, he's on his deathbed. I have no words, no letters. What do I say when I feel so responsible?

I arrive at Bill's room, and I see him on the bed, like a skeleton dressed in an unfitted suit of flesh. Of all the stages of cancer, they say Bill's at the final one. There's no other way to put it.

This is the end of his third act.

There's not going to be a sequel.

No prequel.

This is it.

What the hell do I even tell him?

I stand by his bedside, but the nurses have him doped up with medication.

I want to tell Bill I love him, that he meant—and will always mean—the world to me, that I wish I was more like him and that he's the greatest father on the planet, one who nurtured me as a child, who taught me the way of right and wrong, who encouraged me to expand my knowledge by asking more questions or surrounding myself with all walks of life, who always put me before himself.

I want to tell him he's been a good friend—my best—who's had my back after I didn't want to live anymore. I want to tell him those things, especially how grateful I am to be his son, but I can't even find those words. Then, the negativity sets in, and then I start thinking about how controlling he was and how he often put work before his family and how, like many fathers, had his share of issues. He wasn't perfect by any sketch. But who is these days? And who the hell am I to judge?

Peggy tells me to go back home and get some rest while she stays at the hospital. I take her advice. I don't rest, though. Instead, I do some research on pancreatic cancer. I spend hours reading cancer stories, as well as going through a maze of forums on my computer. It doesn't look good for Bill. His cancer is a death wish.

I shut off my computer and take a pill to help me sleep. I drift off into a dreamless sleep for a couple of hours before I'm wakened up by trumpets.

Peggy's calling me.

I answer the call.

Her voice sounds frail on the other end. She only gets through *two* words before I already know the news. She tells me that my father is dead. Bill is dead. He didn't even make it through the night and I'm left wondering about the goodbye I never told him. Overnight, the cancer crawled throughout his body like a spider. Peggy says that she has to take care of some things at the hospital, as well as some "legal" issues with Bill's lawyer, and a neighbor, Eugene, is stopping by with food later this morning. It all happens so quickly: other people whom I haven't seen in years stopping by to check up on me, as if I've become a concern; then, the phone calls; the pop-in visits; flowers, so many carnations; cards in the mail. Peggy says the funeral will be a closed casket. Even after Bill's death, she has no time to grieve. She's extremely busy with a lot of work, like gathering old photos for the visitation or writing an obituary for the papers. I didn't realize how time-consuming funerals can be until I walk-in on Peggy making one phone call after another, pen held in hand, scribbling words on paper as if she's cramped inside an office cubicle, pushing numbers and pulling hair.

A lawyer with the nose like a toucan, who can pass as Mr. Burns from *The Simpsons*, stops by the house a couple of times with papers for Peggy to sign. I already know about the papers and the thought of a shifty lawyer sitting at the same table where I eat makes me want to snap, and I'm trying to think about something other than smashing that briefcase over his head. Christian comes back home from State, and he's a lot more mature than I last saw him. He also has a whole new haircut; his clothes are different; even the way he talks is different. It's like I don't know him anymore. Peggy's family flies in from New York. Gabe's changed from the last time I saw him. He's shot up at least five inches and his face looks thinner, as if the chubby kid I once knew had been stretched out like Play-Doh. Peggy and her sister, Marlene, go through old photo albums and pictures of Bill, but I want no part of the process. Why the hell is Marlene even here? I overhear Marlene talking about watching someone close to her die. Her lifelong friend died of breast cancer. Now, all of a sudden, Marlene acts as if she's an ambassador of death, like she knows every single thing there is about death, as well as the grieving process. Just listening to Marlene talk about herself makes me sick. Watching the way she gloms onto Peggy makes me want to say something to her. She's been calling all the shots ever since she arrived. Marlene should be ashamed of herself. They *all* should. Every single one of them makes me sick, including Gabe, who acts as if Marlene dragged him here. Most importantly, Peggy makes me sick. Just not too long ago she was in bed with another man named Raphael and now, she's ready to bury my father in the ground.

8

The next morning, I wake up to the sound of the doorbell. I roll out of bed and hurry to the window. Two cruisers are parked on the street. No sirens. Engines are turned off. The sight alone of cops causes my heart to beat fast enough to feel each beat throbbing against my chest. My face goes pale. Palms sweaty. I grab the car keys from the desk, slip on my socks and shoes, then ease from my room.

I creep down each stair as if the stairs have been iced over. Peggy's talking to two cops on the front porch. I eavesdrop on the conversation. Someone has broken into Bill's house. Relief washes over my body. Yet, I'm still curious as to why someone would want to break into Bill's house considering it was, in many ways, a step down from his crummy apartment. They didn't take any furniture or TVs or stereos, says one of the cops. They ask Peggy if Bill had any enemies. She tells them no, not that she's aware of. They talk about Bill's cancer. One of the cops lost a loved one from the horrible disease. The conversation slams on the brakes for a moment, then it shifts directly back to business. As far as the cops know, the intruders didn't take anything. Instead, they vandalized the place. Most of Bill's stuff was thrown around the house. The cops leave the same way they came in.

I surface once the cops drive away, and Peggy already knows that I've been listening in on the conversation from the frustration on her face.

She asks me why someone would break into a house and not steal anything.

I don't know who would do such a thing, but I have an idea who it might be. Peggy assumes that it's foolish kids who had nothing else better to do but go through a dead man's things.

I want to agree with Peggy, but I can't find any reason.

9

Bill's neighbor, Charles, who's around Bill's age, maybe a few years older, pulls me aside after the funeral and tells me how Bill was acting strange a couple of days before he found him unconscious. He tells me that he came by Bill's house to help him move. I tell Charles Bill wasn't moving—at least, if he was going to move, he didn't tell me. He doesn't tell Peggy about Bill's behavior. He only tells me and when I question him, he accidentally reveals that Bill lost his job last year as a guidance counselor. According to Charles, he failed to show up multiple times for work without giving the school any notice. I tell him I don't know what he's talking about and I certainly don't know why he's telling all these things that Bill has been hiding from me, especially right now.

If Charles is, in fact, telling the truth, then the cancer wasn't the only thing Bill was keeping secret.

13

Striving for a clean slate – Beyond t#e grave – Easter eggs and caterpillars – _Zeitgeist_ – The photo – Men in black – Busted – Glitch – Discovering a cure for cancer – The perfect drug

---

ONE day after the funeral I receive an envelope from Bill in the mail. The first thing that comes to mind is another fly lure and that maybe he mailed it out before he was hospitalized. Maybe preparing for another fishing trip?

With all these unanswered questions swirling around my head, I eagerly open the envelope and inside is a piece of crinkled paper attached to the black rock. The only thing holding the paper in place is a rubberband. I carefully remove the rubberband and unfold the note. It's Bill handwriting.

I read the note: "Josh, _don't_ be afraid to <u>cross</u> the line in order to seek the truth - Bill."

Immediately, I'm confused by the obscurity of the note.

The more I think about each word, which, I realize, is significant and deliberately written for me to interpret, I become angry at Bill. Even in death, he still haunts me. I push aside the anger and try to make sense of the note. I don't exactly know what he means by crossing the line. He's aware that I attempted suicide—maybe he simply forgot about the whole thing when Peggy discovered me clinging to life in a bathtub filled with my own blood. Why would he use those exact words _cross the line_ and most importantly, underline the word _cross_. Why would he do this to me? On top of dealing with his death, now he's alluding to a wild goose chase or, even worse, a treasure hunt. Maybe it's his way of telling me to move on with life and don't waste time grieving over his death and to pursue my dreams and take risks. Maybe it's Bill's way of saying: "Everybody dies. *My* death is no different than the next." Or, maybe he did mail the envelope from the grave and his ghost is telling me something different. I stop thinking about the words and concentrate on the rock for the rest of the afternoon. I gumshoe the rock and try to find pictures that closely resemble the rock and after a few minutes of searching, confirm that it's a piece of slate, a type of metamorphic rock, which some people use to decorate their gardens or pathways. Metamorphic, according to *New Oxford*, means transformation. "*My* transformation." Is this what you mean, Bill? Maybe I'm over thinking it. I study each detail of the rock. One side is rougher than the other side and appears as if it was chipped off with a chisel from a large piece of rock. Then, I study the note. *Seek the truth.* What truth? The truth about life and death? What was Bill hiding from us? Seek means search. Search where? Back to *cross the line.* First, *cross.* The very first thing that comes to mind, of course, is a railroad cross. A letter X. X marks the spot? Does the note have something to do with the Hate Train? Has Bill been following me to the Basement? And if so, does he know the members of the Mawb? Maybe he counseled a couple of them? How about the strange cars that have been camping outside the house? Did Bill send them to the house to watch us? Who are they? What do they want? Or, what if he means the religious cross? Bill was a Baptist; Peggy, a Catholic. We used to go to church and all. When Bill and Peggy started to go through their issues and whatnot, we skipped one Sunday morning. Then, after that one week without church, we stopped going period. Me, I was baptized a Catholic. I don't remember anything about being baptized when I was a baby, only pictures as proof. A gray-haired priest dipping my fragile body into magical waters. My tiny arms and legs wiggling around like worms that surface after a rainstorm, my body squirming over the priest's papery palms, my sponge of a brain soaked in sheer terror. I could only imagine how horrified I might have been at the time. Then, again, can babies comprehend fear or even death? A few years ago, I denounced my Catholicism and ever since then, I haven't been practicing any religions.

Finally, the second word: *line*—What line?

Does Bill mean the line between right and wrong?

What are you trying to tell me, Bill?

2

I steal Bill's house key from Peggy while she's cleaning her bedroom and drive to Bill's house, which, depending on traffic, is about forty minutes away in a city called Sandy Hill. The inside of the house is exceptionally clean and doesn't look as though it was broken into, either, except for the damage along the panel of the doorway from what looks like a crowbar—knowing Peggy, she already has someone on the job, ready to make repairs—which makes me wonder if Peggy stopped by and tidied up the place without telling me.

I search the entire house but don't find anything that's "truth" worthy. No great unveil. Not "special" box hidden in the closet. I notice the place also seems less cluttered as it did the last time I was here. Lastly, I check the attic. It's empty. Not one box. I wonder if Charles was referring to Bill emptying out the attic. Bill wasn't moving. He was just clearing out clutter. Bill did that from time to time. Or, was someone else doing the *decluttering* for him?

As I'm about to switch off the lights to the attic, I find an old photo on the floor. Bill's in the photo and so am I. I was only six years old at the time the photo was taken. We spent the weekend in the Badlands of South Dakota at a dinosaur graveyard site. I was into dinosaurs at the time. Had all the toys. Watched all the movies and cartoons. I'll officially go on the record: I was a straight-up dinosaur buff. I gobbled up everything there was to learn about dinosaurs and could name every single one from Aardonyx to Zupaysaurus. While spending vacations at Phantasy Worldz, we used to arrive early in order to beat the crowds and visit the Paleotours first, and I remember how much fun I had learning about dinosaurs while at the same time riding the dinosaur-themed rides.

I study the photo and can't help but wonder: Did Bill intentionally leave this particular photo here for me to find?

Is this a clue?

3

As I'm leaving Bill's house, I spot an unmarked car parked three houses down. A black Crown Vic, possibly a government vehicle.

A strange man dressed in black is camped inside the car. He's wearing black shades. Very 1950's. Incredibly suspicious.

I keep my head down and drive away, as if I don't see him.

4

It's dark when I get back to the house. All the lights are turned on inside. I step inside and close the door behind me. I head straight to the kitchen for a bite to eat.

Once I make it to the kitchen, I notice all of my trophies laid out on the kitchen counter.

Over fifty pieces of artifacts, from the swimmerets on the iconic statue at the gates of Phantasy Worldz to the severed hand, foot, or even head of famous yet controversial statues of past generals, former presidents, or trailblazers to photos of vandalized Civil Rights monuments and empty spray cans. I don't realize how many things I've destroyed, defaced, and collected in order to turn people against one another until I see the entire spread before me.

Out of the box.

Busted.

Peggy quietly strolls into the kitchen and then plants herself behind the counter. The look on her face is one of disgust and disappointment. Her eyes are red and watery, and I can tell she's been practicing a venomous speech inside her head. The first words to come out of her mouth: *What are these?*

"So you've been snooping around my room?" I say.

"No, Josh," she says. "I wasn't 'snooping.' I was putting away your record player and came across these things." She points at the maimed face from a George Washington statue. When I was looking for schools in Virginia, I destroyed part of the statue, then afterwards, the beam of a flashlight cut across my vision followed by a man's voice and I was chased for a couple of blocks by a chubby, out of shape security guard who watched way too many 80's cop movies when he was a kid.

And now, the gig is up.

My very own prologue for war, over.

The armies have retreated.

The battleships sunken.

"I want to hear an explanation," she says loudly. "What have you been doing behind my back?"

I don't answer Peggy. Too embarrassed.

"Do you know the trouble you've gotten yourself into?" Peggy yells. "You can go to jail, Josh! Is that what you want? You want to have your *entire* life ruined? For what? To prove a point? To destroy what others have worked so hard to build? Answer me! What the hell are you doing? Huh?"

I don't answer Peggy. Too ashamed.

"How many hours have *you* spent working to keep a roof over your head?" she asks one of the many questions on her mental list. "How many hours have *you* spent working to keep food in your mouth? Answer me—"

"—You're seriously going to do this now, after everything that's happened?"

"I need to know, Josh," she says, as if she's not going anywhere until she receives an explanation from me. I can't weasel my way out of this one; however, I can't find the right words. She'll never understand.

"I want you to leave," she seethes, pointing at the door. "I don't even want to see your face right now. . . "

I don't budge an inch.

"*Leave*," she says.

I don't leave.

"*Right now!*" she screams and slams her palm against the counter. "Get outta here! Now!"

I leave with a heavy storm. I make sure to let Peggy know that I mean business by slamming the door behind me. I think I broke the hinges on the door, but I don't care. I can tear down the entire house with an excavator. I don't care. Who does she think she's messing with? I'll destroy her.

I get back in my car and peel away.

I truly believe that'll be the last time I'll see Peggy. She'll never understand why I did those things; and the fact alone is why I can't go back. I'm never going back.

Only one place to go.

5

I wait until one of the Meme twins shows up before making a move. She makes her rounds through the restaurant, making sure everything is turned off, like the stove, the ovens, soda machines, and finally, lights. I'm left wondering where the other one is, considering they usually act as if they're joined at the hip.

Once she locks the doors behind her, I make my move and sneak around back. The back entrance in the alleyway is unlocked. I open the door, run my finger across the duct tape over the latch bolt next to the door handle, and can't help but wonder: Did I put that piece of tape there? The tape wasn't there before. Somehow, I knew the door would be open, though. I ignore the creeping suspicions and gently shut the door behind me. I sneak into the dark club, which reeks of hot sweat and urine.

Before starting up the game, I check the restaurant upstairs and make sure the place is empty. One of the Meme twins is closing the door to the restaurant. She punches in the code to the alarm and locks the door behind her.

I go back downstairs and turn on the Hate Train. I put on my headset, as well as my gloves, and play the game, Free-for-all.

I scroll through my weapons until I come across my weapon of choice: brass knuckles.

I choose Atlanta as my level, a dimly lit Peachtree Center Station appears around me.

The train arrives.

With my hands curled into fists, I board the train. My first NPC happens to be a middle-aged man with a five o'clock shadow. He's decked out in the clothing of his favorite football team. Every single garment on his body from his hat down to his socks matches the blue and orange colors of his sports team: The Engineers.

The mascot being an old-timey railroad engineer dressed in pinstriped overalls and a ticking front brimmed cap.

I approach the sports fan, who puffs out his chest from my presence. He says to me, "What you looking at, creep?"

I rear back and punch him in the face with the brass knuckles. Several teeth spit from his gaping mouth. He falls to the floor and I beat his face in until I feel and hear the bones of his skull cracking between my fingertips.

I take out the next person who's carrying a boombox over his shoulder. I yank the boombox from his hands and smash it over his head.

Then, I take out the next person, then the next.

My next three victims happen to be from a gang of thugs tearing off the clothes of a young girl and doing the gangbang on her while other passengers loll around, watching with intense gratification by licking and biting the edge of their lips. The thugs see me and then slam the young girl's head against the railing, knocking her unconscious. I break each one of their arms and legs, as if their bones are made of dried pasta.

I break a lot of things.

Each lowlife who comes faster and stronger at me I drop as quickly as the next.

Behind me, a mean-looking man with a shaved head and a tattoo of a swastika on his forehead throws a punch but I dodge his fist at the very last second and shatter the side of his face over the window and when I pull back his head, tiny shards of glass are embedded into his eye and cheek as if he stuck his face into a cactus that bears spines made of glass. I bring him to the ground and slam his face over and over and over against the floor until there's nothing left of his head but a handful of bloody skin that hangs from my fingers like a wet mop.

Once I'm through pulverizing flesh and bone, I spot someone in the back of the train. He's sitting in the seat with his head facing the floor. He looks as if he's not supposed to be here—a glitch?

He's wearing a black overcoat that appears as if it's been stuffed into a garbage disposal. The side of his face is pale and vampiric. I step over the pile of bodies and stomp my way through the puddles of blood pooling over the floor. I approach the mysterious man. I get about ten feet away until he turns his head toward my direction. It can't be him. . .

"Bill?" I say in awe. "What are you doing here?"

He stands up and approaches me. He looks skeletal. His posture is extremely weak. His cheeks are sunken in. His eyes are like two glossy, black marbles lost in the darkness of his deep eye sockets.

"What are you doing?" I say.

He doesn't answer. Yet, he continues to teeter toward me.

"Don't come any closer," I tell him.

In a phlegmy voice, he reaches out his boney hand and says to me, "Come, Joshua. Join us."

He takes another step closer. His eyes roll over white like the eyes of a shark. I strike him in the face with a crippling haymaker. His head violently snaps to the right, then mechanically turns back around as if he's possessed by a demon who enjoys banging up his cheap ride, and I'm merely Bill's exorcist trying to rid the evil puppeteer within him. The flesh around his left cheekbone has been peeled away from the blow. The bone underneath is exposed; and now, the flabby piece of flesh hangs over Bill's face like a loose piece of thread. Bill smiles a hideous smile, the devil's smile with his teeth coated with bright red blood. At that point, I realize the sickly man floundering before me isn't Bill at all but a *thing* that has taken over Bill. Once more, I strike him in the face with a right hook. I strike him two more times. While back-pedaling from each blow, his heel snags onto the leg of a seat, causing him to fall backward. I pounce on top of his body and repeatedly pound away at his face until my brass knuckles cave in his skull. All the hatred I feel inside me is all concentrated at the cusp of my metal knuckles, and the whole time I'm thinking about a heavily medicated Bill lying on his deathbed. In that cold, stale hospital. Withering away from the thing that has taken over his body.

I hate cancer.

I hate what it did to my father, how it settled inside his body like an unwelcome guest, then it consumed his body the same way a spider did to the meal it caught by the very silk it spun, slowly nibbling away at pieces of its catch, a wing one day or a leg the other, until nothing was left of it but tasteless scraps for the foul creatures below.

I hate cancer, not because it didn't hate my father but because it was the greatest swindler of them all who had its own weaselly team of accomplices, the doctors, nurses, and pharmaceutical companies that somehow chose Bill for laughs, as if he was a worthy candidate turned gullible contender, who was unaware that he was stepping into the ring to square off against an opponent with a nearly impeccable track record, and yet despite the glimpses of hope or pats on the back or being welcomed like a new family member with warm smiles and the gentlest of embraces or even the gracious offerings of experimental drugs and promising trials, those odds, whether or not Bill was up for the challenge, were always stacked against him.

Not once did cancer ever show any remorse for why it decided to migrate into his body. Cancer didn't care who my father was or what he did. Whether he was decent or corrupt.

I continue to pound away at the mushy pile of his face.

Each blow, each thought flashes before my eyes; and I'm thinking about scientists who can't come up with cures to eradicate cancer once and for all!

I hammer through brain with my fists, blood showering my face. I didn't act quickly enough. I could've traveled the world, seeking a cure in remote regions of the world, tropical rainforests, barren deserts, the farthest reaches of the abyss.

I feel the bones break in my hands, but I keep pounding. I can't stop. I *won't* stop until I no longer feel anything.

Finally, I turn my thoughts to all of those despicable people out there sharing their "Cancer Story," the shameless ones who've exploited their loved ones by posting pictures of their sickness in order to receive awareness or attention or, even worse, a LIKE.

I don't hate them. I hate what cancer has done to them. I keep punching through flesh and tissue.

Manmade viruses or diseases, processed foods, nitrates, carcinogens, air pollution, insecticides, pesticides, chemicals, like fluoride being dumped into rivers or water supply, greenhouse gases, choking smoke, toxins, and metals, carbon emissions, oil drilling, fossil fuels: disturbing images of a once lush and green land being violently beaten, stabbed, lacerated, pared, maimed, raped, then poisoned, crippled, destroyed!

The hate runs through my veins, like a series of hashtags forming railroad tracks throughout my body. Each hashtag, each track, connected. Running deeper and deeper.

Now, I'm not beating my father. I'm beating the sickness inside his body—or so I think.

14

What is real anymore? – Working while sleeping – Old blood – Runaway – Crossing the line – Clue revealed – Searching for truth – Longer hours

THE rest of the night plays out like a drunken blur.

One minute, I'm driving through the dead of night.

The next, I'm standing right beside Gabe on the shores of Lake Cynosor. We're having a spitting contest of who can spit the longest.

I wake up from the black dream with the sun pressed against the left side of my sore face. The other half of the pillow is stained with a yellow substance. I lean closer and sniff the pillow and the yellow stuff smells like stomach bile.

I reach deep and try to piece together the fragmented memories from last night: me getting into a self-inflicted fight with Peggy, then me driving to Atlanta, then me playing the Hate Train all by myself, then, after that, everything's foggy.

I roll out of bed and part of my body feels sticky to the touch. I trudge my way to the bathroom and step over each item of clothing scattered around the room like landmines.

I check myself in the bathroom mirror. I flinch from the sight of my reflection. I'm covered in blood. Both my hands are black with dried blood. The blood is caked over both my wrists and forearms, as well. Even the bottom of my white undershirt, I notice, is stained with bloody handprints. I check my face where I have a laceration on the left side of my cheek. Several red marks—three, I count—run parallel to the laceration. It appears as though I was scratched or clawed last night. I don't remember getting hurt. What the hell happened to me?

I run both my hands underneath warm water and once the water hits the dried blood, the blood comes off more easily. I thoroughly wash my hands with soap. I use a Brillo pad to scrub away the blood from the cracks in my fingernails. Next, I change shirts. I have blood on the waistband of my boxer-briefs. So, I change my underwear, then look down at my shaky hands. They're clean, but I can't find any cuts. My knuckles are red, sore, and swollen, however, *not* one cut. I clean my face next. Then place Neosporin on my face and let the cut breathe. The injury isn't life threatening or anything. The blood could've come from the cut on my face, but it's highly unlikely.

I stare at the red stains in the sink and try to convince myself this is my blood. But in the back of my mind, I know it's not.

As I'm piecing together last night, I feel the house vibrating.

The vibration intensifies!

I rush to the window where a helicopter's flying over the house. The same unmarked car from earlier is parked across the street—a Crown Vic, possible government; however, a different man dressed in black is camped inside. Wearing those same 1950's shades. Incredibly suspicious.

What's he doing? Is he here for me? Most importantly, who is he? A cop? Is he working with the Feds?

I hear a *knock* at the door—

—Joshua!

I move away from the window and check the door where I find a bloody handprint smeared over the handle.

My hand.

"You okay?" Peggy says, pauses. "I didn't hear you come home last night," she says with a tremble in her voice. "We need to talk." She *knocks* again, this time louder. "Josh," she says. "I know you're in there. Please open the door. . . "

"Give me a minute," I tell her, my voice as shaky as a maraca.

I turn on the TV and flip through news channels. I come across a story about yet "another" violent attack at the Peachtree Central Station in Atlanta. Seven people have been seriously injured. Two of the victims hospitalized. Cops have obtained surveillance footage of the attacker. The news only shows a segment of the footage due to the "disturbing nature" of the video. One of the victims has crawled from the train, leaving behind a snail-like trail of red blood along the ground. The attacker, dressed in a black jacket and blue jeans, comes into focus.

I look around the room and find the articles of clothing, both the black jacket and the blue jeans, on the floor. Could be a coincidence? I turn my attention back to the TV. His—or her—face is disguised with a black ski mask. The attacker's hands are dripping with strings of blood. The attacker stalks toward the victim, who is shielding his face.

The attacker towers over the helpless victim and rears back his or her hand and as the attacker strikes down at the victim, the news cuts away.

The bedroom door shakes!

Peggy attempts to open the door, but it's locked. She's jiggling and turning the door handle.

"Josh," she says in a near shout, "open the door. Now!"

I frantically grab the dirty clothes from the floor and toss them underneath my bed. I throw on a pair of clean pants. Then, I slip into my shoes. I reach underneath the bed and grab the keys from my jean's pocket. I head to the window. Open it. In the corner of my eye, I see the note, as well as the piece of slate on my desk. I pocket them both and climb out the window.

2

The lures, I tell myself, the trip, the texts, the slate: it was all precisely planned.

I make a U-turn and drive to the Okeenaw National Park north of the Ford Davie Campgrounds.

Except for an older couple walking their dog, the place is dead when I arrive at the park. I head straight to the Chattooga River. I keep my head to the ground and look for any rock that looks out of the ordinary. I find the spot where Bill and I went fishing last time. I find the log. I search the area. I lift up the log and search underneath. I don't find any slate or any rock that remotely looks like the one in my hand.

I pull out the note and read it to myself once more. Cross the line, I tell myself. *The line* is the river, the border separating South Carolina from Georgia. I roll up the edges of my pants and slog my way through the cold river. The water runs up to my waist. I hold my breath and swim through the deepest parts until I reach the other side. I search the banks of the river but don't find the slate anywhere near the bank. I walk closer to the woods. . .

There it is, the slate caught in a heavenly ray of sunlight spearing through the branches above. Parts of it glimmer from the light. I hurry over to the rock. A small chunk of slate is missing from the top right corner. I compare the smaller piece of slate in my hand to the larger piece on the ground, and it fits like a glove!

Okay, I tell myself. Now, what?

I drop to my knees and search around the slate but don't find anything significant.

I lift up the slate and roll it aside. A glittery metallic object is revealed in the sunlight. I dig through the dirt and pull out a key with the number, 378, on a keychain. I brush off the dirt from the green fob with the words TITAN STORAGE.

I can't help but wonder: What did you do, Bill?

3

According to the GPS on my phone, Titan Storage is a storage facility located in Bradbury, another one of those cut and paste towns just outside Sandy Hill.

I use the passcode on the back of the fob and punch-in the four-digit number on the keypad. The gates open, and I can feel the butterflies bouncing off the walls of my stomach lining. The steering wheel is slippery with palm sweat. I ease my foot off the brake and drive to unit 378. I park and step outside. The nerves cause my legs to weaken, like I'm standing up after sitting for hours. I take in a deep breath, which helps calm the butterflies. Then, I unlock the unit. I slide open the garage-like door, revealing boxes and boxes of stuff—*Bill's stuff*, I conclude. I don't know what I'm looking for. I've already crossed the line. And now I need to seek the truth.

What truth?

Whatever truth Bill mentioned in the note, it has to be in here.

But where?

Only one way to find out.

PART THREE
THE PASSENGER

15

RAM – A world of lost interests – Family ties – The Hollow Soldier – Unearthing a dark past – Cold cases, hot laces – The Belmont Bandit – The life and times of the legendary Richie Lamb – Murky

I'M four boxes deep into old toys laced with lead when all of a sudden I come across the same train set Bill bought me for my fifth—or sixth—birthday. The edges of the tattered box are torn and raggedy and rip apart when I pick it up. The train inside, however, is intact; in fact, it's appears to be in mint condition, except for the locomotive. I rake away at the round stain of encrusted snot on the smoke stack with my finger-nail and run my fingers over my initials, JBL, etched underneath the toy.

Why did Bill move all of this "stuff" in here? If I had to guess, like a shot in the dark, I'd say that he didn't want Peggy getting involved. If Bill left the house to me, she'd most definitely find a way to get her hands in the mix. After all, she was once married to him. Knowing Peggy, she wouldn't dare let Bill's lawyer hand the keys over to me. She'd go in there and auction off his stuff or have a garage sale on a Saturday morning or declutter or, even worse, take Bill's stuff to the nearest dump. I remember they frequently argued about Bill's so-called "problem." He was a type of person who held onto things—a border-line hoarder, some would say behind his back without batting an eye-lash—whereas Peggy was the type to discard anything that was no longer beneficial to her or the people around her, including me, even if it had any kind of sentimental value. But what was so important for Bill to move his stuff in here? What are you hiding, Bill? Show me the way. I keep searching through partially ripped boxes, most of which are filled with memorabilia from Bill's childhood in Port Landia to a galore of photos of him and his white husky named Buck. Nothing "truth-worthy." He's collected *MAD* magazines from the mid 70's well into the 80's. He has boxes full of magazines, including the No. 171 issue from December 1974 called "The Sting" with President Nixon on the front cover. Like the train set, the magazines are still in fairly mint condition—almost. More boxes: *Playboys, Hustler*, and whatnot. Then, other boxes: books from Doyle's *Sherlock Holmes* stories to Fleming's *Bond* pocket-sized paperbacks to Hesse's *Siddhartha* to Joyce's *Ulysses*. Bill can stock an entire library with books. He referred to himself as a "biblio-phile," which, at first, sounded more disturbing than the word actually implied. Every time I spent a weekend with Bill, I'd go through some of the books on his bookshelves. If you look up bibliophile in the diction-ary, you'd probably find Bill's name used in a sentence: *Bill didn't realize he was a bibliophile until he ran out of room for books on his bookshelf.* I rum-mage through dozens of boxes packed with paperbacks and hardbacks. I feel myself getting warmer, not like I'm moving in the correct direc-tion, but warmer, as in closer to the truth.

I climb over more boxes, dig through the contents inside, then pull out unopened packages of game systems, as well as keyboards (a Moog and a Korg synthesizer), old "interests" that he never got around to giv-ing me. I pull out a crisp MANGA from the bottom of the box. I re-member one time I was into MANGA. I never told anyone about it, yet here it is. The pages of the book are crisp and clean, as if it's hot off the press. I pull out a seven-inch doll of a samurai tucked away underneath a stack of MANGAS. I remember I was into samurais one year—maybe eleven or twelve, I think. I used to wake up extra earlier every Saturday morning and catch an anime called *Saul the Samurai*. Yet, here is Saul. Untouched. I should feel sorry for myself, but I don't. I feel angry instead.

I close the box and keep searching through the storage unit. I come across a wired shelf with boxes so old that even the dust has started to change colors.

I wave my hands through mushroom clouds of dust motes and rummage through mounds of photo albums, crinkled birth records, baby books with envelopes of baby teeth, and wood-brown newspapers. Somehow, I feel as if I'm on the right track. I don't know how or why I know these things. I *just* know.

I grab the first item: a worn, flimsy shoebox with the word *Florsheim*. Inside are photos as old and discolored as the shoebox itself. On the back are dates from the middle nineteen hundreds.

I sort through the photos, mostly natural landscapes, including farms, countrysides, remote villages or uninhabited cottages, woods, groves, mountain ranges—one being the Appalachians perhaps—then, desolate streets stretching into blurry horizons, small cut and paste towns which once had character, like Spartacus, before corporations gradually started to replace Mom and Pop shops. Each photo I flip through becomes clearer and more distinguishable, as if they were taken with a better camera. More photos: deserts, as well as desert life, cacti, more desolate roads, empty gas stations. That's where the photos end, in the sleepy desert. I put aside the shoebox and pick up an album with the gold word *photographs* over a green leathery surface. The first thing that comes to mind when I hold the album in my hand is the photo I found in Bill's attic, the one with us standing next to a digging site. I open the album and skim through each photo. Some of them are black and white and appear as if they were taken during the war—World War II, I think. The photos consist of men dressed in uniform, soldiers posing at a camp or standing in organized groups, all bundled together like a colony of combatants. I pull out random photos, the color faded, and they appear from the wrong time period. The words *fas foto* are written on top of the photos, which, I think, is French. Photos of an older couple on an airplane, then photos of the same older couple seated with the perplexed and perturbed faces of foreigners inside a room covered in floral wallpaper. I pull out more photos and read names written on the backside of photos. The first: "Mildred Lamb," my great grandmother, a petite lady who gave birth to her first, "John," when she was in her late twenties—John Junior, my great uncle. Bill never spoke about these people, his family. I often wondered if the characters he wrote about in his stories were like these twisted impressions of the people he knew. I wondered if Bill ever thought about me whenever he was creating a character. Whenever I did bring up Bill's family by asking him questions about them, he'd always dodge the questions by saying, "I don't know," which, I think, was his way of saying, "I don't want to talk about it."

I keep flipping until I come across a partially ripped landscaped photo: a group of boys huddle around a tall man with quite a mean slouch in front of a hilly pasture. The Lambs. There's John Lamb "Senior," my great grandfather, holding the hand of his eldest son, as if his hand was the handle of a walker or cane to keep him upright. Then, there are his three sons: John Lamb "Junior," his eldest (who is "15 yrs." in the photo), David Lamb (who is "12 yrs."), his second eldest. My two great uncles. In the middle: Bill's father, my grandfather, Joshua Christopher Lamb ("10 yrs."). Christopher doesn't look anything like his two older brothers, John or David. I see John Senior in the bottom of Christopher's face, but not much. After my great grandmother, Mildred, died in 1923 at the age of thirty-two from complications while delivering David, John remarried a couple of years later. From the photos, the second wedding was much smaller than the first. I can't find any description on the back of the photos from either wedding; however, the difference in the weddings is uncanny. I come across other photos of John Senior when he was younger: photos of John Senior standing among other sooty-faced men with the mountains at their backs. The faces in the photos are harder to make out. I flip the photos over: "Jorge, Harold, and me." John Senior was a coal miner who "passed away from black lung at the age of forty-eight," reads an obituary. Other photos: one of John Senior's family at the cemetery and another, at John Senior's wake. I come across another photo, one of an intense woman, hard to look at, yet, at the same time, hard to look away. The back reads: "Eleanor Goodson," who later changed her name to "Eleanor Lamb," and then, later, after John Senior passed away, changed her name back to Eleanor Goodson. Christopher favored Eleanor more so than John. I can see more of her in his face from the nose-up. Eleanor is my great grandmother, not Mildred. I remove a photo of Eleanor sitting on the lawn with a flowing black summer dress speckled with white dots, her brunette hair flowing over one of her shoulders, her head cocked back and she's giggling at a gangly awkward-looking shadow mimicking a monkey behind the camera. I search for more photos of Eleanor, especially ones of John Senior and Eleanor together, but I can't find many.

The next page is a newspaper clipping about John's remarriage: "Two years after Mildred's passing, Mr. Jonathan Lamb of Williamson took Eleanor Góodson as his wife at the Palm's Meadow in Cleaverland yesterday evening."

Most of the photos appear as if Eleanor raised the boys, as well as another child—or neighbor (I can't tell who the strange, ghostly boy is in several of the photos because his name is *not* written on the back along with the others). Eleanor and Christopher were close, I can tell from the photos of them goofing around together. Then, I find a later photo of Christopher in his twenties in an art studio: looking over his shoulder at the camera, brush in hand, hands looking as if they have been dipped in paint. I find another one with Christopher dressed in an oversized boxy-looking suit, shaking the hand of a businessman with a pencil-thin mustache. In between the two is a painting of a coal miner on his knees, hands spread out beside him as he gazes up at the sky. I find other photos with other paintings, then, a photo of Christopher holding a "5 month old" baby in his arms—baby Bill, my father.

I stop and count the years on my fingers.

Christopher was around thirty-seven, I believe, when the daughter of a wealthy broker, Evelyn Kroger, his wife, my grandmother, gave birth to William Isaiah Lamb.

I come across a couple of newspaper clippings.

Christopher died at the age of forty-five, which means Bill was around eight years old at the time, not even a teenager. Christopher's death was unknown, as far as I know; however, the newspaper article states that he died from "natural causes." The first headline: "Local Man Found Dead in Train Tunnel."

I keep reading: "Saturday morning, two boys found a dead body lying in the middle of the train tracks."

I continue to read the article. The cops determined Christopher died of "natural causes" since there were no signs of a struggle. Bill never spoke a single word of his father's death. Christopher was the youngest of the three; but I haven't met any of them because they had died long before I was born. And Bill *never* spoke about any of them, not even John Junior, my grandfather's older brother who, from most of the photos, seemed share-worthy. Apparently, after skimming through photos, John fought in World War II.

I find a photo of John proudly standing in front of "the Statue of Jeanne d'Arc at Orleans—" I think it says, but the words Orleans is marked through with a pencil, "taken October 1944."

A note underneath reads: "*You can see where bombs have damaged it. Please show David.*"

Another photo with John in front of a statue that, I think, reads: CHANZY. The note on the back reads: "Le Mares, France. Dec. 1945."

Another photo with two French ladies riding bikes down a street made of cobblestone.

The back reads: "Royal Palace at Versailles near Paris. Taken October 1944."

I remember while I was rummaging through the boxes of books I came across an encyclopedia. I fish it out from the box and flip to the W section.

I find World War II (1939-1945).

I find other photos of him posing in front of other historical statues or cathedrals, "Cathedral at Seuliss." Or is it Saulis? I can't make out John's cursive, but I think it says that the cathedral is located "somewhere around Paris." The photo was taken "Oct. 1944 by me."

Other photos, I discover, with John standing with his major (not once does he mention his major's name).

More of those *fas fotos* with the older couple mixed in, as well.

More blank postcards, including one from the CHARTRES - La Cathédrale and another from ETRETAT - L'Aiguille, then La Manneporte. An entire photo album of family and war.

I open another album with photos of John Junior and his wife, Laurie, a French nurse whom he met in France. The photo album is filled with the aftermath of war: John and Laurie's two children, a boy named "Luke" and a girl named "Michelle," as well as an old newspaper article. The headline reads: "Sgt. Lamb's French Bride Arrived Sunday." I read the article: "Many residents who remember Sergeant John H. Lamb will be extremely interested in learning of the Sunday arrival of his French bride, the former Mlle. Laurie Moreau of Le Mans. Mrs. Lamb, a nurse, was met last Sunday as she descended from Train No.

16 and was taken to the home of her mother-in-law, Mrs. Regina Ferguson, at Martinsville."

Bill has a book of maps called *Atlas*. I climb back over the boxes and pull out the massive hardback. I go back to the photo albums and plant myself next to the shelf and search through the M cities. I find Martinsville, West Virginia, which reminds me: Peggy mentioned Bill's side of the family being from West Virginia.

After Christopher's mysterious and untimely death, Bill and his mother, Evelyn, hopped from one town to another until they finally settled in Port Landia, South Carolina. I continue reading the article: "There (Martinsville, West Virginia), the bride of less than one year will wait for the arrival of Sergeant Lamb, who is due in the states soon from Le-Havre, France." The article states that they married "in a small military chapel near Rennes, France, on March 21, 1945."

I come across a photo of a guy around my age wearing overalls, his hands in his pockets. I remove the photo from behind the plastic film and read the back: "David, 19 years old." He looks identical to me, a spitting image. I place the photo aside and keep rifling through photos.

Eventually, the photos become more vivid and clear. The photos are no longer black and white. Yet, they have color. Each page after Laurie reunites with John back in America shows the following twenty years of their lives from raising their children—photos of Luke and Michelle playing in the back yard of a one-story house or washing their Ford Coupe—to standing with them after graduation to John shaking hands with Luke, who is dressed in an Air Force outfit. I find a photo of Luke standing outside a jet, helmet tucked underneath his armpit. However, I can't find any recent photos of Michelle or Luke, except for the photos of Luke in the Air Force. I keep flipping. Each photo shows the bond of a family—dare I say, a family that appears at peace with the world despite being in the grip of war. Why would Bill hide them from me? Was he ashamed of these people? I keep digging through albums. Another album: John and Laurie in the later years of life. I read the back of several photos and realize they were taken in France. They're visiting Laurie's family in Nantes, France. More of those *fas fotos*—that's where they're from, France, and the elderly couple in each photo is John and Laurie; however, I notice there is a significant gap in time from John and Laurie raising their two children to the golden years traveling around the world.

Then, I discover more photos of John's middle brother, the one who looks like me. His was name David, a minister. More photos are missing from the pages as well, only round sticky residue where photos once rested. An entire photo album is dedicated to David, a lanky man with wide telephone pole-shoulders, building a church from laying the foundation to placing the cross on top of the chapel. The last pages show

David and his congregation—David standing in the very middle of the group with a grin stretched across his entire face.

Underneath the album: more newspaper clippings.

According to an article, David's "body was discovered by a caretaker between the Oinky-Doinky (the store that John Junior managed), and Ruth's Hardware," and according to the authorities, was pronounced dead at the scene. His death was reported as "died of natural causes." That's two mysterious deaths: both bodies discovered by two different types of people who never gave statements—at least, none that I can find in the papers.

Then, finally, the last article: "One Member of Veteran's Family Slain in Middle of the Night."

Then: "Home Invasion Tragically Ends with Two Deaths." A man disguised in a black mask broke into the war veteran's house during the late hours of the night. Mr. Lamb's daughter, Michelle, was discovered unconscious at the scene of the crime. Mr. Lamb shot twice at the per-petrator with a twelve-gauge shotgun, the last shot left the perpetrator "unable to identify" at the scene. The perpetrator was pronounced dead at the scene."

Then, another article days later: "Housebreaker Identified as Local Convict, Sherman Tolbert."

Another: "Investigators Find the Murder Weapon."

I keep reading: The murder weapon used to murder Michelle Lamb was a "bird's beak knife."

Then: "Mr. Tolbert shot while trying to flee from the scene."

According to John's statement, he heard a noise coming from Luke's bedroom down the hallway. He went to check on his two children in their bedrooms, first starting with Michelle's bedroom where he discov-ered her unconscious. John tried to stop the bleeding, but she was al-ready gone. That's when John caught Sherman Tolbert sneaking into his son Luke's bedroom. According to John, Sherman was going to pay for what he did to his daughter. I start to question whether or not these murders or "natural" deaths are somehow related. I start to question whether or not the papers are right.

Finally, I pull out the last album in the bottom of the box. The al-bum is much different from the others. The surface is smoother, not as a chapped or cracked. The edges are together, as well. The album ap-pears as if it's brand new. Once I open the album, I find a photo of a guy who looks like Eleanor, yet nothing like John, David, or Christo-pher.

I turn over the aged photo and read a name: "Richie."

I flip to the front of the album and find a baby photo: "Richard An-thony Lamb, born 1930, 9 lbs." The "other" brother, the fourth and last brother, the brother whose photos had been removed from the other albums and placed in this very one. I find a partially ripped photo, which looks familiar. A young Richie—no older than four or five years old—is standing alone in a familiar field, his head in the daises below, as if he's in his own little world. I grab the first album and grab the ripped photo of the Lambs and compare the two photos, and they match. I connect the two ripped photos like a puzzle piece.

Why was Richie ripped away from the family?

I flip through photos of Richie with his brothers, John, David, and my grandfather, Christopher, who are much older than Richie. Eleanor must've had Richie with another man before John passed away from black lung. Not sure what went on during the time, but the photos tell a story of an outsider. I come across less photos of Richie and more newspaper articles, each one about a notorious outlaw named the "Belmont Bandit," from Williamson, West Virginia. I find a "WANTED" flyer of an unfavorable sketch of a man who looks like Richie, then professional-looking photos of Richie posed with an assortment of guns, as well as posters saying: "THE BANDIT WANTS YOU!" The articles state that the Bandit started his crime spree in Belmont, branding him the name, "Belmont Bandit." He continued south of the coast where he hit up over thirty banks and killed thirteen people, including two police officers, as well as a Senator from Alabama. He was known for stealing from the rich and giving back to the poor, a character who was adored by the people and yet, despised by those of higher status. Eventually, Richie met his fate in the small town of Marl, Texas, where he ripped off a famous oil tycoon named Brutus Gaffney. I pull an article with the photo of a big-game deputy holding up the head of a dead man lying in a pool of oil, or what was called a "Texas bath." The dead man's jaw is slack with black oil dripping from his yawning mouth. Behind the two stands a sheriff in a superhero-like pose with a wide beam stretched across a weather-beaten face. Marl Police Department officially identified the body as *the* Belmont Bandit, "Richard Lamb, son of Hester Eleanor Goodson."

I pull out the damp note from my pocket. The ink is smeared but legible. *Cross the line*, I read to myself. What if Bill means *another* line?

I run my finger over the tear in the family photo, the tear running crookedly down the right side of the photo like a fault line.

Then, I remove the photo of David holding a wooden cross upright with his fellow worshipers. What exactly are you trying to tell me, Bill? I put the albums and photos aside and grab a fresh breath of air outside the unit. I can't stop thinking about Bill's relatives—my relatives— Richie, and how Richie was killed. For the first time in my life, the truth feels so gray and murky.

16

Still life - The branches don't fit - Preserving history - Opportunity strikes - Unpublished works - Wasted and Waning - Pound, Pound, Pounding on Heaven's Door - Zeta Ursae Majoris - Gone.

YEAR'S worth of photos. An entire century of the still memories of a once loving family disbanded all kept concealed between binds of dusty photo albums.

So much love and joy, sorrow and pain, heartbreak and demise.

Tragic events cloaked by unexplainable mystery.

Questions unanswered.

What do I even do with all of them?

Is this Bill's last gift to me?

Or, is Bill luring me into a secret darker than my very own?

I manage to track down the owner of the storage facility in the main office. I ask her about unit 378. She stands like a doe that's spotted a human, staring at all of the cuts and bruises, especially the scratch on the left side of my face. She inspects my face until I give her an excuse to separate herself from me. I emphasize the unit belonged to my recently deceased father, William Lamb, as she's leafing through a filing cabinet. As if reading from a script, she shares her condolences for my loss. She pauses once more and studies my current state. Then, pulls out a manila folder and flips through several pieces of paper. She informs me that Bill paid two years rent for the unit. She shows me the form, as well as the receipt, stating that Bill left the storage unit to his son—me.

Two years, I tell myself.

It makes sense.

Sort of.

But again, why two years?

2

I grab a flashlight from the trunk and head back to the storage unit where I fish out a lamp, as well as an extension cord from one of the boxes. I run the cable into a hallway outside the unit and plug the lamp into an electrical outlet, then close the door to the unit behind me, grab an armful of photo albums, and place them along the shelf. Then, I clear out one half of the room by stacking boxes; and eventually, I clear out enough space on the floor to place every photo in chronological order, starting from the photos of a younger John Senior during his days working as a resilient coal miner to the childhood photos of Bill. Grandfather to grandson. I use the list of descendants written in perfect cursive on the torn piece of notebook paper and get to work.

3

The timeline is complete. I've managed to sort through all of the photos from the photo albums, including all of the newspaper clippings, and to the best of my ability, place them in correct order according to the dates provided.

I take a step back and observe the timeline from a wider angle. One person stands out the most: *Richie*, also known as the Belmont Bandit, a modern day Robin Hood, the incarnation of John Dillinger, Public Enemy Number 1. He may or may not have been a decent person— possibly misunderstood—but one thing is for sure: he was definitely the outsider, the black sheep, the *bad seed*, the phantom among the Lambs. Photos of a younger Richie suggest that he was an okay kid, I guess. He reminds me a lot of myself when I was younger, playful and most importantly, curious. Based on the photos, he doesn't come off as the bad son. I think—if I had to guess—the family *made* him bad by rejecting him; however, Richie had a choice, I guess, and he chose the path of a criminal.

I step away from the photos and another box catches my eye. I make my way past the shelves and open the untouched box. Inside are unpublished manuscripts. I pull out each manuscript from the box and stack them on the floor. Some of them date back long before Bill wrote *A Decent Man*. I remember Bill mentioning that he started writing when he was around twelve years old. He wrote his first book when he was seventeen. A horror story in the vein of the classic creature-features called *Red Special*, then another, *The Darker One at the Landing*. I skim through other recent manuscripts and drafts for his eleventh novel.

One called *VVV*. More manuscripts: *The Crippler; Member's Only Book Club; Children of the Night; Killing School; Midnight in an Anything But Perfect World; Parody of Paradise; Mr. Glass*—

"Glass?"

The name sounds familiar.

Then: *Hardback; The Perfect Beast; The Sportsman; Modern Jazz; Point of View; Lemon; Fisticuffs Friday; Better at Night; Life on Pause; Storm Port Landia*—which, after skimming, I learn is a story about Bill's childhood growing up in a small town living next to a paper mill.

In one excerpt, the main character, Page, describes the smell in the air as "rotten eggs" and whenever she takes in a deep breath, it "hurts my (her) lungs." "*Youthful years,*" she writes, "*spent playing in a chicken coup of the dead. The odor so foul and pungent it attached itself to everything, including myself.*" The list of stories goes on and on. So many manuscripts. So many words. So many hours of hard work, anguish, and discipline. The writing is superb and much sharper. Bill 2.0. Most of the stories are not short enough to be short stories but not long enough to be novels. I think Bill once called them "novellas." Somewhere in between a short story and a novel. I pick up one of the manuscripts, much thicker in size—a six hundred pager, single-spaced, twelve font. The title reads: *A Better Man*, a sequel to *A Decent Man*, which I believe to be his eleventh and final novel. I pull out more manuscripts, at least thirty to forty manuscripts. The date on one of them is only a couple of months ago.

4

It's already night when I finish loading Bill's manuscripts into the back of my car.

Since I'm not too far away from Sandy Hill County Cemetery, I decide to make a pit stop at a gas station. I wait until some twenty-something goes inside to pay for gas, then I give him the old "Mister" with the tap on the shoulder. I ask him if he can buy me a case of beer. He doesn't mind. I hand him money. He meets me behind the convenient store and returns with a case of Pabst.

I tip him with a five-dollar bill and tell him thanks.

"If you get caught with that—" he says fatherly.

"—I know, I know," I tell him. "I don't know you."

"We *never* had this conversation."

"What conversation?"

5

Two beers down, and time has completely vanished.

I pound away another beer. Smash it over Bill's headstone like an accordion. Then, crack open another one.

I've already gone through three beers, and I'm starting to feel a buzz creeping behind my eyeballs. The night sky is clear, bright, and I can count every single star and constellation, like a map of the stars has been laid out above me.

I point out certain stars, famous ones, and put them together as if I'm connecting tiny dots.

One group of stars catches my eye the most, seven of them.

The Big Dipper.

Every since I was a kid, the Big Dipper was like my starting point whenever I stargazed, my compass, my beacon, my very own North Star; and whenever I located it, I could find my bearings among the darkness of the night. But, of all the nights, why does the sky seem so bright?

While staring at the Big Dipper, I can't help but wonder where Bill has gone.

Where are you, Bill?

What are you doing right now?

Are you looking down on me, flashing a light on me?

Or, darkly, are you looking up at me?

I used to think that once you die, that's it. You're gone. Forever stained with blackness. Now I don't know anymore. A part of me wants to believe Bill's somewhere out there. Waiting. Watching. I *want* to believe he's here with me, even though he's not really here. I want to believe there's still a chance for me.

I pound my way through two more beers and squash each can into a disc.

I pick up a flattened beer can from the ground and stare at it for the longest time.

I think about all of that garbage my teachers taught me in elementary school about how, if I try my very best in whatever I do or if I put in enough effort and hard work, I'll never be a loser, or that time at summer camp I received a red ribbon even though I didn't deserve one, or the whole MOST LIKELY TO SUCCEED (JOSH LAMB) bullshit in the front of the middle school yearbook. I want to pay a visit to each one of those teachers who put these ideas in my head, and I want to shake the truth from them. I want to know why they filled my head with these ideas. I want to know why they set me up for failure or why they didn't tell me, not what a kid like me wanted to hear, but what a kid like me needed to hear. And that whole being born into this world alone is bullshit. The second we enter this world of piss we are given something as precious as light; and then, we're greeted by two hands of a stranger to nurture us in the wake of our fearful state of disarray, and the strangers assure us that this messed-up world we've entered is a safe place, a place where we are welcome to be or choose whoever we want to be: a teacher, businessman, retail worker, athlete, entertainer, writer. Anybody. We are given faces too, each one more unique than the next, and these faces may look strange to us at first, and we don't know anything about these faces at first. Soon, though, we get to know these faces. We get to cherish them, adore them. We are given all these things only for them to be taken away. No matter what, we *all* lose something or someone. We're all losers. Each-and-every-one-of-us.

I pound away another beer and the beer helps rid each drunken thought from my head. I drink until nothing remains upstairs but a soggy dark void. My head starts to feel like an elevator slowly rising through each level. Then an invisible weight suddenly crashes over my shoulders. One minute I'm floating, and the next, I'm surging out into a sea of shit. Another discarded interest. Why didn't you tell me? You could've gotten treatment, you son of a bitch. You could've still been here. With me. Fighting. I would've been there for you. I would've— *Why, Bill?* Why did you do this to us? Why did you do this to me? I curl my body into a ball and I want to cry until I'm compost—at least that's how I feel right now, like there's no more hope for me. I'm already gone.

17.

A caw – Hungover – Sup, homey – Cancel me this – A Killer Next Door – Pick-Me-Up – Finding the right words to say to Peggy – Scab – *The Man with Glass Eyes* **– History can be a revolving door – The Fifty Year War – She speaks – Evidence**

"WAKE up," a soft, tender voice inside me tells me.

Above me looms a sickly-thin man drenched in oil. He's leaning over my body and studying me, despite having no eyes.

I peer closer at the strange man and study him. His eyelids peel open, revealing the eyes of a madman: the irises of his eyes as black as a raven's, and the whites sharp and brilliant like the sun wrapped in white silk.

The oily man reaches his oily hand toward me.

I pull myself away and open my eyes to a red sky.

I'm gasping for air.

I calm myself by taking several deep breaths, then acknowledge the headstones around me. I wonder how in the hell I ended up in a cemetery; but I soon find out after I find smashed beer cans scattered everywhere. I hear a car door slam shut from behind and locate the noise, as well as a middle-aged woman dressed in all black walking toward a headstone about five headstones away from Bill's. She can't see me or, at least, I don't think she can. My body is concealed by the headstone, and I'm making sure to stay hidden. The wind is blowing, not a strong gust, but strong enough to cause the loose garments of her black clothing, like the black-latticed veil over her pale face or the black dress, to flap around her in a stoic villain-like fashion. She carries a certain grace about her, something that doesn't seem of this world. She kneels down and places a bouquet of red roses next to the headstone. I quietly collect the beer cans, including the ones that are still full, toss them in the closest trashcan, and leave the cemetery before I make a scene—if I haven't already.

As I make it back to my car, I start the ignition and drive away; and it's not until I'm well outside Sandy Hill I hear those dreadful sounds of Maximus breaking down. On the dashboard the red needle along the gauge slowly rises like the thin second hand on a clock moving from 6 to 12. The hood smokes, gradually at first, but then worsens as I continue to drive. I pull off to the side of the road and as I've done from time to time, especially during long drives across country, I fill the radiator with bottled water, which normally helps whenever Maximus overheats; however, this time, I manage to get only a few miles before the engine starts smoking again.

I hate myself for not using coolant instead of water or not taking Maximus into the shop for a basic tune-up like Peggy insisted time and time again.

Even worse, I can't get a decent signal on my phone.

In other words, I'm on my own.

Fortunately, I'm not too far from Bradbury; however, I'll have better luck finding service the closer I get to Sandy Hill, which, according to GPS before the app froze, is roughly six miles away.

I hate to leave the manuscripts in Maximus while I'm searching for a signal. But what other choice do I have? I turn back around and start walking in search of a signal.

2

Believe it or not, the walk actually helps relieve the hangover.

Eventually, I make it into downtown Sandy Hill.

Dehydrated and exhausted from the walk, I stop at a convenient store next to an underpass and buy three bottled waters with added electrolytes and down two of them and keep the other one for later.

Finally, I'm able to get a decent signal on my phone.

I use the ride share app, Pick-U-Up. The driver is located about ten miles away, which gives me, according to the app, an estimated twelve minutes to kill.

As I'm waiting on the curb outside the convenient store, a man, whom I presumed is homeless based on his raggedy clothes, as well as the garbage-like smell emitting from his body, walks right by me. I catch the profile of his face, and he can pass as Bill's twin.

Thinking my eyes are deceiving me, I peer closer at his face and again, except for the dirt and blemishes on his face, he looks identical to Bill. I slowly stand to my feet to prevent a dizzy spell and follow the homeless man to the underpass where dozens and dozens of homeless people are gathered.

"Bill?" I call out to the homeless man.

He turns his shoulder and faces me; and again, even examining his face, now in its entirety, he looks incredibly similar to Bill; however, his nose is slightly wider.

"Sorry," I say. "You just look like someone I knew."

I turn around and as I'm about to walk back to the convenient store and wait on the ride share, the homeless man says in a smooth and intelligible voice, "Perhaps we were related. . . "

That voice grabs me, and I can't help but turn around and face the homeless man.

"This person you speak of?"

"Maybe," I say, thinking if Bill had any other relatives whom he was keeping from me.

"You know," he says, "sometimes, we only see the things we're searching for, and at times, it's the only things we see."

I glance at the other homeless people hanging out next to empty oil drums where a low fire burns next to various camping tents and beds made out of cardboard.

The homeless man waves and walks back to the campsite.

As he joins other homeless people, I walk closer to the underpass for a better look and what was once a few dozen is now hundreds of homeless people.

I stop, take it all in, and in that moment, I visualize Bill in each one of their faces: Bills camped inside collapsed tents; Bills standing over flames inside oil drums, keeping warm; Bills aimlessly wandering through aisles of trash; Bills combing through garbage for food or whatever; Bills passed out on cardboard boxes; Bills shooting up drugs inside a dark tent.

Engulfed by a gagging stench in the air, I snap from my trance. As I focus, those familiar faces change; and over the warm beating fires and underneath shadowy hoods, I see the altered faces of tired, desperate souls moving like phantoms and yet, when gazed upon by the living (drivers, pedestrians, onlookers, etc.), they're treated like an ink smudge on society. Once these people had jobs. Once these people had loved ones. Once these people had a country that they fought for and one that they could call their own. Now, after whatever faults, mishaps, or reasons that led them to a place of constant rejection and looks of disdain, from being laid off to being divorced to being abandoned to being ostracized, banned, or canceled, I see raw pain on their faces, real and rancid, a pain, nonetheless, that makes mine feel so insignificant.

Most of all, I can see the helplessness like an exaggerated expression, once worn as if it was a tremendously heavy and irremovable coat, and now, it weighs on skin and bones, absorbing that irremediable poison into the blood supply, only to spawn a new kind whose only purpose is to adapt to its stale and unnatural surroundings.

Dirty on the outside and even dirtier on the inside.

Isn't this what we all eventually become?

The filthy product of an American Nightmare?

For years I knew that Sandy Hill had a major homeless problem and the city's mayor, who somehow kept getting reelected, acted as if he didn't give a shit about it. Now, witnessing it with my own two eyes, that utter helplessness, it was worse than I could ever imagine. The news channels, which once covered the stories on Sandy Hill's homeless problem, stopped reporting them.

My ride share arrives. During the entire trip back to Spartacus, I can't stop thinking about what I just witnessed in Sandy Hill.

3

During the trip home, I try my best to keep myself from dozing off in a car with the strange Pick-U-Up driver by coming up with a legitimate story in my head but end up scraping the story the closer we get to Spartacus.

By the time the driver pulls into my neighborhood, I have absolutely no stories for Peggy, whom I can only assume is worried sick about me. I know that, as much as it kills me, I need to be upfront with her, clear the air, in essence, and maybe, by doing so, she will understand; otherwise, if I don't, I may leave Spartacus and never come back. I can't leave angry, and I certainly can't do that to myself. Most importantly, I can't do that to Peggy.

When the driver pulls onto my street, I witness at least a dozen cop cars parked in front of the neighbor's house and immediately, I know they're here for me. I stay low in the backseat, tell the driver *not* to slow down and to keep driving.

As soon as the Pick-U-Up driver drives past my house, it's clear that the cops aren't here for me. They're here for one of my neighbors. Two plainclothes DEA agents escort the strung-out neighbor from his house while I believe his biker girlfriend, as well as his son and his girlfriend, both a couple of years older than me, wait with a police officer and a detective. Walking behind the neighbor is what looks like the neighbor's scruffy-looking friend, whom I've seen hanging around his house before. He wears a chained necklace with a police badge around his neck.

The neighbor appears furious with his friend, as he's escorted to the back of a cop car.

Then, I witness the same shady car that I once saw parked outside the house. Then, I witness the man wearing those same 1950's shades standing on the front lawn. He's chatting to what looks like another DEA agent. After the Pick-U-Up driver drops me off on a street behind my house, I later find out from Peggy, who knows the scoop on the neighborhood drama, that the neighbor was part of a sting operation

that had been in development for many weeks. Apparently, our neighbor was a drug dealer, as in top of the pyramid kind of dealer, who had
been supplying nearly the entire East Coast with fentanyl smuggled into
the country via the US-Mexico border. Surprisingly, I'm relieved by
the story and if I didn't know any better, the issues between Peggy and
me, at least for the time being, are not important—that is, until I break
the news about poor ole Maximus. Peggy doesn't care about the car,
nor does she care about my whereabouts last night. She's only glad that
I'm okay.

4

After informing Peggy of the broken down car, she springs into action
and takes care of the situation. She calls a tow truck to pick up Maximus and drop off the car at the nearest repair shop. Once the car is
fixed later that afternoon—turns out, it only needed coolant and some
minor patching up but several major components of the engine, which
will cost a fortune, need to be replaced in the near future—Peggy drives
me to the repair shop. We don't speak a word to one another throughout the entire drive, except for, of course, Peggy verbally trying to wrap
her head around living next to a drug dealer, who was responsible for
selling death to those with heroine addictions. Peggy's left in a state of
shock by the whole ordeal. She doesn't say it, but I know that it's on
her mind because it was on my mind the moment I saw cops parked
outside the neighbor's house; in fact, it's still weighing heavily on my
mind.

5

Fours hours of sleep, and I'm back to my old self again. It's late afternoon, and as soon as I wake up from taking a nap after returning home
with my car, I check the driveway. Peggy's car is gone. I go downstairs
and check the kitchen, the living room. She hasn't left a note, as she
usually does. No money. I go back upstairs and check my phone. I
have no missed calls. No messages. I have nothing.

6

I decide to take advantage of the empty house by clearing out my car,
starting with the manuscripts from the back and hauling them up to my
room.

On my last trip, I come across an older photo next to the wheel well,
like the one from the photo albums, protruding from one last manuscript; however, I don't remember taking any of the photos with me before I left Bradbury. Or did I? I remember clearly loading manuscripts

inside the car. Then I left and got wasted. I don't remember anything from the time I went to the gas station and did the "*Hey, Mister*" tactic for booze to the time I woke up against Bill's headstone with a gorge running down the middle of my skull.

I pick up the photo and carefully examine it: a group of masked kids are breaking the windows of a cop car with bricks and baseball bats; around the kids are other people cheering on rioters.

The photo appears recent, only a couple of years old. I grab the manuscript and more photos trickle from the pages. I turn over the manuscript and read the title, "*The Man with Glass Eyes*." I set down the manuscript and open the centerfold where many more photos are crammed into the spine held together by three brass fasteners. I turn over the manuscript and the photos rain down over the lining of the trunk. I flip through a few photos, which look familiar to the ones inside the shoebox. Some of them old while others more recent. The recent ones were taken at protests and rallies: snapshots of violence, irate red-eyed people screaming to the top of their lungs or people crying or people tossing Molotov cocktails through storefront windows or people filling up streets while marching for "Equal Pay" or basic "Human Rights." The last two send chills down my back: one, a photo of Bill and an older man with a faded black fedora sitting on a porch; and then, another, Bill and that same old man standing outside a rundown convenient store with hazy mountains at their backs. I can tell the photos were taken about a year ago. Bill's face appears much fuller, and he's healthy-looking. The old man is probably pushing early eighties.

I flip over the photos, one of them reads with fresh ink: "Me and Richie in Williamson, West Virginia."

Richie is, in fact, dead. Died by being drowned in oil, according to the newspaper clipping—a "Texas bath," read the article. I grab a random photo, a much older one: a black and white of a quaint town in a valley. The date reads: May 17, 1954. That's eight years before Bill was born. Only two people first come to mind, and both of them are "presumed" dead.

7

Next thing I know, I'm back at the storage unit in Bradbury.

I head straight to the shoebox with the word *Florsheim* on it. I compare the older photos from *The Man With Glass Eyes* manuscript to the ones inside the shoebox. The photos appear as if they were taken by the same person. I scatter the photos along the floor and flip over each one. Each one dates back to the early 1940's (the first one, a photo of a mountain range, June 11, 1942) to the late 1970's (a photo of an abandoned house, August 2, 1979). Most of the photos from 1942 to 1948 are taken around a small town in the mountains. No photos are taken during the 1980's; then, the most recent photos are *not* landscapes or empty towns or minimal shots of nature, but photos of people, such as the rioters, protesters, or looters from *The Man With Glass Eyes*. Yet another timeline, I realize. I arrange each photo in its proper place along a new timeline, starting from 1942 to 1992. Fifty years. I remember seeing a young cameraman in a photo of John and Eleanor—John Junior, that is. I grab the photo album and find the photo of John—just around my age—standing in front of a military base. He's dressed in uniform. Next to him stands my great grandmother—Eleanor. Not too far away from the two stands the same young cameraman in the background; however, he's *not* a cameraman but a kid—no older than eight or nine years old—with a camera. I flip over the photo. No date. I sort through the shoebox photos until I come across a black and white photo of a military base, the *same* military base from the photo of John and Eleanor. Again, there's no date on the back. I pull out a photo of a younger Richie from one of the photo albums. The kid taking pictures behind John and Eleanor looks identical to Richie.

I take the shoebox, as well as the article about Richie's death, back to Spartacus with me and research the dates on my computer. I start with the photo of the rioters. I type in the date, "1992," and the first thing that comes up on the search engine: LOS ANGELES RIOTS.

I scroll through images: looters, rioters, buildings up in flames, including stores and small businesses, civilians armed with weapons, police scrambling around the city, chasing down looters; even National Guard troops are stationed throughout the city. It's complete chaos on the streets, nothing like what happened in Kernelson.

I rifle through other photos inside the shoebox.

I type in the dates on the back of each photo, first starting with May 17, 1954.

On May 17th, Brown vs. Board of Education declared the separation of public schools for blacks and whites unconstitutional.

August 28, 1963: Martin Luther King, Jr. delivered his "I Have a Dream" speech.

I type in other dates from the back of the photos.

I pull up videos on YouTube. I watch them, as well, including famous speeches and addresses.

Later that year, in November 1963, I learn President John Fitzgerald Kennedy was assassinated in Dallas, Texas. A man named Lee Harvey Oswald was the "alleged" assassin.

Each photo holds a significant date in American history, from the attack on Pearl Harbor to the bombing of Hiroshima and Nagasaki, to the many dates surrounding World War II to the Korean War in 1950, to a black lady named Rosa Parks who refused to give up her bus seat to a white passenger, thus inspiring the Civil Rights movement, to the Civil Rights Act of 1957, to the Space Race, to the Equal Pay Act of

1963, to the Vietnam War, to the Selma marches, to the assassination of Martin Luther King, Jr. in 1968, to the first man landing on the moon (July 20, 1969), to Watergate, which led to the resignation of President Richard Nixon, to the 1973 oil crisis.

I get about halfway through typing in the dates from the back of each photo when I realize I'm doing exactly what Bill wanted me to do. I stop gumshoeing and shut off my computer. I pull out the article about Richie's death—the "Belmont Bandit" drenched in oil.

Texas bath.

I carefully read the article.

Every word.

Then, I read it again and again.

Three times, I read the article from start to finish. Could the article be wrong? I guess the question I should be asking myself: If that's not Richie in the newspaper, then who is it?

8

Peggy and I spend most of the dinner inside a globe of tense silence. I hardly touch my food. I know Peggy has many questions built up inside, questions about the scabbed over cuts, as well as bruises on my face, my trophies, and what I've been up to lately. She starts to talk, but I immediately cut her off—*I'm sorry.*

"For everything," I tell Peggy. "I screwed up. I know. I don't know what I was thinking. I *wasn't* thinking—"

"You realize how much trouble you can get into?" Peggy says as she places her fork aside.

"—I know," I interrupt her. "I'm sorry. I want to make things right for myself, for you, for Bill. . . "

Just saying his name out loud brings tears to my eyes; however, I never shed one tear in front of her.

Stay strong, I tell myself. That's what Bill would've wanted.

We don't talk that much after my apology. Peggy changes the subject by telling me she could use an extra hand at the store. She says that she can use another cashier.

I tell her that I'll think about it. It's not quite the answer she's looking for, but it's better than giving her a flat-out no.

9

I'm rinsing the dishes in the sink when Peggy says my name by the doorway. I stop what I'm doing and turn around.

"Your father was a good man," she says. "Best I've ever known. He always wanted you to become your own man. He *never* wanted you to follow in his footsteps. Yet he wanted you to make your own story,

175

Josh. To create, *not* destroy. He wanted you to be whoever you wanted to be."

My eyelids grab the tears in my eyes and keep them from falling down my face. I stay strong in front of Peggy. I don't display any kind of weakness. She hasn't mentioned his name to me ever since his death. Did something happen?

As Peggy's about to leave, she turns back around and tells me, "Walking away from a fight doesn't make you a lesser person, Josh. It's what you do with your life and the positive impact you make on others that makes you a better person. I *believe* in you, Josh. Always have. Always will."

It's not until nightfall when I'm cutting my nails in the bathtub that I realize Peggy must know something that I don't know.

I place the clippers aside and rush from the bathroom and check the windows.

I search the dark streets, but I don't see any suspicious cars.

Who's gotten to her?

18

Mashed Potatoes - Dull Boy - Ultimate fantasy - Back to the drawing board - Not out of the dark just yet - And yet another attack! - Scheming and dreaming - Peggy's promise - Gl⊙ck 21 - The Seed

---

FOR the remainder of the night, I stare at the TV in my bedroom, mostly flipping from one channel to another.

I stop on one channel.

Someone's getting raped against a tree in the woods.

I flip to another.

Someone's getting eaten by a herd of zombies.

I flip to another.

Someone's aiming a revolver at the face of a wounded person, who is pleading for forgiveness.

Before I flip to yet another channel, the helpless person's face is blown off by a close-range gunshot.

I flip to another channel.

Someone's singing about "clapping" a cop while doing donuts in an empty parking lot and waving around a green plastic water gun outside the window.

I flip to another.

Inside an investigation room, someone's confessing to a murder while Good Cop fetches the murderer coffee and the expressionless Bad Cop stands against the tinted glass.

I flip to another.

Someone's being thrown against a rope wrapped in barbwire.

I flip to another.

Someone's head is being crushed like a watermelon by two massive hands of a giant robot.

I flip to another channel airing a special coverage on the Halloween-masked bank robbers who've been branded with the name, "The Spooky Robbers."

I flip to another channel.

Someone's getting raped again, but this time in an alleyway.

I flip to another.

More carnage and gore.

Someone's getting eaten again, this time by a pack of wolves.

I race through every channel: sudden car explosions; someone's standing against a backdrop of flames; Demolition Derby; more extreme wrestling; Internet videos of people jumping off rooftops; the #WHATABOUTUS movement looting in the streets of St. Louis; bare-knuckle fighting; soft porn; two heavyset people clawing, then ripping each other's hair out as a rowdy, barbarous crowd behind them chants, "Fight, fight, fight!"

I flip to another channel where a pretentious Olympian swimmer is doing a toothpaste commercial urging viewers to reduce water usage by making sure to turn off the faucet in order to save water while brushing their teeth while on the contrary he used to swim in gallons of water, which could've been used for more important things, like drinking or transported to areas that are suffering from major droughts such as the West Coast.

I flip to another channel.

Someone's mowing down an 80's themed nightclub with an assault rifle.

I flip to another.

Someone's being slapped in the face by a dildo.

I flip to another.

Someone's strangling a cat.

I flip to another.

Someone's hanging upside down on a bloody meat hook while being gutted by a doctor with a wicked smile painted in lime green over his surgical mask.

I flip to another.

The Spooky Robbers have hit yet another bank.

I flip to another.

Someone's slowly cocking the hammer of a pistol while sticking the barrel inside *his* mouth.

I change the channel before the kid pulls the trigger and flip to another channel.

Someone's puking into a microphone.

I flip to another.

Someone's being suffocated by a grocery bag.

I flip to another.

Someone's flinging a white miniature poodle across a posh great room furnished with gold.

More channels: a scammer selling counterfeit goods from China over infomercials; a mainstream artist breaking storefront windows; a dull not-so funny late night TV show host turned surrogate for big pharma making snarky remarks at a politician's facial features—the camera does a close-up on a hysterical crowd—then more destruction; more blood; more people getting raped; more killing; more cannibalism; more protesting; more carnage; more fire.

I mute the TV.

I can't help but wonder if society is crumbling or if I'm the one who's crumbling and every fiber of me is falling into oblivion, as if my body has become an hourglass and each grain of sand is a piece of life falling into that inevitable darkness.

2

After hours of flipping through channels, I finally doze off.

Distorted faces flash in a pulse-like rhythm behind the underside of my eyelids.

The faces fade into oblivion, and now, I'm walking into Meme's with an M4 Carbine with a mounted M203 grenade launcher.

Along my vest are STANAG magazines.

I first take out the robotic clerk with a gunshot right between the eyes. She doesn't fall to the floor; yet, she stands there like a robot, as sparks pepper from a smoking hole in her forehead.

Someone rushes at me.

I take out the assailant, a cook holding a butcher's knife, with a shot to the head.

I make my way down to the Basement.

There, I see the Mawb.

I plant myself in front of a wall in order to prevent any assailants from sneaking up on me.

Then, with my M4 gripped in hand, I shoot every last one of the members of the Mawb. I unload each magazine. Then, reload the assault rifle and unload a magazine. I unload. Then, reload.

I do this several times until they're all lying in puddles of blood. My hands shake with electricity. My body looms over dead-dying bodies. My eyes watch final breaths escape their lungs.

Distant police siren wail outside, growing louder and louder.

Above, I hear an army of footsteps approaching.

I rush from the red-lit hallway to the alleyway where I'm greeted by the spotlight of a helicopter.

Bright sirens are flashing all around.

I rush to my car.

Get inside.

I rev the engine.

Then, I floor it through downtown Atlanta. I'm weaving through traffic. Through the rear view mirror, the cops are closing in on me. I hit the brakes as soon as I approach a sharp curve. The brakes aren't working! I repeatedly pump the brakes, but again, they're *not* working! I check the rear view once more. The cops are closing in.

As I turn back around, I find a young boy who's no older than five years old standing in the bend of the curve.

I slam on the brakes, but, again, the brakes do not work!

At the very last second, the boy raises his head. The headlights shine over his face as if he's standing on center stage.

The boy standing before the car is Richie, and he's staring at me with these narrow, glaring eyes.

The dream freezes, and I'm staring back at him.

We stare at each other for what feels like an eternity, while the world around us nearly stops. In that very moment, I see a younger version of myself staring down at the stranger behind the wheel.

Just as I'm about to run over myself, I bolt upright to the booming sound of a *knock* on my door.

I'm sweating profusely. Bullets of sweat race down my forehead.

The upper part of Peggy's body oozes through the crack of the door.

Josh—

I try gathering myself.

My heart is racing, and I'm having trouble catching my breath.

"Yeah," I say, coughing or choking. "What—"

"—You were screaming," she says.

"What?"

"Do you want me to get you some water?"

"No," I say and finally relax. "I'm fine."

"You sure?"

I nod my head.

"Yeah," I tell her. "Fine."

Peggy leaves the door cracked and walks back downstairs.

I roll out of bed and splash my face with cold water. I take a pill to help me sleep and tell myself that it's only a dream. I turn up the volume of the TV, sit against the headrest of the bed, and wait for the darkness to set in.

3

Peggy's starting to hang around the house more, and I know it has something to do with me. She's about to make a run to the grocery store. I tell her that I'll grab the groceries. She's surprised by the comment, but she's glad I'm willing to step up and help out around the house, even if it's a task as common as running an errand. She hands me cash, but I pocket the cash and decide to use my credit card on the groceries.

The self-checkout is backed up with a line of people; however, only one person—an older lady with a purse about the size of a duffel bag—is checking out in the express lane. Clearly, the sign above says no more than ten items, and the older lady has an entire buggy full of groceries. I let it slip and tell myself that she's old and maybe she can't read the sign.

While I'm waiting to checkout, I flip through the magazines and books on the racks.

I flip through one magazine after another.

Tabloid trash.

Sex scandals. . .

Someone boned someone who was married with children.

Someone boned so-and-so, which led to so-and-so's contentious divorce.

Someone boned this amount of people and lived to brag about it in a no-holds-barred interview, only to commit the act of "kissing and telling," which, to tabloids, was like handing over next month's issue on a silver platter.

Someone boned a celebrity, whose true identity of being an undercover Russian spy was exposed via released text messages.

Someone boned someone on camera and in return, the sex tape was leaked all over the Internet.

Someone boned himself, which I don't think is physically possible.

More magazines.

More people boning and finding new ways of screwing over one another.

More gossip: famous realty TV show celebrity, Chalice Saffron, posting a saucy topless photo of herself, which was called the "Selfie heard 'round the world in 80 days." Monica Estevez, former child actress from the hit TV drama, *In Good Company*, underwent a facelift at the age of thirteen—"against her own will," the shocking article reads, "carried out by her vampiric parents," who were trying to wring every penny from their child.

More mystery novels: covers of silhouettes holding guns, posing with guns, aiming guns, shooting guns, or even boning guns.

Glossy-print romance novels with shirtless meatheads with silky blonde hair like a Swedish model posing in front of California sunsets.

Novels with a BDSM torture devices and sex toys on the cover.

More smut.

More death.

I can't escape the carnage.

It's like a stalker who's following me everywhere I go.

4

As I'm leaving the grocery store, I pass a newspaper dispenser.

The headline on the *Spartacus Herald*: Car bomb kills 38.

The suspect parked a van next to a crowd of protesters in Tucson, Arizona.

Homeland Security has claimed the incident as an act of "terrorism." Terrorist organizations are claiming responsibility for the massacre. It's never going to end, is it?

5

On the way back to my car, I pass the local guns and ammunition shop.

I stop and look over a display case of handguns behind the storefront window. I look over the price tag on each gun.

I find one that I like: a Glock 21, Gen 4, .45ACP caliber, two-tone dark earth.

The price: "$499.⁹⁹."

I take a mental note of the price and then head back home before the groceries spoil.

6

Later that night, I go online and research different pistols and semi-automatics. There are so many to choose from: a Glock, Beretta, Smith and Wesson. Each one has its own personality. Each one is special. I compare the prices from the local gun shop to ones online. I find that same Glock 21 for four hundred and fifty dollars. I write down the make and model on a piece of paper, then turn on the TV, and flip through channels until I finally fall asleep.

19

Helping hand - No escape - A slow but deadly virus -
Don't *Overlook* - Where the hell do we go from here? -
This ain't no fairy tale - The Woman Who Wore a Mask -
An unforgivable crime- The most beautiful people in the
world

THE following day Peggy stops me while I'm heading out the door and asks me if I can do her yet another favor and grab a thing of ricotta cheese. By "thing," I think she's referring to a tub or a container of ricotta cheese. I don't ask. I know what she means. Plans are that she's making a pan of lasagna with ground turkey tonight, and she doesn't have enough ricotta to complete the dish.

Without giving the errand much thought, I make a quick run to the grocery store for her like the little helper I am.

I pocket the five dollar bill Peggy hands me—the ricotta should cost no more than three dollars and I don't expect her to ask for the change—then I stop at the bank first. I withdraw five hundred dollars from my savings account. I secure the money in the centerfold of the car owner's manual and place it underneath a stack of wadded receipts and fast-food napkins inside the glove box.

Next, I stop by the store where two kids are standing outside arguing over a phone. One is yelling, "You fuck! Give it here!" The other one's laughing and pushing away the other kid.

An older lady passes the kids, and they act as if she's an object, a passing figure, a background actor filling up a scene, and continue to yell out every curse word from the alphabet.

I ignore the two kids and grab the store's brand of ricotta from the fridge section of the store—Peggy's "thing."

The self-checkout is backed up yet again, whereas all the other checkout lanes remain barely empty, which is no surprise.

Only one person's standing at the checkout in the express lane.

As before, I walk to the same express lane and check out each of the magazines on the racks.

The magazines and books have changed since my last visit. I flip through one magazine after another.

More tabloids.

More sex scandals.

I pick up the latest issue of *Tasteful*. Last week, a video taken by a drone captured famous pop singer Kool Kellie and her producer Max Richards having sex in Max's multi-million dollar mansion in Malibu. The sex tape—or "illegal video"—leaked onto the Internet and before the video could be removed and taken off sites or social media pages, the video had already spread across the Internet like a wild fire. Professional examiners were called in to do thorough investigations after the pop singer claimed the person in the video was *not* her but a look-alike. On the cover of the magazine is a blown up still of a birthmark in the shape of Michigan on the left cheek of a woman's ass while she sits in a rather suggestive position on the white leather couch. *Tasteful* compares the birthmark to Kool Kellie's left cheek from footage of her music video, "Detox," and in the video, Kool Kellie doesn't bare any birthmarks whatsoever; however, some professional analysts indicated that the photo in *Tasteful* was photoshopped. Contributors from the magazine reached out to Max Richards from one of his studios in Bel Air and he agreed that he was "the guy" in the sex tape. He also claimed Kool Kellie was, in fact, the young woman in the tape as well, despite the investigators final report stating Kool Kellie was *not* the young woman in the video.

If Max Richards was lying in order to gain publicity for Kool Kellie's new LP, *Orange Juice*, which drops next week through Max's record label, Salvage Yard Records, then who was the mysterious woman in the sex tape?

I guess we'll never know.

I flip through other magazines, more books.

More sex scandals.

More half-naked men posed in front of a backdrop with a falling sun.

More Barbie-doll faced women with glossy skin and puffy duck lips.

More botched face jobs.

More grotesquery.

More alien abductions.

More smear campaigns.

More false-accusations.

More long distance photos by paparazzi.

More rumors.

More gossip.

More controversial chirps and chirp wars.

More pregnant women: "*Who's the real baby daddy: Chad or Ben?*"

More carnage.

More fire—*Sir?*

I turn to some girl's voice and find a cashier patiently waiting for me to step forward with the groceries. Another person—the same older lady from the entranceway—files in behind me with a basket of milk and white bread and a worried expression on her face.

I place the ricotta on the scanner and as I'm about to reach for my wallet, I come up empty. Shit. I must've left it in the car.

"Did you find everything you needed?" the cashier asks me.

"Ah—yeah," I say, frantically digging through my pockets.

I pull out the crinkled five-dollar bill that Peggy gave me. I turn to the line growing behind me. I can't go back to my car, I tell myself. I'm already here. Ready to pay for the ricotta. I turn all flush and sweaty.

"Do you have a *Market* card?" the cashier asks right before she scans the ricotta.

"I don't," I say.

She slides the ricotta over the scanner and places the ricotta inside the bag.

"Your total is two dollars and ninety-five cents," she says.

I hand her the five anyway.

The cash register springs open. She reaches inside and pulls out two dollars and five cents. She freezes. One of her brows lowers a degree from the sight of a nickel in her palm. She thoroughly looks over the coin before handing it to me.

"No way," she says with strange enthusiasm. "It's a double die."

"Huh?"

"A double die buffalo nickel."

She hands me the cash first, then, lastly, the coin. On one side is an Indian head, while on the other side, is a bison.

"It's your lucky day," she says closely. "If I were you, I'd have a collector look at that. They'd probably pay a fortune to own a double die."

I ask, "What's a double die?"

"You know, a double die," she says, as if I'm supposed to know what a double die is supposed to be.

Clearly, I don't.

She leans over the counter and points to the bottom of the coin.

"Yeah. . . "

"You see the date?"

"1916," I read the date out loud.

"That's right," she says. "You see underneath the number. It's been double-died."

The date 1916 appears as if the same date has been shadowed underneath the date.

Which makes it look three-dimensional in its design.

I ask, "What's that?"

She says, "It's when the printers transfer an additional image to the coin because it didn't work the first time. But in these cases, the print is misaligned, and sometimes, they had to do multiple impressions, like three or four times, in order to get the correct result they wanted."

I ask, "So, what's so special about this coin?"

"I think there was only like two hundred of them out there," she says. "It's a very rare coin. It's worth *a lot* of money."

I glance at the cashier, then look down at the coin, then shoot another glance at the cashier.

"You know your coins."

"My father," she says flatly, her tone slightly changing when she speaks about him. "He collected them."

"I see," I say, looking over the coin once more. I turn to the line and people are all staring at me. One of them sighs and gives me a "while-we're-young" kind of expression. I ignore the people in the line and hand the cashier the nickel. "Here," I tell her. "You can add it to his collection—"

"—I can't accept that," she says, leaning backward as if I reek of something awful.

"Take it," I say, trying not to make a scene.

"Really?" she whispers.

"Really," I say. "It's yours."

While nobody's looking, she grabs the nickle from my hand and pockets it. She rips the receipt from the register and writes something down on the receipt. She says clearly as her manager starts to walk over, "If you go to our website and fill out a brief survey, you have a chance to win a fifty-dollar gift card."

She hands me the receipt with her name, as well as her number written on the bottom. I look over the name, *April*, on the receipt.

"Have a nice day, sir," she says, her face glowing.

"Yeah," I say, as the manager approaches the checkout counter. "You too."

I leave the grocery store feeling strange.

What's happening to me?

2

I pass the same gun shop.

Strangely, I find myself slowing down yet speeding up.

Eventually, I stop for a second and look over the various models of handguns and pistols on the front display case.

I go back to my car and grab the money from the owner's manual.

I glance over the money.

What am I doing?

Why do I even need a gun?

What's the point?

They don't give a shit about me when I'm alive. Why in the hell will they remember me when I'm dead? Here today. Gone tomorrow, right?

I'll be no different than those people on the covers of magazines or tabloids.

Another sad face in the paper or on TV.

I'll turn into a two-dimensional puzzle that's incomplete.

The pieces of the puzzle lost or hidden underneath couch cushions. Pieces mistakenly thrown away.

Like something invaluable and replaceable.

Expendable.

Even worse, I'll turn into something that's entirely disposable.

Reduced to ones and zeroes.

Buried among the dead forums of the Web.

What am I doing, Josh?

I think long and hard before buying the gun. Once I buy it—that's it. There's no coming back. It's such a big purchase.

So, I decide it's best that I sleep on it another night.

I ask myself, What's the rush?

I put the money away and drive back home where Peggy's waiting for me to return with the ricotta. She's acting strange as well, as if something has recently happened. She informs me that she has good news. Someone has made an offer on Bill's house.

"That quick?"

She asks, "What do you think? Keep it or sell it?"

I think over Peggy's comment. Mostly, I think about the storage unit in Bradbury. I think about all of the things Bill left me. I think about his manuscripts, all of them now in my possession. Most importantly, I think about the cashier, April, as well as the rare buffalo nickel.

"Sell it," I tell Peggy. "That's what Bill would've wanted."

I hand Peggy the thing of ricotta, as well as those two dollars of change.

She asks for a receipt, but I tell I threw it away.

I make my way upstairs. Halfway up, I stop and turn to Peggy, who starts pulling pans from the drawers.

"Mom. . . " I say.

She stops and looks at me. She seems confused.

". . . it's just a house."

"I know it is," she says and gets to work on the lasagna.

I head back to my room and contemplate calling April.

3

After the sun goes down, I fill up my tank, make sure I have enough coolant in Maximus, and then I drive straight to Atlanta.

I camp outside Meme's for about an hour before each member of the Mawb shows up. From where I'm parked across the street, I can hardly recognize their faces; however, I know it's them based on their movements and postures—take for instance, Wage, who's always slouching and looks like an old, arthritic man, as he ambles his way into Meme's. They look no different than those characters on the paperback novels in the grocery store: a group of these dark figures without any expression who are standing around Meme's, as if they're lost. One of them is pacing back and forth, like a tweaker itching for a fix.

Eventually, once they're all there outside—I count eleven altogether—they head inside. A couple of minutes pass before one of them steps outside and lights up a cigarette. I can't tell if it's Double-A or Mayhem.

Whoever it is, he or she is staring at me, the banished one, with glowing cat-like eyes while taking slow drags from a cigarette. It's as if he or she can sense the presence of a banished one. Like, in a way, I carry a certain look and smell to me.

What I'd do to hack into New Jack's username when he's sleeping or passed out and under his avatar, run down his score from the leader board, his name falling faster than an avalanche—thoughts of disrupting the Hate Train come and go and before I know it, my mind shifts toward the thought of April. I wonder what she's doing right now?

I hang around for a few more minutes until I grow tired of waiting. I make it back home before midnight.

I spend the rest of the night flipping through channels.

What else is new? There's nothing on TV.

I flip through one channel after another.

Someone's getting raped by a giant octopus.

I flip to another.

Someone's getting stabbed in the back with a dirty shank made from a toothbrush.

I flip to another.

Someone's getting eaten by a werewolf.

I flip to another.

Someone with a badly scarred face is crying in a dimly lit room with a black backdrop—"What was your initial reaction?" says a soft-spoken journalist from behind the camera.

I stay on the channel.

The certain someone, a woman, reveals part of her face underneath her hand. At first, I think it's a glorified drama queen, some crybaby who's trying to get attention or, even worse, sympathy in order to get money or publicity in front of a camera.

The woman removes a balled-up tissue from her bloodshot eyes, revealing a, not badly, but severely scarred face that used to be the face of a young and attractive woman. Her skin is pink and flaky, as if her skin has been turned inside out. The woman looks as if she has been burned by what looks like a corrosive liquid.

I turn up the volume on the TV.

Next, I push the INFO button on the remote: "Scarred For Life: Model Natalie Hagen sits down in an exclusive one-on-one interview with Gloria Beal four years after she was viciously attacked in Winnipeg."

Natalie clears away the tears again, sniffles, and then, finally, answers Gloria Beal's question: "First, the burning," Natalie says, her voice trembling. "I literally felt the skin melting from my face, my eyes on fire, my entire face felt like it was on fire. I could feel the acid eating away at me. The pain was tremendous. At the time, I didn't know what was happening to me. One minute I'm walking to my car, like any other normal day. A young, happy girl with a great job and a great life—and I worked so hard to get where I was. *Nothing* was ever handed down to me," Natalie emphasizes. "And I felt like nothing could stop me. I was, as cliché as it sounds, on top of the world. Then, the next minute. . . " she says, wiping away the tears as soon as they roll down her scarred, wrinkled cheeks, ". . . a strange woman approaches me with a cup in her hand. She flings the acid in my face. Next thing I know, I'm in ah. . . like a horror movie. Thankfully, someone was close by and called an ambulance. When the paramedics informed me that I had been burned by acid, I thought it was all in my head, like I was in a nightmare. I was in so much pain, I remember. Even the air pressed against my face hurt. It was so bad that when I arrived at the hospital the doctors had to put me in an induced coma. But I don't remember anything after the ambulance ride. Later, when I came to, the first face I saw was Dad's. I was blind in my left eye, everything was blurry out of my right eye, but I *knew* he was there with me. I could *feel* his presence. I could *hear* him talking to me, and he was telling me that I had a long journey ahead of me but everything was going to be okay even when it felt as if the world was coming down all around me. Dad grabbed my hand and said, 'It's not your time, Natalie. God didn't betray you. God loves you. God will make you whole again.' I didn't know what Dad meant until two years later when I tried to take my own life."

I lean closer to the TV. Turn up the volume.

Gloria asks, "Describe those moments before you attempted suicide?"

"I lost a lot of friends after I was attacked," she answers. "Most of the friends I lost turned out not being friends at all. I made a lot of enemies. I remember, after the attack, I was afraid to leave my flat. I was afraid to show my face in public," she says with a pause. "I was mad at the world. I was incredibly angry. I was angry with the person who turned me into this hideous person. I *hated* everything. I *hated* the way people looked at me. I *hated* how they pitied me. I *hated* everything and everyone." She takes in a deep breath, calms herself. "Only one person came to visit me and that was my photographer, Alejandro. We texted each other back and forth from time to time because I didn't like to talk whenever I wore my mask. And Alejandro didn't live too far from my flat. So. . . every now and then, he'd stop by, check on me, and ask me if I needed anything."

Gloria puts in a word: "He sounded like a good man."

Natalie says, "Alejandro was a great man. Honestly, I wouldn't be here if it wasn't for him. He saved my life."

Tilting her head to the side in thought, Gloria asks, "According to police reports, a man named Elijah Karlsson, one of the tenants in your building, was the one who found you unconscious on the kitchen floor."

"That's what police told me but I've never heard that name before," Natalie says hesitantly. "I remember Alejandro texted me earlier that night. I didn't respond."

Gloria asks, "Why didn't you respond?"

Natalie says, "I was sitting on the couch, watching TV, thinking: This isn't life. I don't wanna live anymore. Here, doing this to myself. I went to the bathroom and grabbed a bottle of painkillers— Percocets—the doctors prescribed to me and I remember placing a pill on my tongue." Natalie motions placing an invisible pill on her tongue, then closing her mouth and swallowing. "Swallowed," she says. "I placed another one on my tongue. Swallowed. Then, another. Swallowed. Another. I kept cramming pills in my mouth like they were M&Ms, one after another. This wasn't a cry for help or a cry for attention or whatever. I really *wanted* to die. I wanted to be with Dad. The worst part about it was the waiting, knowing I was about to die at any second. I rushed to the kitchen, grabbed a bottle of vodka, and I remember chugging the whole bottle. Then, I must've blacked out after that. I woke up in the hospital. Alejandro was there with me. The doctors pumped my stomach. If Alejandro didn't stop by, then I would've been dead. I believe God had sent Alejandro to my flat that night."

Gloria asks, "When the police questioned you about Alejandro, did they believe you?"

"No," Natalie answers. "O'course not. They thought that I was crazy—"

"—Because Alejandro Gómez died in a plane crash a year after you were attacked?"

"Yes," Natalie says. "He was there. I *saw* him with my own two eyes. Nobody believed me."

She's crying again. She's wiping the tears from her face again.

Gloria asks, "Have you seen Alejandro Gómez ever since you tried to commit suicide?"

"The last time I saw him was at the hospital the next morning when I came to," she says.

Gloria states, "In your book you wrote, 'when I was a little girl, my dad was the three M's: Mentor, Motivator, Mom.' What did you mean by 'Mom'?"

Natalie laughs, her smile is crooked and her lips are stretched across her face like taut rubberbands.

She says with reflection, "I used to joke with him about how he did all of the stuff a mom would normally do when I was growing up since he raised me all by himself. Cleaning the house. Cooking the food. I used to call my dad 'Mr. Mom' like the one from the American comedy."

Gloria asks, "What was your relationship like with your father? Your. . . mom? Were you two friends or was he strict and parental?"

Natalie says, "He used to always say that he couldn't be both, but, to me, he was a parent first and a friend second. There were some things I couldn't share with him and others things I could."

Gloria asks, "Like what?"

Natalie thinks, then says, "Like the first time I had my period. I was devastated. I couldn't share that stuff with my dad. I think he was 'more' devastated when he found out. I remember he brought home one of his lady 'friends.' She helped me through it because Dad didn't know what to do. He was in complete 'panic' mode."

With a stern expression, Gloria states, "You were nineteen years old when your father passed from Hodgkin's disease. You had just appeared on the cover of *Le Chic*. What exactly was going through your mind at the time?"

Natalie says, "He had been battling the disease for a while, and I remember preparing myself for the worse. I remember, before he passed, he told me not to mourn. He told me to 'keep doing' what I'm doing. Don't stop. 'Don't give up,' he said. He wanted me to keep living my life and not spend my life grieving over him, if he died. That was the kind of man he was. He was the most selfless man I had ever known. . . "

My eyes start burning.

I don't realize what's happening until tears start streaming down my face. I'm not talking about a couple of tears but a full-on waterfall. I haven't cried so hard in years.

". . . Two weeks after Dad died," Natalie says, as I try to control myself, "I was back at work. I did a photo shoot in Panay, then another one in Santo Domingo. One after another. Work was that one thing that got me through his death. And that attitude later rubbed off on me. Now, I still work but for a better cause."

"In 2015, you started a charity called Beautiful People, with all of the proceeds going to victims of attacks and domestic assaults," Gloria says. "You've opened up dozens of new schools in poverty-stricken neighborhoods around the country and the world. You've spent hours helping out children with special needs and disabilities, as well as the elderly. You've also been known to anonymously donate money to other charities besides your own—"

Natalie interrupts, "—If I donated money anonymously, then it wouldn't be anonymous."

Gloria follows up: "But for the record, you have been known to anonymously donate money to certain organizations?"

Natalie says modestly: "Yes."

Gloria: "How has your own charity changed, not only your life, but also the lives around you?"

"When I first started helping out other people," Natalie says, "I started to feel good about myself again. I think it was the first time since the attack that I felt like my old self again. Like I was on top of the world again. *Beautiful People* made me realize being a model was the best yet, at the same time, the worst thing that happened to me. When I was modeling, I was projecting an image for the way a woman should look in society. By looking this way with a perfect body or staying fit and healthy, a woman should feel way more confident about herself. Now, thinking about the modeling, I knew I was only making society worse off. I think about how I was responsible for pushing these young women to look or try to look the way culture or the mainstream wanted them to look by starving themselves or doing all this cosmetic surgery to their face or body. I felt torn up inside for what I did. I felt ugly."

A follow-up from Gloria: "Are you saying you have regrets for being a model?"

Natalie straightens her shoulders and sharpens her posture.

"I have so many regrets, Gloria," Natalie says. "I still feel guilty. Whenever I feel this way, I think about what Dad said to me before he passed. 'Don't stop working, Nat,' he told me. 'Don't give up.' *Don't give up on people*: that's what he was telling me. And work, of course. I work and work and work. I never stop working. I hardly sleep. But people, I remember Dad loved people so much, and he held them to such high standards. Now, I live through Dad—or he lives through me. I'm always looking for that next project where I can put my time and energy into helping other people. Why spend so much time and energy in a gym or watching what we eat and focusing on our bodies when we can be doing productive things in the world like helping people who are less fortunate or improving living conditions and our children's education? By rolling up my sleeves and helping people, I can set an example for the next generation to come. I'm not saying we should all stand in a circle and hold hands and sing songs like a cult. The world, it's what we make it. Don't talk about the change," she emphasizes. *"Be* the change."

4

I turn off the TV and gumshoe Natalie Hagen on the Internet.

From the IMAGES tab, I pull up a before and after image of her. The two pictures are like day and night. In one picture, she's wearing a mask made up of silicone called a "compression mask," which helps lock in the moisture. I hardly recognize her face beneath the scars and disfigurement. Even the irises of her eyes—especially her left one, which received the most damage—look as if the acid had somehow changed them from a once tiger's eye-brown to a smoky color.

I click on other websites and skim through more information on Natalie, her charity, Beautiful People, her many contributions, her involvement with other communities such as a non-profit organization called "Hand Over Heart," which brings in teams of volunteers dressed in the patent lime green T-shirts to help restore and rebuild areas which have been damaged by either natural disasters or, get this, riots. That one photo in particular of Natalie in a green Hand Over Heart tee planting a new tree in the ground stays with me as I continue to come across more photos and articles of Natalie and her loyalty to "helping people," as she talked about in the interview with Gloria Beal, then, lastly, her social media pages. She's not a part of the Hashtag Generation and the holy circle jerk of morality. She has around three thousand followers on her Chatterz account and a few thousand on other social media pages, including her PhotoBag page where she has the most followers. She mainly posts pictures of different landmarks and attractions around the world. Believe it or not, she's a very private person who doesn't post gazillions of photos, especially about herself and even the ones that include a shot of her face without filters or makeup, which, surprisingly, make her appear way *more* attractive. She's not the type to share everything on the Internet—let it all hang out, in essence—even though Natalie shared one of the most revealing conversations on TV with a rigid woman who has quite a nose for a story. Natalie isn't the type to post photos of herself and the ones with her face in them look like, more or less, a mistake, like someone had taken the photos without her knowing, sort of like the ones Christian used to take of me all the time. He'd wait till I was distracted, then sneak up behind me with a camera, then take a photo of my dumb face as soon as I turned my head toward him—my jaw slack, mouth crooked, one eye half-opened—then, afterwards, we'd both share a laugh at my own expense. It's hard to make sense, especially coming from a woman who was considered one of the most famous models in the world.

I come across an image of Natalie before the attack: a centerfold from the magazine, *Le Chic*.

I take a mental image of her and attach that voice from the TV to the image and imagine Natalie sleeping next to me in bed. We share what it feels like to lose a loved one. We share our most intimate secrets with one another. We share a lot of things.

20

Vicious cycle – Flipping the world the Bird – Their hand revealed – A decent meal – Those who survived the fire – Hand Over Heart(z) – Rebuilding a symbol – Strategic Acts of Kindness – Josh finds his Pacific – Leap Year – Old friends

FOR the first time in a very long, *long* time, I actually get a full eight hours of sleep without any interruptions. REM sleep without the dreaming.

After learning last night that Hand Over Heart is going to be in Kernelson, I wake up energized and refreshed, as if it's the first day of my new life. The skies are like glass. Strangely, the sun appears brighter than usual. The air even has a familiar freshness to it, like mountain air.

I roll out of bed and hop my way downstairs where Peggy's fixing herself a cup of coffee in the kitchen. She asks if she can make me breakfast and I tell her that I can make my own. She leaves the kitchen and gets ready for work while I make a warm bowl of oatmeal. I throw in a handful of fresh blueberries.

While the oatmeal's finishing on the stovetop, I turn on the TV and check the local news.

The report says there's been yet another massacre.

A shooting at a community college campus in Washington State.

Thirteen dead.

Many hospitalized.

Shooter blew out his brains as the cops were closing in.

"Not a terrorist attack," they're saying, but a disgruntled student who attended the college last year.

I flip to another news channel.

Someone in a homemade TV studio inside a living room is talking about the shooter's background and all of the information he's obtaining comes from the Internet.

I flip to another.

Someone's at the crime scene and with a trembling voice, telling a reporter about what happened the moment the shooter started to unload on bodies.

I flip to another.

More news is still coming in.

More causalities.

Now, they're saying fourteen people have died.

I hear a *sizzling* noise from behind me!

The pot of oatmeal starts to smoke.

I hurry back into the kitchen and remove the oatmeal from the stovetop before it burns completely. I manage to salvage whatever I can by covering the oatmeal with milk, then head back to the living room and tell myself that I'm not going to let some "disgruntled student" whom I don't even know ruin such a beautiful day.

Optimistic about the day, I turn off the TV and take my breakfast to the table where I skim through a news feed on Peggy's tablet.

Nothing has changed.

Each headline and article consists of the same back-n-forth politricks mixed with a dash of celebrity boning gossip, then a sprinkle of angsty "delete-or-destroy" campaigns on Chatterz, one involving a *Children of the Corn*-like cult carrying out a deadly crusade against a public figure I never even heard of who posted an insensitive chirp ten years ago that, at the time, wasn't at all insensitive but now it is, resulting in a swift termination of his cushy, six-figure broadcasting job, thus hours later causing the public figure I never even heard of doing a swan dive off the Sunshine Skyway bridge with a hundred feet of cable cord tied around his neck, hanging himself, then another involving that same bloodthirsty cult bringing down yet another public figure I never even heard of by baiting him into a fight at a local diner, then posting the brawl on the Internet, which resulted in the public figure I never even heard of to lose all his sponsors and issue a lengthy apology statement to the press saying how pathetic of a person he is, a generous helping of over-the-top publicity stunts and the exploitation of a perverse gratification for sitting upon the holy throne of victimhood followed by a decent-sized dollop of overwhelmingly large factions of Internet dwellers deriving pleasure from basking in the misfortunes of others—which I believe the Germans call *"Schadenfreude"*—then a small pinch of violent protests, unrest, and turmoil throughout an algorithmically divided country where its national bird, the once keen, graceful, and skillful hunter of the bald eagle has been replaced by a weak, sarcastic, and often pouty-faced Tweety

Bird, then (*The hell with it!*), dump in widespread Chatterwarz and abra-
cadabra into that boiling pot, stir all of it in before it bubbles to the top,
and then *shazam!*

The quiet breakfast gives me time to figure out what I'm going to do
for the rest of the day. So, I do exactly that, I plan.

2

After breakfast, I put on decent clothes—not too flashy or anything
that'll draw attention to myself but something I don't mind getting dirty
in, like a not too tight but not too loose pair of blue jeans as well as a
flannel shirt. If it comes down to getting sweaty or dirty, I can always
roll up my sleeves.

I wait till Peggy goes to work and pace around my room until finally
making my final decision.

Once she leaves, I drive to Kernelson. According to the organization's homepage there's going to be a team working at Fellowship For
All today and for those who are interested in lending a hand, all are welcome.

I stop once to use the restroom. My stomach's acting grumpy this
morning, not from hunger, but from the bundle of nerves unraveling inside me. I haven't felt this nervous in a while. But, I tell myself over
and over it's those "good kinds" of nerves, the ones that eventually taper
off as the day goes by.

I drive through Main Street Kernelson. Nothing left of the destroyed businesses but a burnt pile of bricks and rubble. I don't see any
improvements from the last time I was here; in fact, most of the town
looks dead and forgotten.

As I arrive at my destination, I notice a bunch of action outside Fellowship For All—or what used to be the rehabilitation center for those
who struggled or are struggling with addiction. Like the small businesses in Kernelson, nothing much remains of the facility but a burnt
pile of rubble; however, the place is thriving with people who are all
working and helping remove debris. Lots of people. Pockets of them, I
see, all ages and backgrounds, chipping away at pieces of burnt wood
with axes and picks and dumping the pieces into a wheel barrel, then
taking those pieces to a dumpster, which is nearly full. They look like a
chain gang working in sync, only without chains. I park Maximus and
before stepping outside, take a deep breath and tell myself that I'm doing the right thing. I'm first approached by a spastic lady wearing a
purple bandana wrapped around her forehead, who threads her way
through a group of volunteers and seeks me out. The very first thing
she asks me is if I'm here to help out with the Hand Over Heart
organization.

"To help rebuild Fellowship," she adds.

I ask her, "What can I do?"

She walks me over to a man named Robert Townsend who has a deep and resonant voice like one in a TV commercial, says I'll be in good company; and in return, Robert walks me over to the back of a truck where extra tools lie in a bed.

I sort through tools, mostly shovels and hoes.

I grab a hoe.

Before she leaves me with Robert, she extends her callused hand and says, "Name's Claire."

I shake her hand and tell her my name. She flashes a smile and says, "Thanks for coming out."

She acts like a person on a mission, a straight shooter.

I like her.

As Claire walks away, I ask Robert, "What do you want me to do first, Robert?"

"You can call me Jack," he says. "Or 'Old Jack,' at least that's what everybody calls me around here."

Old Jack?

I stop and pause and think more about the name.

Even his face, his eyes especially, it's like I've seen him before or known him in another life.

"Joshua Lamb, huh?"

"Josh," I say, as I walk beside Old Jack to a pile of burnt rubble. "Call me Josh."

His eyebrows rise far enough to crease his forehead.

"Good name," he says. "*Biblical.*"

"Yeah?"

"Of course." He tilts his head to the side and asks me, "*Have I not commanded you?*"

I'm not quite sure if he's asking a question so I don't respond.

"*Be strong and courageous,*" Old Jack goes on to say to me, "*Do not be afraid; do not be discouraged, for the Lord your God will be with you wherever you go.*"

I ask Old Jack, "What's that? That from the Bible?"

"Joshua one-nine," Old Jack says.

An awkward tension swells over the two of us.

"Sorry," Old Jack says, breaking through silence, "I can't help myself. I'm what my wife calls a walking, talking search engine, full of all sorts of useful—" he says out of the corner of his mouth, "—or *not so useful* information. More like a bookworm or glorified bibliophile. So, what brought you here today, Josh?"

Surprised by his remarks, I say over a slight pause, "Guess I had nothing else better to do."

Old Jack lets out a bellow of a laugh.

"Good one," he says.

"*So*," I say, "how does this work?"

"First time, huh?"

"Yeah."

Old Jack removes the work gloves from his hands and glances at the young lady, Claire, who's frantically moving from one place to another like a water bug.

"Well," he says and lets out a deep sigh, "we basically have one job today and that's to clear away all the debris. Believe it or not, we don't answer to anybody around here because, frankly, that's not really how Hand Over Heart operates. In a way, everybody's in charge. Claire," he nods his head at Claire, "she's the one who pretty much organizes everything around here. Although, I believe she woke up this morning like a woman possessed. Whenever she gets like that, I guess it's best to stay out of her way."

"You do this kind of stuff a lot?"

Old Jack asks, "What stuff?"

"Volunteer work."

"I've been working with Hand Over Heart for about four years now," Old Jack says. "Let's just say it keeps me busy and most importantly, out of trouble." We stop in front of the ruined building. Old Jack squares himself to what used to be the entrance of the rehabilitation center. "No question we have a *long* road ahead of us, but isn't that life, Josh? One very long road with various off ramps along the way? Eventually, we get back on the right road, right?"

"I never really looked at it that way, but yeah, I guess so."

"Besides," he says and turns to me, "from what I was told, it was an old building that needed much repair. At least now, we get the opportunity to rebuild it from scratch; and hopefully, we'll have it up and running in no time."

"That's the plan, right?"

"You got it," Old Jack says and walks to the area where we will start working. "So, where you from, Josh?"

"Me?" I point to myself. "I'm from Spartacus."

"Ah," Old Jack says and puts on his gloves. "Spartacus. Beautiful town."

"It's a'ight, I guess."

"Any brothers or sisters?"

"Yeah," I say. "One. He's off at college. Now, it's just me and my mom. How about you?" I ask, turning the question around on Old Jack. "Where you from?"

"Bellamoore," Old Jack says.

"Bellamoore, huh?" I think about the town. "Nice place."

"It is indeed," he says. "Eventually, after much convincing, my sister got me to move out there." He looks around at the group of people helping out. "But I know. I like it here a lot. And maybe—who knows?—one day, I actually might call this place home."

He places his hand over my shoulder.

I find comfort in his touch.

Old Jack says, "Let's go, Josh." I follow him to the rubble. He tells me, "We have a lot of work to do."

I pick up the hoe.

Old Jack grabs a sledgehammer.

We get to work.

3

After spending hours chewing through the burnt wood with a hoe, I work up quite a sweat. I remove the loose undershirt from over my nose and mouth and grab a cup from the water cooler.

Robert, who's been breaking down walls with a sledgehammer and going to town on what used to be a recreational room, looks as if he can use a break as well. I ask him if he'd like to take a break, and he agrees and grabs himself a cup of water himself.

While we're cooling off and hydrating underneath the shade of a large oak tree, Robert introduces me to two other volunteers, both of whom are around my age.

One guy is named Brandon, who looks and dresses kind of like me and probably has a closet full of similar clothes.

The other is Julia, a girl with a short, wavy bob cut that's dyed orange. She's extremely bubbly with a personality that can light up a room, and she sports several tats on both her arms and shoulders; however, only parts of the tattoos, like the gnarly arm of a Xenomorph-looking alien or the wing of a mythical fairy or the exaggerated profile of a Japanese anime character blowing a kiss from the edge of her fingertips, are revealed underneath her faded black T-shirt that has as many holes as a slice of Swiss cheese. It's fair to say I'm attracted to her, not necessarily her looks—don't get me wrong, she's cute and she has a fit and rather slim figure that suggests she routinely exercises on a daily basis—but mostly Julia's positive attitude, as well as her overall aura. Honestly, I don't think I've ever met someone with so much *good* energy.

Brandon tells me he's from Riverside.

Julia is a hair stylist from Statesboro, which is only twenty minutes from Spartacus.

I later find out that Brandon was in a similar state of mind as me, and he confesses that Hand Over Heart saved his life last year after he was involved in a near-fatal car accident, which was caused by alcohol. Fortunately, for Brandon, nobody was injured, only himself and his pride. He says that before the accident he was a "lost cause" and got into a lot of trouble and hurt a lot of people, *emotionally*, not physically. I don't know much about Brandon or his background, but when he speaks about himself and all of his past wrongdoings and misfortunes, I can't help but think of myself and how much he reminds me of myself.

Julia shifts the attention toward me and asks me what I'm most interested in.

"Me?"

"Yeah," Julia says ecstatically. Her round eyes light up. "Who else?"

As I look around at the site, the debris, the volunteers, and that family-like atmosphere, I refocus on myself, me actually being here, me making the effort to come out here and lend a hand, me actually finding peace of mind in the work.

I carefully think about my answer.

Confidently, I tell them, "Personal sovereignty."

21

Beating the Hate Train for good – The Big Pull – Just a spur of the moment kind of thing – *Le Chic* – Deep wound investments – Mending alternate timelines – Destroying one world, creating another – The choice – Different roots, same earth – A passenger on a "train that never stops" – If so, speak easy...

WHEN the day is all said and done, it's fair to say, "I'm beat."

Twelve straight hours of breaking down a foundation, which involves lots of digging and dumping, dumping and digging.

The twelve hours fly by, and by the time I said my goodbyes, I am so tired that I'm not even hungry. I ate some of the food Hand Over Heart provided: a squashed patty of a hamburger and a cup of fruit.

During the drive home, I think about my recent experience in Kernelson. Strangely, it felt good getting to know some of the other volunteers, like Brandon or Julia or Thomas or Renee, and somehow, I can see myself hanging out with them. Except for Brandon or Julia, most of them are from the Kernelson area.

Before I reach Spartacus, I decide to pick up some dinner on the way home even though food is the last thing on my mind; however, I know if I don't eat before I sleep, I'll wake up in the middle of the night with a growling stomach.

I grab Peggy some food, as well, and when I make it back home, she's in the bathroom, putting on makeup.

I tell her that I brought home some food. She looks almost upset from the comment.

"Didn't I tell you?" she says. "I'm going to dinner with Bethany tonight."

I go back into the kitchen.

She steps from the bathroom and says from the doorway, "But thank you. That was nice of you."

I never left a note for her. I don't think she left a note for me either. If she did, I never found it this morning. Either way, I don't let Peggy's plans ruin the night.

I turn on the TV.

Someone's throwing out the first pitch at a baseball game.

I leave the channel on baseball and eat dinner by myself. I head to my room after dinner. While I change out of my dirty clothes, the thought of the Mawb suddenly comes to mind. I wonder what they're doing right now, if they're playing the Hate Train. A part of me misses them and that camaraderie. A part of me misses the rush of adrenaline that I felt whenever I was plugged in. But I tell myself those days are over; and by coming to terms with the reality of never playing the Hate Train ever again, I've been enticed, more or less, been given a sample of a whole new world with endless possibilities. I pull out the receipt with April's number. I think about calling her, but that's all I do, really, just think.

2

The next day, I'm back at Fellowship For All. Old Jack is surprised to see me. He's mainly surprised how someone like me, a guy from Spartacus who's in between (*fill-in-the-blank*), has exhibited so much interest in rebuilding the rehab. Personally, of all the places, I don't know the reasons why I chose Fellowship. In a way, I guess it chose me; nonetheless, Old Jack welcomes me with open arms and acts as if he truly cares about me and appreciates me for being. . . me and also appreciates me showing up and ready and willing to put in the hours. I feel all tingly inside, knowing there are people of this new world who find solace in others, including a misfit like me who was once on the verge of destroying the world. Old Jack walks me over to a much older man, who looks as if he's in his late seventies. His name is Al, and surprisingly, he's here to lend a hand. Apparently, Al's a newcomer, like me, and a local of Kernelson. Moved here in '89. Ran a hardware store. Once Al reached an age where he was comfortable enough to retire, he handed down the store to his only son, who eventually sold the place due to the rise in property taxes. Just last year, Al lost his wife to breast cancer. According to Al, her name was Rosé, spelled and pronounced like the pinkish wine, not the flower, and for twelve great years, she fought off the cancer like the great Joan of Arc fighting off the English during the siege of Orléans. After her first battle, the cancer retreated, went into "remission," then some years later, it came back, only to be defeated, then life for Rosé went on like this for years until the fourth time, the last time, the cancer came back and it brought a vengeful army with it.

Despite our age differences, we immediately forge a tight bond, Al and I, especially after I reveal to him that I, too, had lost someone to cancer. I share my story with Al, who, in return, shares his story with me. We are completely opposite in our backgrounds and upbringings and we don't have much in common (In his early years Al used to be a detective before he opened the hardware store, and during our conversations, he tells me about cases he worked on, like missing cases, "cold cases," he calls a few of them, as well as homicides, each and every one as fascinating as the one before—after he left the force, he wrote and published a fictional series of mystery books, compared himself to a cross between Christie and Westlake); however, it's the bond, the one molded and sealed by the death of a loved one and throw in the fact that my loved one happened to also be a writer like Al, that makes whatever differences we have seem so trivial; and oddly enough, I feel much stronger and more open-minded after spending an entire day talking to a wise old man who has lines like highways along his face, a wise old man who morally, philosophically, and politically bleeds a different color than me.

After Al and I spend a majority of the day sharing each other's company, we end the day around twilight. We've cleared out most of the debris and we can't do much else until a truckload of cinderblocks for the foundation arrives tomorrow. Just standing back and seeing all of the work that Al and I have accomplished in one day is impressive and draws the eyes and ears of those who had been volunteering for Hand Over Heart for many years.

Before leaving the site, I spot a familiar face in the crowd. He's talking to Old Jack, who then shakes the familiar man's hand and says goodbye to him. I excuse myself from the others and try to get a closer look at the man's face.

It can't be him, I tell myself over and over as I follow him to his car, which is parked along the street.

He gets inside, and as the familiar man's about to drive away, he turns his head to me and behind the driver's side window I see the face of Sam Glasser—"Glass," as the Mawb called him.

Sam drives away.

I chase after him, but not once does he slow down or stop.

Yet, he keeps driving.

And I keep telling myself over and over, "It can't be him."

3

According to Old Jack, the man's name is Rodney Firehouse, and he's in charge of Fellowship For All. His name is not Sam Glasser, he corrects me. What kind of name is Firehouse? And, even if he's not Glass, then he could be Glass's relative or even his brother—a twin perhaps?!?

I leave the site thinking about Glass and his possible doppelgänger; however, all the progress that I made throughout the day outweighs and eventually, wins over any suspicion or negative feelings I have for Hand Over Heart.

Glass aside, I decided to stop at Freddy's.

I pull into the parking lot of the sandwich shop and park the car in an open spot in the front and lo and behold, the same smelly homeless man is hanging outside.

Before exiting the car, I reach into the glove box and pull out a hundred-dollar bill from the five hundred dollars and stare at Benjamin Franklin's face. I pocket the money and enter Freddy's. The whole time I'm waiting for my food, I'm debating whether or not I should give the homeless man the money. I don't know his story or why or how he ended up on the streets to begin with. A part of me wants to know his story; however, another part of me thinks that by giving him money he'll stop hanging around Freddy's—he'll use the money to purchase new *clean* clothes, perhaps a business suit and a tie, then start applying to jobs, then eventually start earning money on his own. As I'm leaving with my food, he approaches me, as expected. I do as I always do: I ignore him—or, at least, try to. I get back inside my car. Then, as I'm about to start the ignition, I walk over to the homeless man, who, from his stained and crooked teeth and gaunt face, looks as if he hadn't eaten a decent meal since the Great Depression, and hand him a hundred dollar bill.

Behind all of the dirt and grime, I see a man who has nothing.

I look closer and see a reflection of myself in his glossy bloodshot eyes.

"God bless you, sir," the homeless man says, once his oily fingers touch the green paper. He bows his head. "Thank you so much."

I get back in my car and drive away and hope for the best.

4

The next day, I'm pacing around the house looking for two double-A batteries for the TV remote when Peggy decides to help after realizing how frustrated I am and recommends I check the basket of batteries in the laundry room. It was only just a couple of weeks ago that she asked me for double-A batteries—pretty sure it was my last two—and when I questioned her why she needed them, she hesitated and said she needed them for the wireless mouse, which I know wasn't true. I'm insulted by Peggy's recommendation, considering she fills the basket with mostly used or dead batteries; and I start to wonder if she's experiencing the onset of dementia because I can't say how many times I've told her to stop putting used batteries into the basket, but she does anyway.

With no luck in finding the batteries, I let the frustration slide off me and decide to pick up a biscuit for breakfast at a drive-thru before heading to Kernelson. For some reason, I'm compelled to stop by Freddy's. I slow down as I drive past the sandwich shop, and a blot of a figure next to the dumpster catches the corner of my eye.

I pull into Freddy's and drive around the back of the restaurant where I find the same homeless man lying on the ground. He isn't moving and after second glance, I think he's dead. I get out of the car and approach the smelly homeless man, who's alive but barely conscious. He reeks of shit and booze. I kneel down over his body and find track marks all over his arms from where he recently shot up. I pat him on the side of his face, but he's completely out of it.

"Sir," I say, shaking his chin.

He lets out a moan and mumbles something at me.

Something like "Lee'mee lone."

Mindful of any needles he may possess, I peel open the side of his raggedy coat and it's there, in the unveiling, where the causes of his current condition are fleshed out before my eyes. Two golf ball-sized bags of drugs spill out onto the pavement below. I can only assume that there's a needle in one of his pockets and the last thing I want to do right now is stick my hand in a place where it doesn't belong and wind up infected with a disease. I feel awful and the comforting blanket, which had been softly swaddled over my body from the moment I started helping out with Hand Over Heart, is gone, stripped away, discarded; and now I feel naked and angry and the rush that I felt when I first played the Hate Train is back and I can only imagine steam shooting from every orifice of my face. Most importantly, even though I didn't forcible stick that needle into his veins and poison his blood, I feel as if I enabled him, like that tiny voice in the back of his head saying, *"It's just a number."*

As I step away, the homeless man rolls over on his back, which I know is a dangerous position to be in, considering his current state. I carefully roll him back onto his side to help prevent aspiration if he starts hurling chunks, and while doing so, the needle is revealed behind his shoulder.

I draw my eyes back to the infected places along his arms where he had injected the drugs into his veins. I remember the first time I saw him loitering in the parking lot outside Freddy's. I specifically remember those marks on his arms, the cloudy bruises around the red dots, and yet, I completely ignored those marks and the notion that he might've been an addict when I gave him the money.

It's at that moment I know the identity of the homeless man.

I flee the scene and rush back to the house.

I'm back home.

Back in my room.

Confused yet horrified.

On the verge of full-blown panic attack.

As my mind races at what feels like a thousand miles per hour, I piddle throughout the room in order to keep myself from fainting, first cleaning and then organizing, like tidying up a desk or putting up my clothes in their proper places, either folded and placed in the drawers of the chest or fitted with hangers and placed along the bar in my closet. These are chores that I rarely accomplish and are either met with contempt or procrastination and put off for another time; however, they keep my mind from fishtailing and flipping into a ditch so deep and dank and dark that even a sane and chemically balanced person would struggle to claw out of before finally waving the white flag and surrendering to the extended hand of lithium.

While I'm putting away a pair of jeans, I come across the magazine, *Le Chic*, with Natalie Hagen on the cover.

Next, I pull out April's phone number from my pocket and contemplate calling her. I wonder whether or not I can gather enough courage to do it. What will she say? Will she be surprised to hear my voice? I spend about a thirty minutes pacing around my room. Wondering what I should do next. I decide to put off calling April and rummage through the closet, searching for what?

I pull out a stack of brochures, pamphlets, and catalogs from potential colleges and universities, which were mostly used as fronts to carry out my plan that would lead to the destruction of the world. I come across one particular catalog from a college located in Tennessee. The college specializes in arts and design, and I remember, of all the schools, it had, by far, one of the most unique campuses. I open the catalog, flip through random pages, and skim through the various programs like, for instance, Animation, Art History, Architecture, Film and Television, Visual Effects.

I stop at the section of Illustration and Graphic Design and can't help but lose myself in a full-page photo of an illustration that was drawn by a former graduate, who went on to work in a major studio in Hollywood. It's a 3D image of a red haired, don't-fuck-with chick decked out in post-apocalyptic getup and in the zany font below her are the words *"Create your own mayhem!"*

I drop the catalog and dig through a box of random junk that I once had on my desk before my last "decluttering." I come across a crinkled flyer in the bottom of the box.

Old Jack?

On the flyer is Old Jack's name, as well as two others, who are spoken word poets. According to the flyer, Old Jack is going to be performing "poetry slam" at an upscale café located in Bellamoore. I remember grabbing the blue flyer from a street post, then pocketing the flyer, then contemplating whether or not I should attend the event. The date on the flyer is from two years ago, which would've been a few months before I decided to go full nuclear in my end of days campaign. The name on the flyer, Old Jack's name, stays with me. Even though he's wearing glasses in the dark and grainy photocopied picture, his face, Robert's face, stands out the most.

I draw my eyes to the piece of slate next to The Leaning Tower of Pisa-like stack of Bill's manuscripts on the desk.

I place the flyer aside and then crumble the receipt with April's number and toss it in the trash. I grab the rock from the desk and in a sudden fit of rage, I rip my computer from the wall, the monitor, the keyboard, and load them into my car. I grab all of the keyboards, synthesizers, synth modules, the 8-track recorder, the MIDI controllers, drum machines, distortion pedals, the seven EPs on CD and cassette tape that I created during a tumultuous phase when I dabbled in music, only to later make a mistake of releasing the EPs on the Internet for free, as well as the various music equipment that Bill gave me from the very back of my closet, and load them into the back of Maximus. I grab every electronic device, including the TV set, the remote, my mp3 player, my phone, and cram them into my car. Finally, I grab the shoebox of photos with me. More confused than concerned, Peggy asks me what I'm doing.

Once she sees Maximus packed full of my stuff, the look on her face changes, and she becomes worried about my well-being.

With clarity, I reassure her that I'm fine and I tell her that I'm doing what I should've done a long time ago; then, before she has a chance to question my behavior, I leave without telling her where I'm going.

Where I'm going is none of her business.

6/7

I pick up a rental truck somewhere in Sandy Hill and drive to the storage unit in Bradbury.

I spend the next two hours clearing out the entire storage unit. I manage to squeeze every raggedy-ass box, every piece of memorabilia, every trace of Bill, inside the back of the truck.

Last but not least, after the storage unit is empty, I transfer all of the equipment from my car to the truck. The TV, CDs and cassette tapes, the musical equipment, and all the junk from my room.

With the truck packed to the brim, I drive to Lake Rama before sunset. In the middle of nowhere I find an open field next to one of the many coves in the lake and unload the contents inside the truck into a large pile. I grab the aluminum baseball bat—another item Bill had given me when I was young and dumb—then I go to town on a monitor first, then the tower, and beat every inch of my computer until nothing remains but the shattered and pulverized guts of what used to be a computer.

Food for fire.

Toxins for air.

Next, I do the same with the keyboard and swing for the fences. The keyboard strikes the side of a rocking horse; every key explodes from the board and showers over the field with letters and numbers.

I work my way from synthesizers to electronic devices, the TV, and pound away on the screen with the butt of the bat.

In the cool silence of twilight, I make my own music, a new kind that resonates for miles.

The sounds of materials being crushed and shattered.

My Song.

I destroy my phone next, and it feels, in a way, as if I'm slaying The Beast and then as it lays dying in its flickering demise, yanking out the cancerous tumor from its insides by cutting off its food supply, allowing it to wither and wilt and starve, and no longer giving it the attention it so desperately desires. The feeling is like biting the very hand that had been feeding you; however, this cold and rotten hand wasn't providing me with valuable information, nutrition, or a greater knowledge and understanding of current events, but rather forcibly jamming poison down my throat until I cowered into submission.

As the warm metal eats through each device, I pound away until the tears come freely. I embrace the tears running down my face. I embrace the anger, rage, and sadness, like a wheel of emotion spinning round and round before landing on the needle of euphoria.

I embrace the freedom to let it all pour out of my body. For the first time since that young boy was ready to explore the world, I feel my chest open up like a book; and finally, I take it all in. The smell of dewy air and the freshly cut blades of grass from a distance. The sticky grip of leather in my hands. The sweet sounds of birds singing one last song before nightfall. For the second time in my life, I feel one with the world.

Once everything is destroyed beyond repair, I remove two photos, one of David standing with a faithful congregation and another of a young Richie, from the photo album. I pocket the two photos and dowse the entire pile with gasoline. I throw in the shoebox of photos as well, including the two photos of Bill and Richie together. With a match, I light the pile on fire and stand back away from the fumes. I watch it all burn: the photos, the electronic devices, everything.

Finally, I pull out the two photos and look them over once more. I toss the photograph of David into the rising flames but, after second thought, decide to keep the one of Richie.

I watch that photo burn until nothing is left of it but ash. Lastly, I walk to the cove and fling the piece of slate into the lake.

Even after everything's destroyed, I still feel as if the anger—that hatred—is still inside me, not boiling or thriving but sleeping like a virus that has gone dormant over a cold winter, and I can't help but wonder if the hatred will always be with me, a mutual friend, a lifelong companion, a perfect little parasite who consumes more than it deserves, a neglectful partner who only resurfaces whenever it's the most convenient, and I, its one and only vessel, passively give in to its many triggers, thus freeing itself from the perfect little cage it has constructed along the edges of my cortex, only to then spread and mutate from host to host, vessel to vessel into something incurable. How will I be able to live with such poison?

Three Months Later

Or, eighty-seven days to be exact: that's how long it takes us to rebuild Fellowship For All. To see the finished building, once smothered in charred ruins, now resurrected from ash, makes me feel as if I'm finally part of, not a movement or organization, but a functioning body, like an organ or a gear in an engine, coalescing with one universal purpose, which is to erect, not a structure per se, but, more or less, an idea.

It's easy to see the relief, as well as that sense of accomplishment soaked on the faces of those who worked with Hand Over Heart. I can see the change in myself whenever I find myself alone, and so too can Peggy; however, ever since I silenced those dispatches from the other world, we have very little to argue about anymore, which, I guess, isn't at all a bad thing.

While we put the final touches before the grand opening tomorrow, Old Jack stops by to check up on our progress as Julia and I plant the last Southern magnolia in the courtyard.

"Don't you ever go home?" Old Jack teases and pulls me aside.

I excuse myself from Julia, who covers the roots by filling in the rest of the hole along the base of the tree with topsoil.

"What's on your mind?" I ask Old Jack.

He moves the cup of coffee to his other hand and holds out his free hand.

"I just want to say how proud I am of you," he says and invites me into a handshake.

I remove the dirty gardening glove from my hand and shake his warm hand.

"Thanks, I guess."

"No," he says. "Thank you."

"Sure."

"Everybody's talking, you know?"

"About what?"

"You?"

"Me?"

"Yeah, you."

"Oh-kay."

"If it wasn't for you, Josh," he says, "honestly, we wouldn't have finished this project as quick as we did."

I don't know what to say to Old Jack.

It's been awhile since I've been recognized for my contribution; in fact, I can't even remember when someone has gone out of his or her way to voice an appreciation for me. In a way, after all of the pain and damage I've caused, I don't feel as if I'm worthy of Old Jack's appreciation. Before I can wipe the thought away, it finds its way on my face and as much as I try, I can't hide how I truly feel.

"What's a matter, Josh?" Old Jack asks. "You should be proud of yourself."

"Yeah," I trail off. "I guess, it's just. . ."

"Yeah?"

"For the longest time," I tell Old Jack, "I've felt like I was carrying this weight inside me—this bottomless anger—and at times, it'd show its ugly face and drag me down to the gutters, especially when things didn't go the way I intended. I felt utterly powerless, and I felt like the only way I could obtain power was by hurting others. I was wrong. Now, whenever you flip on the TV and read the headlines in the news, it's all you see. The anger," I say clearly. "*The hatred*," I say, clearer. "In a world with so much anger and hatred to the point where it begins to spread like a popular trend, it's easy to fall into that spell and join the crowd. *But*," I pause, "I remind myself of the path I once took and how much pain and sorrow lies at the end of that path." I shake my head. "I don't want to carry around this weight anymore."

"It's trying times for all of us," Old Jack says reassuringly, "but just remember, Josh: Sometimes, the concerns of a man who truly cares about those around him and strives to make things better for *all* of us can often come off as superficial and be mistaken as an arrogant attempt at doing God's bidding. What's important is that we find ways to push forward without tearing down the entire system. After all, a man can only do so much."

I agree with Old Jack—or at least, I want to agree.

"Lead by example," Old Jack says, pointing at me. "You can be an example, right?"

"I dunno," I say unsurely and think more about my past crimes. "But what I do know, for sure, is that maybe I had to hate in order to love, and what you love is definitely worth fighting for."

"Absolutely," Old Jack agrees, and we both look around at the newly constructed Fellowship For All.

Thinking, I say to Old Jack, "Maybe I had to carry that weight until there came a time where I no longer needed to carry it."

Old Jack places his hand over my shoulder. His touch alone is comforting and reassuring.

He walks me back over to Julia, and together, the three of us get back to work.

#

I'M back on the train riding to a new job interview.

A commotion breaks out to the right of me.

Some woman is arguing with some man about another woman.

Another man, glasses, heavyset, is coughing up what sounds like part of his lung. He's not covering his mouth. Yet, he coughs and sneezes and spreads his germs and droplets of spittle everywhere.

Next to him, a couple is taking selfies with a smartphone.

Some woman not too far away is stuffing her drunken face with French fries dipped in a heavy sauce.

Not too far from her, some guy is talking on a phone, broadcasting his entire conversation for everybody to hear.

Next to the blabbermouth more people have their heads stuck in their smartphone, their eyes glazed over and glossy, fingers moving like the legs of a centipede over the touch screens.

The clouds of steam pour out of the headphone jack like a steam locomotive.

I clench my teeth together almost to the point of shattering. I feel the tendons in my hand tighten like wires.

As I curl my hand into a fist, I feel a soft pinch on my left leg.

A young woman sits down next to me.

Mayhem?

She's smirking at me.

"Long time, no see," Mayhem says.

At first, I'm at a loss for words.

She's cut her hair much shorter. Her eyes are clear, bright, and incredibly vivid.

"Yeah," I say, surprised by her appearance. "I've been sort of busy."

She tilts her head to the side and says from the corner of her mouth, "Too busy for me?"

"Where's New Jack?"

She points at another car.

"He's talking to a friend," she says.

"Are you two, you know, together?" I ask.

"Serious?" She furrows her brow in a wicked V. "Let's just say New Jack has a particular type, if you know what I mean."

I don't know what she means by the comment.

She leans closer and says to me, "Poor guy's been trying to hook up with Candy for like as long as I've known him?"

"Candy?" I utter and glance over at New Jack, who's flirting with a shy and voluptuous girl, whom I suspect is Mayhem's friend, Candy. As New Jack's eyes move up and down what Candy adamantly describes in multiple online dating profiles as her curvy and full-figured body, he can hardly make eye contact with Candy, "I see. . . "

A small part of me is relieved that I no longer have any competition, considering Mayhem, who's on the thinner side, was never—I mean, *never*—on New Jack's radar.

Yet, a bigger part of me feels absolutely terrible for not only breaking the number one rule while playing the Hate Train, but also leaving the Mawb on such bad terms.

"We've missed you, Gaud."

"Really?"

Mayhem's words surprise yet confuse me.

"Of course."

"Thought I was banned."

"You are," she says, "but there are exceptions."

"Yeah?"

"Yeah," she says.

"I'm sorry for what happened back there—"

"—Don't sweat it. So," Mayhem says and slides her hand over my knee, "what game shall we play?"

I think about the next game that Mayhem and I should play. I tell her that I'm through with playing games.

She says mischievously, "No more games? Really? Where's the fun in that?"

"Maybe I'm ready for something new," I tell her.

"New, huh?" she says. "Interesting. . . "

I release my hand from the seat and hold out my open palm in front of her.

"What do you say?"

She asks, "Where to?"

I say, "Why don't we go for a walk?"

"At the next stop?"

"Let's ride for a little bit longer," I say.

Mayhem doesn't say anything, not even a word.

Her eyes study mine, and I picture each thought speeding through her brain like glowing beads of electricity racing through wires.

She grabs a hold of my hand.

Together, we ride the train in silence and ignore the couple arguing beside us.

We ignore everybody riding the train.

We ignore the entire world around us.

At the next stop, some kid slips his frail body underneath an elderly woman wearing a planet Earth T-shirt and takes her seat right before she's about to sit down. Her right foot folds underneath her weight, causing her ankle to twist.

The leather heel of her slip-on cracks in half from the dry rot.

She trips but manages to catch herself along one of the handrails.

With a straight face, the elderly woman regains her composure and tries her best to ignore the kid, who, if I had to guess, is only a year or two younger than me; however, from the redness clouding her wrinkled cheeks, it's evident that the kid's actions have her both flustered and frustrated.

Yet, she remains graceful and *doesn't* make a scene in front of the passengers; and despite the young and fiery girl inside her who wouldn't dare hesitate to snap at the kid and in essence, put him in his rightful place, she doesn't even direct or voice that frustration at the kid, who acts as if he has done no wrong.

I can't help but take notice of the kid's laid-back behavior, the blaring, throbbing music seeping through those oversized headphones like a distorted pulse, as well as the black ski mask hanging from his back left pocket.

My ski mask.

He drags from a vape pen, thick white clouds of vape filling the entire train.

The elderly woman waves away the vape from her face.

Several other people on the train take notice, but none of them utter a word to the kid.

I stand up from my seat and tell the elderly woman she can have my seat while the train proceeds to the next stop.

She declines my offer and conceals the ache of old age, but I insist she sit down.

Eventually, she sits but doesn't thank me.

I don't expect one from her.

Staring at me with that same glint in her eyes, Mayhem cracks one side of her mouth in a smirk.

She's impressed, I think.

So too is everyone else riding the train.

I turn my attention back to the kid before me.

He lifts up his head from his phone and the sides of his cheeks are burning red with passion.

We acknowledge one another, my gaze cutting right through his murky bloodshot eyes.

The kid deliberately rolls his eyes at me and looks away, shaking his head while mouthing *words* underneath his breath. Both of my hands curl into fists. Each muscle in my body flexes so taut that I find myself shaking with an uncontrollable rage.

All of a sudden, the shaking stops.

The train comes to a stop and at that moment, I see my tiny reflection in the kid's eyes.

I'm going to do it.

I'm *finally* going to say something.